QUEEN OF THE UNDERWORLD

A DARK MAFIA ROMANCE

STASIA BLACK

LEE SAVINO

Cover Design by Jay Aheer

"Both her mind and her appearance quickly were transformed . . ."
Ovid's Metamorphoses, Book V

ONE

Cora knew the moment her husband came through the grand doors. His power rolled forward, enveloping her.

Standing in the midst of the party, with her back to the entrance, she felt rather than saw him cross the threshold into the ballroom. Her hands immediately started shaking.

Not now. Gods, please, not now.

Along the edges of the gorgeous room, men in black suits took their places quietly, blending in with her serving staff. Marcus's personal cadre of bodyguards. She recognized them because they'd once guarded her.

The guests mingling near the entrance all turned, the men bowing and women fluttering as they greeted the man who secretly ruled the Underworld of New Olympus. Marcus Ubeli.

It had been two months since she'd seen or spoken to him, beyond the text she'd sent telling him she was leaving him as she fled his Estate. Of course she'd known that wouldn't be the end of it. This was Marcus Ubeli they were talking about.

She'd spent the last two months laying low, knowing he

could come for her at any moment. He hadn't, though. He'd respected her wishes...

Or it had been some sort of game to him. One she didn't want to play. She was tired of games. Done with them. Done with *him* and his world of shadows and violence.

Marcus's dark head was still barely in the ballroom. He was surrounded by people, couples in tuxes and ballgowns who would pay homage to the King of the Underworld, men with solemn faces who wanted to shake his hand and whisper in his ear. Same as always.

Of course she'd known that eventually they'd run into each other. It was inevitable. She'd tried to brace herself for this moment. She'd gone over it a hundred times in her head. A thousand times.

She thought she'd be ready.

She'd been wrong. So, so wrong.

Marcus raised his head. His storm colored eyes swept over the crowded room. He was still surrounded by people, but he hadn't forgotten her.

He'd never forget. He was on the hunt.

Goosebumps rose all over her skin and her heart raced. He was more gorgeous than ever and even a ballroom away, she could feel the wash of power that always preceded his intimidating presence.

Get out. She had to get out of here now.

She glanced around, feeling frantic as she looked for an escape. But she was surrounded on all sides by beautiful, glittering people who were all but caging her in between the giant bouquets of peacock feathers and tables laden with crab and puff pastries.

Armand had opened another spa, and, to celebrate, talked one of his many admirers into opening their house for the extravaganza. The party was totally lush. He'd told

Cora to spare no expense and she hadn't. But now the excess was completely screwing with her need for a quick escape.

There was the staircase on the far side of the ballroom; she could probably wind her way through the partiers to get there...but it would leave her exposed. Marcus might be able to approach her before she could get away. Still, she had to try. She couldn't stand here like a lamb waiting for the slaughter.

She looked up at the tall guest in a white tux who'd been talking to her. "I'm sorry," she interrupted him, having no idea what he'd been saying.

She'd passed off the behind-the-scenes responsibilities to Sasha, her assistant, about an hour ago and had been out among the guests ever since, at Armand's insistence.

The tall black man smiled, showing perfect white teeth. He was bald and cut an unusual figure in the party. He reminded her of Sharo, the dangerous underboss in her husband's business.

"No apologies necessary," the man said in a light tenor voice that belied his height. "I've been babbling far too long. I was excited to meet the woman who made all this happen." He frowned down at her in concern. "Are you cold?"

"No." Cora wanted to rub her arms to quell the goose-bumps but instead lifted her hand self-consciously to her hair. Did she look as harried as she felt? Her hair was a shade lighter than it had been two months ago, worked into an intricate braid around her head. Would Marcus like it? She wanted to kick herself the second she had the thought, but still couldn't shake it.

Tendrils were already escaping around her face. Her fingers smoothed them back, and drifted to her ears. She was wearing the diamond earrings Marcus had given her. The studs hadn't seen the light of day for two months, but Armand had given her the dress and she'd wanted something to match.

Of course, she'd picked the one night Marcus showed up and would see her wearing his gift. Sighing, she pressed her hand to her temple. At least she wasn't still wearing her wedding ring.

"You sure you're alright?" the guest in white asked.

On the far side of the ballroom, the DJ on the dais started a song the crowd recognized. A flock of the younger crowd rushed past, knocking Cora into the giant man. His large dark hands reached out to steady her.

Cora smiled weakly as she looked up into the guest's concerned eyes and tried to remember his name.

"Philip Waters!" Armand swooped in, looking dashing in a black velvet tux that contrasted nicely with his dancing black eyes and swarthy skin. "So glad you could come to our party." The boyish designer and spa owner threw his arm around Cora, cutting off her escape. "Are you enjoying it?"

"I am, thank you," Philip rumbled. "It's been awhile since I've been to a party off ship."

"Well, you've come to the right one. Cora helped pull it off." Armand squeezed her. "Have you heard of her new event planning company? She just started it. It's called Perceptions. A lovely name, if I say so myself."

Cora resisted rolling her eyes. Armand had thought up the name. He'd also called her up weeks ago and strong-armed her into starting the business, helping her file the right paperwork, and loaning her a generous amount of start-up capital.

"Tonight's her inaugural event," Armand was telling Philip Waters.

"Is it?" Philip rumbled, his eyes crinkling as he looked down at her. "Congratulations."

"Thank you." Cora forced a smile. She was happy, she really was.

Or maybe not happy. Content. Happiness was a lie. It seemed to her that everyone was simply trying to get by the best they could. So she did, too. And she stayed busy. That was key. When she was busy, she didn't have time to think. Which was why this event had been perfect.

She barely slept the past week and had almost had a heart attack when the caterers tried to change the menu on her at the last moment. But she'd called around to every fish market in the area and gotten them enough fresh salmon to make their piccata bites right in time. And then she had to fight with the florists to get the arrangements she wanted even though they'd agreed a week ago—

Cora shook her head to clear her thoughts. "I should probably check on the buffet..."

She started to pull away but Armand shook his head. "Cora, darling, the buffet is fine. Quit acting like Cinderella and enjoy the ball. Champagne!"

A waitress wearing little more than a purple bikini and headdress of peacock feathers sashayed by and offered her tray out to them. Cora had a glass pressed into her hand before she could protest.

"A toast—" Armand hesitated.

"To the hostess," Philip Waters supplied.

"To the hostess with the mostess. To Cora," Armand whooped. Cora tried to shush him; if Marcus didn't know she was here before he certainly did now. She was about to extricate herself from Armand's embrace when Olivia broke into their circle.

"Hey guys, what are we toasting to?"

"Olivia!" Armand greeted her. "We're toasting Cora."

"Roger that." Olivia was a hacker Cora had befriended in the past few months and her friendship had turned out to be a lifesaver. Especially now since they were roommates after Cora had moved out of Marcus's penthouse. Olivia relieved Cora of her glass and downed the rest of the champagne.

Cora craned her head slightly and tried to scan the room to see if her husband was circling closer. Armand still had his arm around her shoulders and was doing introductions. If she moved now, she'd appear rude. At least Marcus hadn't approached them yet. Maybe there was still time for her to escape?

"Philip, this is Olivia, resident tech genius who owns Aurum, the tech company. Olivia, Philip runs a shipping business and owns—"

"A bunch of toys that can only be run on water," Philip interrupted, capturing Olivia's hand and kissing it.

"Awesome," Olivia said, looking down her sharp nose. Olivia's face wasn't unattractive but Cora didn't care for the way she wore her hair parted down the middle, black sheets falling to a blunt cut jaw. The whole hairstyle resembled a helmet. After two months of advising her friend to get her hair cut in softer layers, Cora had given up, suspecting that Olivia preferred to look striking rather than pretty.

Of course, that theory didn't jive with the way Olivia flirted. Right now Olivia was fluttering her dark lashes at the shipping mogul. "Do you share your toys?"

"I'll share mine if you share yours." Philip smiled.

"Right on. I'm heading out of here soon, but I'll look you up." Olivia looked Philip over, from his bald head all the way down to his wing tip shoes. "You're what, six one?"

"Six two." Again, Philip's smile showed two rows of

very white teeth.

"Nice. You know what they say about tall men." Olivia looked pointedly at the guest's crotch.

"Olivia," Cora choked out, but wasn't sure why she was even surprised anymore. Olivia was smart enough to realize her rudeness—she simply didn't care. "Philip was commenting on how nice this party is."

Even as she said it, her eyes were darting around. Where had Marcus gone? Had he seen her?

"Oh, for sure. Great party," Olivia agreed.

Armand, now hanging on Cora, had somehow grabbed a second champagne. He pointed with his new glass, dangerously close to slopping liquid onto Cora. "See that guy in the corner? That's Max Mars, the movie star."

They all studied the handsome blond holding court in front of the staircase, surrounded by an adoring audience five people deep.

"Hot. I'd fuck him," Olivia pronounced. Armand snorted in Cora's ear, leaning more heavily on her until she was surrounded by the scent of his cologne. It smelled good but was a little overpowering for her taste. Philip's lips jerked briefly into what looked suspiciously like the start of a smile.

Cora closed her eyes as Olivia went on. "Didn't Anna say she was auditioning for a movie that he's starring in? That would be, like, a huge break for her."

"Yes," Cora said, focusing back in on the conversation at hand. "And she's perfect for the part."

"Where is that bitch anyway?" Olivia frowned, looking back towards the entrance. "Anna is another one of our roommates," she told Philip, and then winked at him. "There's only one bed, though. Good thing we're such close friends."

Cora all but choked on a sip of champagne. "How about another toast?" she said desperately. Philip's grin was now ear to ear.

"To friends!" Armand started to toast again, but the hand that held the full glass was still around Cora's neck.

Olivia grabbed the tipsy designer, and helped untangle him. "Gods, Armand, watch her dress."

Cora was almost free when Armand caught her arm.

"Do you like the dress?" he asked. "It's one of my creations."

"I actually need to go fix it real quick," Cora stammered, tugging at Armand's grip. She'd officially reached maximum stimulus overload. She needed a breath.

"Stop, it looks perfect," Armand scolded.

"Very lovely. You're like a mermaid." Philip smiled down at her.

Cora glanced down. The blue sheath was strapless, hugging her sleek form until her waist, where it shimmered into turquoise and then down into a sea-foam green train.

"Turn around," Olivia requested and Armand's hand pulled her into a spin that Cora had no choice but to continue.

Of course, as soon as she twirled, her gaze swept over the crowded party, and Cora looked straight into the eyes of her husband, Marcus Ubeli.

Like in the movies, it felt like everything around them muted and became hazy. Eight weeks hadn't changed much —for him anyway. Marcus wore his signature suit. Everything about him spoke of power, from the set of his broad shoulders to his piercing gaze. He stood in a crowd and rose above it, a man among boys.

He stood a little inside the doorway, flanked by two men dressed all in black. Shades, they were called on the street.

One glance, and Cora stopped mid-twirl, letting her dress continue without her. She stared at her husband, the sight of him hitting her with earth-tilting force. His eyes locked with hers and there was a fire burning in their depths. Searing her to the core.

With time and space, she had convinced herself that she'd imagined the potency of his effect on her. Surely she'd exaggerated how, with a look, he could pin her in place and have her begging.

A half whirl later and she had her back to him, but no relief. She knew his eyes were on her and she could all but feel the ghost of his hands on her body.

More than that, a million other memories were flooding in. Him holding her at night, his body spooned behind hers. Him finally saying the words that she had waited so long to hear, whispering over and over that he loved her.

And that last night before she'd left him. The terrifying sight of him letting the leash off of his control and watching him brutally bash a man's head in. Over and over and over again, even after the man was dead. Marcus hadn't known she was there, hiding in the shadows, but she'd seen. She'd seen and she'd never forget.

Cora stumbled backwards. "I have to go."

Olivia frowned and Armand's head whipped around. They both realized the cause of her panic at the same time. For the past two months, Cora had been Olivia's roommate, and Armand was a frequent visitor to their tiny loft. They'd listened to her rant, hugged her when she cried, and plied her with ice cream when she moped around for days. She'd never told them the extent of it, though. She'd never told a soul about that last night and she never would.

"Oh darling—" Armand began, his Adam's apple bobbing as he swallowed convulsively.

Olivia was more blunt. "Go."

Philip Waters straightened to his considerable height. His eyes narrowed and Cora froze at the mask of hate that settled over his regal features.

Cora didn't want to know the reasons why the man in white despised her husband. Marcus's whole world was filled with darkness and vendetta. She wanted nothing to do with any of it. And she certainly had no interest in confronting Marcus tonight.

Lifting her dress so she wouldn't trip on the mini-train, Cora fled. Damn it, why had she let Armand talk her into wearing these five-inch heels? She couldn't go too quickly or she break her neck.

"I'm sorry." Armand caught up with her, sounding sober again.

"You told me he wouldn't be here," she said through gritted teeth.

"I know," Armand sighed, and she almost stumbled.

He steadied her, then held her back as she snapped at him. "You knew? You knew he was coming, and you told me…"

"Look, I didn't know he was actually going to show up. I may have let it slip that you were working on this event with me. I didn't invite him."

"You dangled me like bait in front of him! That's an open invitation to a man like him."

She glanced back, and, sure enough, Marcus was on his way towards the ballroom, moving closer to them. People seemed to magically clear out of his way. *Shit.*

"It's been two months, Cora belle. Don't you think you should at least talk to him?"

"I *have* talked to him." Okay, she'd texted. She couldn't bear to hear his voice, although she'd saved his voicemails.

"I mean face to face." Armand sighed again. Cora felt a twinge of guilt. Her friends hadn't been anything but supportive, although they did point out, gently, that talking *to* her husband might be a teensy bit better than just ranting behind his back.

They didn't understand, though. And they never would because she'd never tell them about that night.

Keeping busy was the only alternative to curling up in the fetal position underneath her bedspread. Over and over, waking and sleeping, she heard the *BANG* of AJ's gun going off and the endless images assaulted her—the blood, those brief moments between life and death when she'd bowed over Iris's prone body and begged her to hang on, still believing that true love conquered all.

But it didn't. True love and happy endings were a lie. Iris's eyes had gone glassy and that was only the beginning of that night's violence and bloodshed.

So yes, Cora had run.

And in the last two months, she tried to build a life for herself. One she could actually call her own for the first time, not dictated by her mother or her husband. She was finally doing what she dreamed of all her life—she was living independently and starting to make her own way in the world. But gods, none of that mattered because Marcus was here. She couldn't avoid thinking about him anymore. He'd force a confrontation. It was his way.

"I can't," she said, pushing Armand away and rising up onto the first step of the staircase. He frowned but let her go.

"It's too much tonight. I can't. I won't." She was now talking to herself, climbing the stairs carefully because of the damn heels.

Halfway up, though, she made a mistake. She looked down.

Marcus was standing amid the crowd, looking right at her. Was there sadness in the beautiful hollows of his face, in the shadows under his eyes? She'd expected anger.

Too late, Cora realized she'd been staring. Marcus saw her hesitation, and it was enough. Oh shit. He made his living among the criminals of the underworld, where the slightest weakness could be exploited. So of course he read hers. And, like a siren's call, it moved him.

Holding onto the banister with both hands, Cora watched him prowl through the glittering masses. He kept his eyes on her, and she read in them a promise. He was the hunter; she was the prey. And Marcus Ubeli always got what he wanted.

Under her beautiful dress, her knees wobbled. With what—fear, desire, anticipation?—she didn't know. All she knew was that she was glad she had the banister to steady herself.

Run. Get the hell out of here.

But she stayed rooted in place. Because maybe, secretly, she wanted him to get what he wanted.

A wild card saved her. A curvy young woman walked in, her golden skin glowing against her outfit of pure white. Anna. The people around her formed an admiring circle and Anna smiled, basking in the light of their attention. But behind her, a server lifted a full tray of drinks and staggered under their weight. Cora gasped as she saw what would happen.

The server stumbled and the glasses crashed down, sending liquid in a shining arc, splashing all over Anna's white clad form. Anna paused for a brief moment, looking down as the yellow stain spread all over her white outfit.

But Cora should have known Anna could roll with any situation.

Further in the ballroom, the DJ had taken a break and the music was quiet, so people were turning to see this new entertainment. No one else would be able to pull this off, but Anna was a performer, and now she had an audience. She threw back her head and laughed.

With a practiced movement, she let the bolero slide off her shoulders, and tossed the garment onto the surprised server's tray. Every movement was part of the dance, and it was hard to look away. Her undershirt, a complicated camisole done up her front with little hooks was next. With quick flicks of Anna's fingers, her top started to split down the middle as the audience held their breath.

She sashayed her hips, stepping forward. The people around her cleared away as she moved towards a buffet table. Her hands busy with her top, she still managed to step lightly up onto the table.

Now most of the room was watching. Anna remained mostly in place, moving her hips to a silent song.

The DJ filled the room with a throbbing beat. Now some of the younger and rowdier crowd came around the table, and Anna worked with them, blowing a kiss to her new admirers. A few fans started to holler.

Her top came off slowly, teasingly, until Anna dropped it and revealed a pale bra holding up an amazing pair of breasts. If the crowd hadn't been excited before, they certainly were now, and someone clued the DJ in. He turned up the music, bellowing into the mike, "Ladies and gentleman, please welcome—*Venus!*"

Anna was down to her heels, a sexy thong, and a half slip made of tulle that had underwired the poofy skirt she'd been wearing. Not much more than she wore to work at the strip club where she had her show. Even half-naked, she looked elegant, the mesh skirt around her hips flaring out like a ballerina's.

On the edge of the ballroom, Max Mars left his throng of admirers and glided across the parquet to the stage where Anna was dancing. He stepped up, the spotlight gilding his famous profile.

He held out his hand. Anna took it.

Cora sucked in a breath. Her roommate was laughing, holding hands with the biggest star in New Olympus, and blowing kisses over her shoulder to her adoring fans as Max Mars stole her away.

Taking advantage of the distraction, Cora's staff cleaned the champagne and wet clothes away. Crisis averted.

Not quite. All that commotion, and Marcus was still looking at her. Cora staggered backwards, nearly falling on the steps under the weight of his stare. The promise in the stormy depths of his eyes.

Fate had one more ace up his sleeve. While his eyes had been locked with hers, Marcus had forgotten to survey the crowd. The DJ's music ended and the crowd crush forward to cheer. And amid the waves of people, as if pulled by some magic tide, Philip Waters washed into Marcus's path.

From her vantage point, Cora could see her husband's sober expression falter as he looked up at the man who blocked his progression to her. She waited long enough to see the recognition flicker across Marcus's features as he stared at the giant in white.

Another second and surprise left Marcus's face and hatred flooded in.

Cora didn't wait to see what happened next. Slipping out of her shoes, she whirled and ran up the stairs.

TWO

THE HOUSE WAS A MINI PALACE, big as a hotel. At the top of the stairs, Cora slipped past the sign marking the hall beyond as "Private."

Oh well, she'd ask Armand later who owned the palace so she could beg forgiveness for trespassing. Escape was more important at the moment. She hurried down the hall, testing a few of the doors to see if one could lead to a safe hiding place.

None of the doorknobs turned. Cora ran barefoot from one to another, imagining Marcus stalking up the stairs, the victor (of course) of whatever faceoff he might have had with Philip Waters. He'd pause at the top of the stairs, order his Shades to wait, and come for her.

Finally, the door at the end of the hallway opened and Cora walked out onto a balcony. The air was cold and crisp but did little to cool her overheated skin. Hurrying to the balustrade, she leaned over and looked out over the garden, heaving in a deep breath.

Second floor. No way down. Nowhere else to run.

She blinked rapidly as her heart raced, looking over her

shoulder. Maybe he wouldn't find her? But there'd been that look in his eye. He was done waiting.

Two months ago, riding in Maeve's car away from the Ubeli Estate, she'd texted him: I'VE LEFT YOU. I'M SOMEWHERE SAFE. PLEASE DON'T COME AFTER ME.

She'd turned her phone off, and Maeve had dropped her off at Olivia's apartment. After kissing Brutus goodbye (and getting a doggy lick in return), Cora had gone inside to Olivia and Anna, to hug and cry. Armand had shown up an hour later bearing wine. Armand hadn't chastised her, but hugged her until tears came to her eyes. They drank until dawn.

The next day, she turned on her phone and stared at the six voicemails Marcus left her. And one text: WE NEED TO TALK.

After saving the voicemails without listening to them, she'd texted him back. She was a coward, but she was resigned to being one.

I CAN'T RIGHT NOW BUT WE WILL SOON. I PROMISE. I NEED TIME.

She'd left out what she really wanted to say. His reply said it for her. I'LL WAIT. I LOVE YOU.

He'd kept his word. He hadn't sought her out for two months. Oh, Cora knew he checked up on her, and every week flowers were delivered to Olivia's apartment that Anna and Olivia swore weren't from any of their admirers. But no phone calls, no texts. No showing up on her doorstep. Nothing until tonight. His patience had run out.

Cora took her now freezing hands away from the stone and rubbed them together. The truth was, as much as she'd been dreading this day, she knew it needed to happen. Closure, right? Everyone said it was important. If only she was strong enough.

She and Marcus were wrong for each other. From the beginning they'd sparked like fire but what was it worth if it burned the whole world down?

She'd told herself that she needed the past two months to think. But the truth was, sticking her head in the sand was the only way she knew to become deaf and blind to his charms. Seeing him again now, she knew the truth.

She wanted him. She...liked succumbing to the pull he had over her. If she was being honest with herself, and this was very, very hard to admit...she always had. She wanted his overwhelming strength to roll over her and fill her with desire. She wanted him too much.

And she hated herself for that. Her desire for him, her weakness. She wanted to be able to stand up to him and prove she was strong enough to live her own life.

She had to break the cycle. It was up to her.

Footsteps sounded behind her.

And now was her chance.

THREE

FINALLY, she was here in front of him. Marcus stepped through the grand doors and out onto the balcony with her. His wife. They were reunited at last.

The last two months had been hell. Ask anyone who'd been around Marcus. Sharo, the Shades. They'd all learned to steer clear of him other than when absolutely necessary.

Cora's back was to Marcus but he knew she felt him. She always could. They were connected, no matter the miles that might separate them. Nothing could sever their bond.

So he'd given her the time she asked for. She'd been scared. Everything that had gone down...it was bad. She thought she needed space, so okay. Every single day he'd wanted to drive over, tear down the door to her friend's apartment, and drag her back to the Estate where she belonged. At his side.

For her, though, he'd fought his less evolved nature and let her be.

But enough was enough. She was his wife and it was time for her to come home.

"Cora." Her name was a sensuous caress on his tongue. He'd never wanted anything as much as he wanted her.

She turned and the string of connection between them pulled taut.

She was so fucking gorgeous, he almost lost his breath. She was statuesque and beautiful, delicate, with pale skin that glowed in the moonlight. The dress she wore molded to her curves but it also highlighted the fact that she'd lost weight.

A hundred disjointed thoughts ran through Marcus's head. He wanted to punish her for leaving him. He wanted to fall at her feet and beg her forgiveness. He wanted to grab her, flip her against the wall, and fuck all the frustration of the past two months out between her quivering thighs.

Her hands fisted at her sides as if she could read his thoughts and was forcing herself not to reach for him. He all but growled in satisfaction at the sight. He affected her as much as she did him.

Her eyes narrowed and she squared her bare shoulders, lifting her chin. Whatever statement she hoped to make by the posture was undercut by the fact that her nipples had clearly hardened, completely visible through the tight fabric that clung to her breasts. It was a good thing she'd retreated here for their reunion to take place because now Marcus could enjoy the sight all for himself instead of concerning himself with blinding any fucker who dared to stare at what was his.

"Leaving the party so soon?" he finally fired the first volley.

Her eyes flared and she crossed her arms over her chest. More was the pity. "I'm not much of a party person."

He couldn't help smiling at that. "I remember."

He lifted his hand, holding out her ridiculous shoes that she'd abandoned midflight.

"You left these on the stairs."

Her eyes went wide for a moment and little pink spots appeared on her cheeks. "Yes, well. I've had a long night."

He stalked forward, his eyes capturing and keeping hers. She backed up until her legs hit the balustrade. He knelt. So it was to be bowing at her feet after all. He lifted up the silky material of her dress and exposed her perfect ankle. Gods, to touch her skin again...

"Marcus," she breathed, and he looked up the length of her. Her chest was heaving and he grinned. She seemed to lose track of whatever she'd been about to say. Oh yes, her body remembered his command over it and soon the rest of her would too. He'd make sure of it.

But even as he thought it, he knew he wanted more. He didn't want unthinking obedience. Not from her. No, what he wanted from her was so much more complex.

Lifting her foot, he slipped the first shoe on and fastened it, caressing her ankle and her calf. The chance to get his hands on her again was too tempting to pass up.

He worked on the other one while Cora leaned on the balustrade. She was silent, but by the occasional hitch in her breath, his touch was affecting her.

When he finally straightened and stood, she swallowed hard before finally managing a tremulous, "Thank you."

"My pleasure." Their eyes caught and held a moment before she dropped hers and took a small step back from him. As if any amount of distance could stop the blazing furnace of their chemistry.

"Armand tells me you helped him with most of the preparations," he said. She was like a skittish bird and she'd flee if he wasn't careful. "He says you're indispensable. Your company is taking off."

"Well," she croaked before clearing her throat and trying again. "I've been working hard."

"Not too hard, I hope. You need to remember to sleep and eat."

Cora let out a brittle chuckle. "You should take your own advice. I learned my business habits from you."

"I want to apologize." It was suddenly out of his mouth and she looked taken aback.

He might not be on his knees anymore but hell, he realized only now that this was what he'd come here to say. This and more, but it had to begin here. He had so much to atone for where his wife was concerned.

"I need to ask forgiveness for the violence at the restaurant."

Her eyebrow raised, maybe at the bare description of the shooting that had blown out the windows and terrorized at least a dozen guests, killing three and wounding another handful.

"I never thought AJ would be so bold. I underestimated him and put you in a dangerous position. I'm sorry."

"It wasn't your fault." Her eyebrows were drawn together. "But, if it makes you feel better, I forgive you. I never thought you were to blame."

"Then I apologize for leaving you alone at the Estate the next day."

She looked down at the fabric pooling around her feet. "It's alright. You would've stayed if you could've." She took a deep breath. "I accept your apology."

Did she? Did she really?

He still didn't know how AJ had gotten to her the night everything had gone to shit, but in the end it didn't matter.

The responsibility was Marcus's. If he hadn't left her alone, she never would've been taken. She was his wife and his business was never meant to touch her.

He wouldn't say more on the subject, though. He would never put her in that position again. He would protect her and keep her safe. Something he could only do when she was by his side where she belonged.

"Good." He couldn't help looking her up and down again in admiration. "You look beautiful."

"So do you," she said, and Marcus grinned outright. "Marcus—"

"Cora, we need to talk things out. I've given you time."

"Almost two months," she said softly.

"Have you been keeping track? Counting the days?"

"No," she lied. He didn't need her words, just her expression, to know the truth.

Their gaze locked. She looked both a little lost and a little like she hoped she'd been finally found. So much was said, and unsaid, in one simple look. She was his and she always would be.

"I've given you space, as you requested," Marcus said again.

Cora crossed her arms. Almost as soon as she made the move, she dropped her arms again as if aware of her every vulnerable gesture. "You admitted to getting my friend to spy on me. And I'm sure you've had your men trail me."

"Or I could've bugged your apartment."

"You didn't. Did you?" Then her brows came together angrily. "The flowers."

Marcus rolled his eyes. "Cora, I was kidding. I didn't bug the apartment. Have the programmer check."

Cora glared at him, clearly unamused.

"Listen." He ran his hand through his hair. This wasn't

going how he'd envisioned. He wanted to be straight with her for once. No games. No bullshit. "I want to talk to you. To get everything out in the open."

"Everything?"

He thought about it. "Okay, no, not everything. You know some of my secrets are better off kept. It's not just about me, it's about my business—"

"Your business is the thing that's keeping us apart."

"Is that why you left?"

She clammed up, shaking her head and looking down again, hiding her eyes from him.

He took a step forward. She stepped back automatically and he stopped in his tracks. "Tell me why you ran. Talk to me." It was infuriating not knowing what was going on in her head.

"Still giving orders." She shook her head but didn't look at him.

"I remember you liking when I gave orders."

When she didn't take the bait, he sighed. "What are you afraid of?"

The silence rose again between them.

"Is it AJ? Because he's gone."

"Gods." She turned her back to him, shoulders suddenly tense.

"I know you felt threatened." If Marcus could kill AJ all over again, he would. And he'd draw it out this time. "But I can keep you safe."

Cora stared across the garden. The wind whipped the tops of the trees; the leaves shivered below them. She leaned forward onto the stone balustrade and Marcus couldn't read her body language. He didn't like it.

He came and leaned on the railing next to her. "When AJ called and said he had you, nothing else mattered anymore. You mean so much. You know that, right? You know you're everything to me."

Her eyes closed like his words pained her.

His arm brushed hers and she flinched away. Marcus pulled back, chest cinching tight.

"Don't ever be afraid of me, Cora." His voice came out more rough than he intended, but hell. "I'd never hurt you. I was angry, but mostly I was worried about you. I tried so hard to keep the ugliness of my world far away from you."

"You failed," she choked out, finally looking at him and there was such pain in her eyes. It sliced him to the bone.

"I'm sorry. I never wanted to put you in the middle of things. And when AJ took you..." He broke off, shaking his head, not able to continue. He still didn't know everything she'd endured that day. She'd come to him covered in blood.

His hands shook, thinking about it. AJ had done something to her, made her witness something—not only brought her into their world but drenched her in it. And of course she'd run. If Marcus were any kind of good man, he'd send her away instead of luring her back.

"It's ok," Cora whispered. The wind blew hard enough that even though she wrapped her arms around herself, chill bumps were still visible on her skin.

Marcus frowned. So much for taking care of her. "Let's go back in. Get you out of the cold."

She made a noise that could be interpreted as negative, so he took off his coat and came towards her instead. At the last minute, she turned around and let him place it on her shoulders.

"I swear to you, Cora, I'm not a monster." Standing so close and breathing in her familiar scent, he could almost believe it.

He'd done great and terrible things to ensure the

stability of his city and they'd rightly named him King of the Underworld. He'd soullessly embodied the title for years, holding the wicked in his iron grip so the weak didn't suffer unduly. It was purpose enough, he'd told himself. It was atonement for failing to protect his sister all those years ago.

But Cora had burst into his black and white world in an explosion of vibrant color. She'd thawed the ice in his heart and he couldn't go back. Not once he knew what it was like to love her and feel her love in return.

He felt her body tremble at his closeness. "Come back to me," he breathed in the shell of her ear.

When she shook her head, he could feel her hair catch on the rough stubble of his chin.

"You're not safe on your own. Without me."

"People don't think I'm safe with you." She squeezed her eyes shut like if she closed them long enough, he'd go away.

Instead, he turned her gently towards him, and tipped her face to his.

"Who?"

"My friends," she replied, a little breathless.

"Olivia Jandali?" Marcus gritted out. He'd looked into both her roommates. "Or the stripper? Your so-called friends who left you with AJ? I don't need to tell you what I think of their judgment."

Cora stiffened. He felt it, and his hands fell away.

"I want you back. I need you close to me, where I know I can keep you safe. I know we can work things out, if we just talk—"

She whirled to face him. "This is why I left, Marcus. You try to control me. You can't let me be."

"I haven't called or spoken to you in months."

"And you corner me and ask—no—*tell* me to come back

to you. I left because I'd had enough of that. You can't control me."

She wrenched off the suit jacket and thrust it back at him. When he didn't take it, she spun around and draped it over the parapet before leaning against the cool stone again. She gazed into the garden, stubbornly angling her body away from him.

Pushing her more tonight wasn't going to get him anywhere. But she needed to know he wasn't giving up. Not even remotely. She'd given him a taste of paradise, him who'd lived so long in hell. He wouldn't live without her. He couldn't.

"You can't run forever," he said finally. "We'll talk again in a few days." Before she could say anything else to contradict him, he turned on his heel and went back through the double doors into the mansion.

He'd allow her the illusion of choice for a little while longer.

FOUR

THE PARTY WAS OVER; the last guest had gone home along with most of the staff. Cora sat in a sea of blue green feathers, packing the decorations away into their proper boxes and trying not to think about Marcus. She felt buzzed, exhaustion pushing her to the point where she didn't feel tired anymore. Sparring with Marcus hadn't helped.

It wasn't only him, though. Ever since that night, she hadn't been sleeping. Work wore her down enough she'd been able to get a few hours of sleep sometimes; today she'd gotten two hours in as a midday nap before coming back to attend the party and she considered that a win.

Armand strolled up, hands in pocket, a leather satchel over one shoulder. Like her, he'd changed out of his formal clothes.

"Still cleaning up?" He smiled down at her, watching her wrap the feathers in tissue paper.

"Trying to get as much packed for the movers tomorrow." She looked up at him, trying to gauge his mood. Standing there, hair mussed and deep circles under his eyes, he looked like a hardworking spa owner, not a devilish flirt.

"You mean today. It's almost dawn."

She nodded.

"I'm surprised you're not scrubbing the floor, Cinderella." Armand jerked his head to indicate the spot where Anna had given an impromptu performance earlier. Then his eyes got a little glossy. "Your friend is really something."

Cora smiled at him. "Yes she most definitely is. Don't worry, my staff cleaned the floor. If the hosts complain, my company will pay for the damages."

"It'll be fine, Cora." Armand squatted down near her, putting his satchel to the side.

She smirked at him. "Nice purse."

"Thanks. It's not a purse though, too manly."

"Right. It's a man purse. A murse." She stopped and scrubbed a hand over her face as a wave of sleepiness hit her.

"When was the last time you slept?"

"I got a few hours earlier today." Cora closed the box she was working on and started filling the next one. Armand scooted closer to help.

"And before that? Are you getting enough rest?"

"I'm sleeping. At least a few hours a night. Usually."

"Insomnia is a symptom of another condition. Probably mental."

"It's definitely mental. I've been getting these crazy dreams." Cora tried to laugh it off but the sound came out pathetic.

"You going to go see someone about it?"

"Maybe." By which she meant no.

Armand sighed. He lifted a peacock feather and stroked down it's spine with a long finger before Cora reached over and plucked it away.

"I'm still mad at you." She pointed at him with the feather. "You colluded with the enemy."

Armand leveled her with his gaze. "Your husband is not your enemy. He only wanted to see you." He grabbed at the feather and Cora danced the frond away. "It was long overdue. You two talk things out?"

"Not really. We're supposed to talk in a few days." Cora lay the feather down and folded it in tissue paper.

"Well, that's progress, I guess." Armand crossed his legs and settled down on the floor facing her. "What did you two do up there, anyway?" He waggled his thick eyebrows at her.

"Stop it, or I'll beat you with your murse," she threatened. "We just talked. Why, were you hoping we went somewhere and he made wild, wild love to me?"

"Yes, exactly."

"Well, all the bedroom doors were locked. Which reminds me. Who owns this place?"

"This old palace?" Armand shrugged. "Belongs to my family."

Cora's mouth dropped open, looking across the acre of finely polished wood squares leading to the plush red and gold staircase. "Are you kidding me?"

"This, my lady, is the original Merche family home." He raised his hand and swiped it as if to dismiss the vast ballroom.

"Merche? Like the company?" She mentally scrolled through the last things she'd read about the telecom company and the family that still controlled it. "As in Louis Merche? The head of the telecom company by the same name." Her eyes widened as she realized something. "Full name Louis Armand Merche."

"The fourth." Armand cocked his head at her. "At your service."

"Oh my gods. You're like—"

"One of the richest families in the world? Pretty much. At least, until the antitrust trials broke the monopoly. But now Merche Ltd. is split into so many companies, and you can be sure my family has private controlling interest in all of them. No one really knows how wealthy my family is."

"I can't believe..." she stuttered. "You're wealthy. I mean, really, really wealthy."

"Not me," Armand corrected. "My family. I've been disowned. The only reason I was able to get this place for the night is through my cousin. If my father found out who this party was really for...well, the only reason he wouldn't kill me is because, to him, I may as well already be dead."

"What? Why?"

"My father didn't like my choice of prom date." Armand lay back a little, leaning on one arm still facing her. "Papa thought I should date a nice white girl who came from a wealthy family. My mother bought a corsage for me to pin on her dress."

"What happened?"

Armand smiled ruefully. "My date was white, and came from a wealthy family. But he brought me a corsage, not the other way around."

"Your date was a boy."

"Yep. Papa didn't like confirmation that his only son is gay. Well, bi, to be more specific." He picked up another feather. "Not that my father uses either of those terms."

"Armand, I'm so sorry."

"I came home that night and my mother was crying. But she and the servants wouldn't let me in the door." His head sagged a bit; his brow furrowed as he studied the feather.

Cora waited quietly, her hands in her lap.

"I spent the night with my date, hiding out in his room. A very different prom night that I had hoped for. He let me stay for a week at his place and then couldn't smuggle me past his parents anymore. So, I was homeless."

Cora sucked in a breath, feeling pain all through her. "Homeless? In high school?"

Armand nodded, his black hair wafting over his face.

"How old were you?"

"Sixteen."

She stared in horror, imagining the beautiful young man alone on the streets. "I'm so sorry."

Armand lifted his head, his eyes meeting hers. "I'm not. If I hadn't gotten out, I never would've gotten on my feet. Would've never gotten double M or Fortune of the ground. I would be someone else."

"And your family?"

"What about them?" He blew out a breath and his silky black hair wafted away from his forehead. "You want to feel sorry for someone, feel sorry for them. They threw away something good. They missed out. And they don't know the best thing about life."

"What's that?"

"It's never wrong to love," he whispered. He shifted, coming to his knees across from her, taking her hands. She let him; it was a rare moment when he seemed his full twenty-seven years. "Let me tell you something about your husband. I lived for two years on the kindness of strangers, and as soon as I was old enough, I started a business."

She couldn't tear her eyes away from his. "Your salon. Metamorphoses."

"I rented a small place and cut hair for ten hours a day. I'd just hired my first employee when some thugs came by and shook us down. That's when I first heard of Mr. Ubeli. I went to him for protection."

Armand shifted back, letting her hands go after a small squeeze. "I'll never forget the first time I met him. I'd heard of all the things he'd done: restoring his father's restaurants, building his own empire. He seemed so powerful for someone barely thirty." Armand looked out over the ballroom as if seeing the moment unfold again before his eyes.

"He's amazing," Cora agreed quietly.

"Yes." Armand rubbed his face with his long fingers. "I wanted more than anything to be him. He gave me protection, and for some reason he asked me what I wanted to do. I told him my vision of the spa, and, after a year of working together, he came and told me he'd be a silent partner. And we've been in business together ever since."

She sat silent for a moment. "Thank you for sharing."

Armand's black eyes were intense. "Your husband is a good man. Marcus plays by his own rules, but he's loyal, especially to those he's sworn to protect. When someone puts their trust in him, he'd rather die than break it. His word is his bond."

Reaching out, he took her hand and gripped it. "Talk to him, Cora. He deserves at least that much. And so do you."

She nodded, swallowing hard.

"Alright." Armand dropped the serious expression, and his features relaxed into the playful flirtiness she was used to. "Let's get you home. I'll give you a ride."

"What about the movers?" Cora looked around at the pile of feathers still left to pack away.

"I'll take care of things tomorrow. I think I want to keep some of these feathers—take them home. My housemate loves peacock colors. Come on." He helped her up, and rummaged in his satchel, drawing out a small plastic baggie that held five white pills. "Here."

"What's this?" She eyed the baggie but didn't take it.

"Crack," he said and laughed at her expression. "I'm kidding. They're sleeping pills. Completely harmless. Come on, Cora, they're barely over the counter," he insisted when she still hesitated. "You need to sleep. Take one when you really, really need it."

"Fine." She took the bag and followed him to a small side door. He paused in the exit, smiling down at her.

"Trust me Cora...you did a fantastic job tonight. Your business is coming together. Model placement, party planning, image consulting—Perceptions is going to be hot."

Cora laughed. "I need to settle into one niche."

"That'll come. You keep working hard and let me know what you need. I'm glad to help, like Marcus helped me." The look in his eye was fond, like an older brother's.

She grinned in answer, but let her smile drop the moment he turned away. Her mind was still churning with the words he'd spoken earlier.

Marcus plays by his own rules, but he's loyal, especially to those he's sworn to protect. When someone puts their trust in him, he'd rather die than break it. His word is his bond.

Her heart squeezed painfully. Marcus valued trust and loyalty above everything else. So what would he do once he realized she had betrayed him?

FIVE

Dawn was breaking by the time Armand dropped Cora off at Olivia's apartment. She wasn't tired anymore, but wired and on edge. On one hand, her head was spinning with thoughts of the party's success, her new business, and finally moving in to her own apartment. On the other, the future held some hard conversations with her husband. Anxiety and elation flooded her with adrenaline.

Pushing into Olivia's apartment, Cora walked into a gale of laughter. Olivia, black hair hanging wet around her face, sat on the kitchen counter. Anna was squeezed beside her in the tiny space, holding up the long black tamper for her serious commercial-grade blender. Despite being at the party only a few hours ago, the two women looked energetic and well-rested, both wearing comfy, casual clothes. Cora tried not to resent them.

"Hey guys." Cora let her purse and bag fall to the oak floor, and started to pull off her boots. "What are you doing?"

"Making breakfast," Anna said in her light yet sultry voice. Cora and Olivia sat around once discussing their sexy roommate, wondering if her voice was really that high or if she was putting it on. After six weeks, they figured it really was her voice.

"She says it's chocolate pudding," Olivia said, "but don't believe her. She's a lying liar who lies."

Anna stuck the black tamper back into the blender's top and turned on the noisy thing.

"Geez, Anna, you might want to wait until people are awake," Olivia shouted over the noise.

Anna stopped the blender. "What time is it?"

"It's like six a.m. Did you guys just wake up?" Cora dropped her bag. For two months, she and Anna had been staying with Olivia in the programmer's miniscule loft. After all the trouble with her former boss, AJ, Anna was laying low, working her escort business, and going to movie auditions. The apartment was a tight fit for three people, but they made it work.

"I just woke up. Somebody forgot their keys again." Olivia rolled her eyes at Anna.

Anna shrugged and smiled a million dollar smile. "I put them somewhere safe; I just don't remember where."

"You're lucky you're cute and can get away with this crap. Did you check one of your client's bedrooms?" Olivia snarked. "Or Max Mars's place? I saw how he singled you out tonight."

Anna shook her head, winking at Cora. Last week Anna had cut her hair and now she had big silky brown curls around her face. With her flawless caramel skin and hourglass figure, she looked as glamorous in jeans and a t-shirt as she did in a ball gown.

In the aftermath of their ordeal, the three of them had bonded. Anna and Cora needed somewhere safe to lay low, and Olivia had offered the apartment as for as long as they needed it. Anna took over the cooking, Cora cleaned, and Olivia bitched constantly even though it was apparent she enjoyed having her friends around.

Because of the long hours they all worked, they could go days without seeing each other for more than a few minutes, which probably made the arrangement work so well.

Cora had never made close friends so easily, but she needed them. And she got the feeling they felt the same way. It had been the first time in her life Cora had been truly on her own and free, and the two of them had kept it from being terrifying or lonely.

"What are you making?" Cora moved past the large couch and leather chair into the kitchen, which took all of ten steps. A tiny bathroom and bedroom the size of a closet were to the left of the living room and entrance. Olivia had moved her computer lab to her office, otherwise there would have been no room to move.

"Chocolate pudding."

"It isn't chocolate pudding, it's sacrilege," Olivia muttered.

"It's raw vegan chocolate pudding," Anna explained. "Raw coconut butter, stevia, raw cocoa powder and an avocado. Sugar free, dairy free, gluten free—"

"Flavor free," Olivia put in.

Anna stuck her tongue out at her black-haired housemate.

"Interesting," Cora offered neutrally.

Anna offered the spatula. "Taste. It's good."

Cora did as ordered, and to her surprise it wasn't bad. "Chocolatey," she said.

"Ha!" Anna looked triumphantly in Olivia's direction.

"Don't let the devil woman fool you," Olivia said, then slid off the counter. "Alright, kids, I got to get to the office and see if Pig is still working." Pig was another tech genius who co-founded Aurum with Olivia and no, Cora had no idea how he'd gotten the name. "We've been pulling these crazy all-nighters lately. Last time I left him alone he fell asleep on his laptop keyboard and his drool short-circuited the network."

"Want to get coffee first?" Anna was licking chocolate off her fingers.

"Didn't you just get home?" Olivia asked.

"I went to bed right after I left the party."

"But did you sleep?" Olivia narrowed her eyes.

"A little," Anna mouth curved into a private smile.

"Ooh, was it good? Was his dick really big?"

"Like the Empire state building," Anna mock whispered. "Unfortunately he has an ego to match."

"Wait, is this Max Mars you're talking about?" Olivia leaned in.

"A lady doesn't kiss and tell."

"Oh, yes, a lady does. Coffee and gossip, now." Olivia jumped off the counter top and ran to put on her boots.

"Let me change." Anna finished putting the last of her concoction away and headed for the bedroom.

"You coming?" Olivia asked Cora.

Cora shrugged. Watching her roommates banter had given her a little burst of energy. "Might as well. I'm not tired right now."

Olivia frowned. "Still not sleeping?"

"I'm going to the spa in a few hours," Anna said as she stepped out of the bedroom, wearing a little black dress that fit her curves like a dream. "I'll sleep there. You could come with me, if you want. Get a massage. That might relax you enough to get some shut-eye."

Anything sounded better than lying in bed for endless

hours replaying every second of her encounter with Marcus. Cora nodded.

∾

AT THE COFFEE SHOP, Olivia pestered Anna for details of her love life while they all waited in line. Letting her friends bicker, Cora looked over the stacks of mugs and bags of coffee beans for sale, and unwittingly, her mind wandered back to last night.

Marcus had looked so good. In their time apart, she'd tried to tell herself that she'd exaggerated his effect on her. She told herself they *weren't* meant for each other. That her body *didn't* light up with recognition of its perfect mate every time he was near.

You're a lying liar who lies.

"Hello, Earth to Cora." Olivia waved a hand in her face and Cora jerked her head up. It was her turn to give her order. Once she gave it, Olivia pushed her gently toward Anna.

"Go grab the couch," Olivia ordered. "Cora looks dead on her feet."

"Come on, honey." Anna took her hand and led her to the back of the coffee shop. Every man's head in the shop turned to watch them go.

They all settled onto the couch and Anna looked Cora directly in the eye. "Talk to me. Why aren't you sleeping?"

"Insomnia, I guess." Cora sagged back onto the couch cushions. "I don't know, I lay awake for hours. And when I do sleep..." She trailed off, shivering at the thought of her last few nightmares—the impression of darkness and blood, always so much blood, and the horrible feeling of responsibility and guilt that lingered long after she woke up.

"Nightmares?"

Cora swallowed. "The worst."

"I've been having them, too." Anna reached out and took her hand.

Cora stared. "You have?"

"Oh yes. The one where there's something awful chasing you and you're scared but can't get away. I've had it a few times since AJ took me." She leaned forward and squeezed Cora's hand, her lovely face serious. "Because the scary thing really did happen, and my mind needs to process it. So I get the dreams."

"What do you do about them?"

"Let them come. Allow yourself to feel scared and to process what happened. The dreams help us sweat it out. If that's what my mind and body need, I'm okay with that." She shrugged. "Anyway, the most important thing is it's over now. He can't get to us anymore. No one's seen him since."

Cora tried not to flinch. No one had seen him because he was dead. She remembered the nightmare scene on the dark lawn of the Estate all too well. Her husband raising his arm and bashing AJ's head in, over and over and over again.

Her memory wasn't a dream. That was real.

I'm not the monster, Marcus had said.

Your husband is a good man, Armand told her.

"You're going to be ok, chica." Anna's smile was warm.

"One tea, one latte, and my five-shot espresso." Olivia set the drinks down and plopped down between her two friends. "Scoot over, you guys. So, Cora how'd the rest of the party go?"

Cora sat back and tried to smile. Her memories were her burden alone. "Fine. I mean, I got no complaints." Cora uncovered her tea to let it cool.

Olivia eyed her over the latte. "Did you tell that husband of yours to fuck off?"

"Olivia!" Cora gasped.

Anna leaned in. "Wait, Marcus was there?"

"Armand invited him and didn't tell Cora. Get this: Ubeli walks in all gangster and he practically threw her over his shoulder and carried her upstairs. Totally hot."

"Oh my gods," Anna said.

"It didn't go that way," Cora broke in.

"You telling me after two months he didn't get you alone and give you the business? He made his thugs wait at the bottom of the stairs and everything. And when he came back he looked smug..."

"Olivia." Cora had her hand over her face.

"Looked to me like Mr. Big Mob Boss Man got some. Just sayin.'"

"Okay, first of all," Cora started, so loud half the café would be able to hear her. She lowered her voice. "You can't talk about Marcus like that."

"What's he going to do? Waste me?" Olivia gave a sassy little head shake. Obviously she saw the whole thing as a big joke. "If he wanted to do that, he could've done it the first week when he nearly gave me a heart attack standing right outside the apartment when I opened the door."

"What?" Cora all but shrieked. The entire coffee shop turned to look their way but Cora didn't care. Olivia glared at them until they looked away again.

"Yeah, bitch. Like, the second day you were there laying low."

"He came to the apartment?" Cora asked.

"Yeah, he's the one who dropped off your clothes. I told him you were out and didn't want to see him anyway. He actually smiled and said that you were lucky to have such loyal friends. He gave me his information in case something happened and I needed to contact him."

Cora's mouth hung open but she couldn't speak. She could feel anger creeping up her neck, flushing her skin red. She'd say he couldn't help himself but that was no excuse.

"Why didn't you tell her?" Anna asked for her.

"Shit, girl, you said you needed to deal, I let you deal. You didn't want to talk about him so I never brought it up." Olivia shrugged and looked at Anna, who'd raised a brow. "What?"

"Nothing. I can't believe you kept a secret for that long, that's all. I didn't know that was possible for you."

"Just because I want to know everything doesn't mean I can't shut up." Olivia went back to sipping her espresso.

"Breathe, Cora." Anna reached behind Olivia to touch Cora's shoulder. "It's going to be alright."

"No, it's not. I'm going to kill him. He said he gave me space. He lied to me."

"About time you wanted to do something about Ubeli," said Olivia. "Armand and I are ready to lock you in a room with him, and see who comes out alive. Or pregnant."

Cora smacked Olivia's arm hard enough for her drink to slosh a bit. "That's it, I'm not speaking to either of you anymore."

"Oooh, silent treatment. So mean," Olivia said as she got up and moved to the other side of Anna, away from Cora. "That's going to be difficult, seeing as we're helping you move in a few days."

"You got the apartment?" Anna chirped, obviously trying to change the subject.

"She did. She's leaving us," Olivia answered for Cora. "And her business is taking off. My little bird is leaving the nest!"

"Oh hush, Olivia," Cora said.

"I thought you weren't talking to me."

"I tried. I can't be mean for long."

Olivia looked knowingly at Anna. "Fifty bucks says next time she and Marcus meet, she winds up pregnant."

Anna pursed her red lips and ignored their blunt friend. She turned to Cora. "I'm going to miss you."

"Me too." Cora hugged her.

"All right, bitches, enough of this mushy stuff or you're gonna ruin my makeup." Anna swiped at her eyes and smiled a dazzling smile. "Who's ready for the spa?"

SIX

"Come in," Marcus barked after a knock at his office door.

Sharo, his second in command, peeked his head in. "You called, boss?"

"Get in here."

Sharo lumbered his large body through the door and shut it behind him. He stood with his arms behind his back until Marcus bit out in frustration, "For fucks sake, sit down. Don't just stand there looming over my desk like the damned grim reaper."

Sharo didn't say anything. He merely sat, one eyebrow raised the slightest bit. Marcus wasn't in the mood for his silent judgment. Nothing was going his way lately and he was sick of it. He ran a tight ship. But there were too many elements that were out of his control and it was threatening everything he'd ever worked for.

"We've got to get that shipment back. I can't believe Zeke Sturm of all people has finally grown a set all these years. But if he thinks getting re-elected mayor suddenly means he's above the laws of the Underworld, he's got another thing coming."

"We don't know what he's thinking," Sharo finally commented. "We can't get a meeting with him."

Another frustrating fact. Sturm's security kept the man all but sequestered. It had been two months but since he'd secured re-election, he'd only been to three public venues—a gala, a play, and a restaurant opening—none of which Marcus had been able to corner him at to get alone time so he could ask where the *hell* his shipment was.

The police had seized the huge shipment at the docks two months ago after tailing that rat bastard AJ there, but Sturm had promised Marcus he'd return the shipment within a week. But then a week had gone by. Then two. Then three. And no word from Sturm.

No shipment got to New Olympus that didn't come through Philip Waters. He owned the seas. At first Waters had been understanding and hadn't demanded payment for the lost shipment, once it became apparent it was going to stay in police custody. Things like this happened and the Ubeli's have been long and loyal customers.

But then suddenly Waters had pulled a one-eighty and said he wouldn't sell any more product to Marcus until he paid for the first shipment after all.

Marcus didn't know why suddenly everybody thought they could fuck him up the ass, but it was high time he reminded them exactly why people used to be afraid to even say his name out loud.

"It's time to put the fear of the gods into Sturm and anybody else who thinks they can take advantage of me," Marcus growled through clenched teeth. "I run this city. No one else."

Sharo didn't say anything for a long moment. And when he did, Marcus wished he hadn't, because it only made him want to deck his longtime friend: "Did you talk to her?"

Marcus glowered at him. It would have silenced any lesser man. But Sharo only sat forward.

"Did you apologize? I know it's not in your nature but women like to hear the words—"

"Of course I apologized," Marcus cut him off irritably. "She's not ready to hear it. But she will be. I'll make sure of it. Anyway, I'm not having this conversation with you."

Sharo frowned. "You can't go in and start ordering her around. You have to be delicate—"

"I'm not taking dating advice from a man who only sleeps with prostitutes."

Sharo stood up, turned his back and headed for the door. Shit.

"Wait," Marcus called. Sharo paused, hand on the doorknob. "I'm sorry. That was uncalled for."

Sharo inclined his head once but didn't turn to look back at Marcus. "She's the best thing that ever happened to you."

"Don't you think I know that?" Marcus all but shouted. And then, because Sharo was the one person Marcus could genuinely call a friend and so he deserved it, Marcus gave him more, in a quiet, tempered tone. "I'm doing everything I can to get her back. Everything and anything. None of it means anything without her."

Sharo gave another simple nod and then exited through the door. It closed softly behind him.

Marcus looked at his laptop but soon pushed back from his desk in frustration. He wasn't going to get any more work done tonight.

He paused for a moment, though, looking towards the door, remembering the first time he'd seen Cora up close. She'd pushed through that very door frantically and shut it again, wet and disheveled, on the run and thinking she'd found a safe place in his office.

Even then he'd been enchanted by her beauty and sweetness. She'd fallen asleep in that chair right there, across the desk from him. He'd lingered longer than he should have, watching her. His beautiful enemy. And then, instead of destroying her like he'd meant to, he'd gone and fallen in love with her. And she'd changed everything.

Life without her was unfeasible. Untenable. He wouldn't go back. He was only getting through each day on the promise to himself that she'd soon be back in his arms. In his bed. Forever.

But standing here mooning like a lovesick teenager was beneath him. So he grabbed his jacket and called his driver to bring the car around front.

He busied himself with emails and phone calls on his way home. It wasn't his normal way, but now riding in cars listening to music only reminded him of when he'd done so with her beside him. So he filled the void with distraction.

At least until he opened the door to his silent penthouse. A place had never felt more empty. He took several echoing steps inside the marble foyer, letting the door shut behind him.

Everywhere he looked, he saw her ghost. In the kitchen cutting vegetables for the salads she was always trying to get him to eat. Lounging in the sunken living area, curled up like a cat on the plush sofa while she read a book.

She'd get so lost in what she was reading, she wouldn't never noticed him at the edge of the room so he could drink in his fill of her. The delicate curve of her neck. Her plump, pillowy lips and the way the top one was ever so slightly fuller than the bottom. That lip of hers drove him mad, the way she'd bite and worry at it when she was thinking about something. He grew stiff just remembering it.

He frowned and dropped his suitcase by the door. He needed a fucking drink.

But instead of going to the bar at the far end of the room, he found his feet heading towards his bedroom. Because no matter how he tried, he couldn't rid himself of thoughts of her. And she'd never been more present than when she'd given herself to him completely in his bedroom.

He pushed open the door slowly intending to linger in the memories.

But then he threw it open with a bang. "What the *fuck?*"

He pulled out his gun from the holster beneath his jacket and swung around, looking for intruders. After confirming the bedroom and ensuite were clear, he closed the door and called Sharo.

"Yes, boss?"

"Security team to the penthouse. Now."

"Sending them." Sharo was immediately at attention. "What's happening?"

"Intruders. They or may not be still on premises," Marcus said, keeping his voice low.

"Team is on their way. What tipped you off? Did they ransack the place?"

Marcus looked at his bed again and the gruesome tableau that had been laid out there. Three bloody, severed dog heads were arranged as if all belonging to a three-headed dog, a likely reference to Cerberus, guard-dog to the Underworld.

"Looks like the Titans have finally decided to respond to our message from a couple months ago. Either that or Waters has decided to up the stakes."

SEVEN

Cora sat on the balcony seats while The Orphan's voice rang out in the hall. It was beautiful. Pure. Perfect. At the same time, everything was wrong. So wrong.

She clutched the railing, shaking her head. No, she had to stop it. She looked around frantically for someone to help but there was no one.

"If you die before I wake," Chris sang, "I'll give my soul; it's theirs to take—"

"No!" Cora screamed but her voice made no sound even as a monstrous darkness rose behind Chris. "Run!"

Iris stumbled out from the other side of the stage, looking dazed and confused. She was clutching her stomach and when she brought her hands away, they were covered in blood.

"Iris," Chris shouted, throwing his guitar to the ground and sprinting towards her.

But the darkness, the monster behind him, it was faster. Cora screamed as it swallowed him up, a title wave of blood drenching Iris as she fell to her knees and—

Cora sat up in bed, hand flying to her mouth to stifle her

scream as sweat poured down her temples and her heart raced.

On the side table, her phone was buzzing insistently. It must have woken her. Thank the Fates. Sometimes she was stuck in the nightmare world for what felt like an eternity.

Cora wiped her forehead with her forearm and reached for the phone, fumbling for the angry little device.

Missed call...four thirty-two pm. She groaned. She'd gotten only an hour of sleep after getting back from the spa.

Her fingers hit the button to listen to the voicemail.

"Mrs. Ubeli," said a familiar voice, and she started at hearing her married name. "This is Philip Waters; Mr. Merche gave me your number. Please call me when you get a chance." He gave his number.

She blinked in confusion for a moment but then remembered her earlier conversation with Armand.

He'd come in while she and Anna were at Metamorphosis, before they'd gone in to get their massages. "Don't mean to interrupt girl's day out. I wanted to let you know I gave Perceptions a referral. You remember the big black guy in the white tux?"

She remembered the intense stare down between the tall man and her husband. "Philip Waters...uh, yes."

"Well, Waters called trying to get in touch with you. Cora, he is raving about how great the party was last night. I sent him to your website but I'll send you his number, too. This is huge! He owns a huge company—I bet he wants you to do something corporate. That's big money right there. I'll help you, of course. We'll get some sub-contractors." Armand's voice had buzzed with excitement but Cora had been beyond exhausted at that point. She'd hoped she'd fall asleep during the massage, but no such luck.

Saving the voicemail, she dropped her phone on the

bedside table with a groan. How long could a person go without sleep before they went crazy?

Hauling herself out of bed, she went tiredly to the bedroom door to stare at the rest of the apartment. No one was home. Olivia would probably work through the night with Pig. Where Olivia was a devil, stubborn and driven, Pig—Cora didn't know his real name—was an angel, sweet and talented. His ideas were cutting edge, Olivia had told her once, but he'd give them away if it wasn't for her push to get them patented, designed, and distributed properly. Olivia was a fiend when it came to business.

Anna was probably getting a private tour of the studio by her new boy toy, Max Mars.

Meanwhile, Cora thought, *I'm slowly going mad.* Grabbing a laundry basket, she started picking up the place.

When she went to clean her purse, the baggie of white pills Armand had given her fell out, and she paused, considering. She hated taking medicine for anything. Even when she was little, her mother would let the fever burn out or feed her chicken soup for a cold. She frowned. Her mom was scarcely a role model, though, considering she was a murderous crime lord. Then Cora laughed humorously. She had a lot of those in her life.

She pulled out one of the little pills. It weighed heavily in her palm, a fair trade for a night's rest.

After swallowing it with a glass of water, she waited a few minutes, then kept packing for her upcoming move.

She was rummaging around in her suitcase when she heard a clink. Checking the small pockets, she pulled out her wedding rings, the plain white gold band and matching engagement ring, unique with both diamonds and red stones. She slid it on her finger, watching the diamonds and garnets catch the light.

She remembered the night Marcus had first but it on her finger. That had been another lifetime. She'd been another woman. A girl, really. She hadn't even known who or what Marcus was yet. She'd been so naïve. And if she could go back in time and warn her former self? She flopped back on the couch and stared at the ceiling fan. If she could do it all differently...would she?

A knock at the door startled her out of her thoughts.

She glided across the small apartment and opened it, expecting Armand or even one of her roommates who'd forgotten their keys. She didn't expect the familiar dark-haired form, with tall, broad shoulders filling the narrow frame.

"Marcus," she whispered numbly.

The next second he was on her, his large hands cradling her face with infinite care as his mouth closed over hers. Firm lips pressing, pulling, dominating hers until they parted.

She closed her eyes, her breath leaving her in a rush. What was she doing? She couldn't just let him— Marcus's hands caressed her cheeks, her shoulders, her hips, guiding her backwards. And she let him. His scent washed over her.

She clutched his shoulders for balance at first, then harder, her fingers digging in and grabbing him. *Yes.* She missed him. She needed him.

He swung her up and her legs locked around his waist. Then they were in her bedroom. On the bed.

Her hips arched upwards, juddering, begging as Marcus braced his big body over hers. His mouth, his hands, were everywhere. His stubble scraped the inner curve of her breast and she cried out in shock at the abrasive pleasure.

Fabric tore and she kicked free of her ruined sleep

shorts. Her hands turned to claws, digging into the solid muscle of her husband's back.

Please, I need—

He reared up, a massive shadow over her. In a moment he'd fill her and all would be well. Everything in the world swirled away. It was only Marcus, Marcus, *Marcus*. She couldn't see his face, but as her body convulsed in painful pleasure, the light silhouetted the curve of his cheek, cruel and confident and everything she'd longed for in the eternity they'd been apart...

Cora woke up with her body shuddering in the throes of her orgasm. Her hand flew to her naked chest as if she could still her pounding heart.

She looked around in confusion even as she checked the sum of her naked limbs. In the cool bedroom light she couldn't tell whether it was night or day. Marcus was nowhere to be seen. Had it been...a *dream*?

What the hell? She pushed her hair back from her face and tentatively felt herself down *there*. No, she hadn't had sex. Sex with Marcus, especially after going so long without —she'd definitely feel it afterwards.

She flopped backwards on her pillow. She wasn't sure which was more unsettling, the sex dream or the nightmares.

Her phone chirped at her from an unruly pile of pillows on the floor. 7:56 a.m., the glowing light told her, over twelve hours since she'd taken the sleeping pill. She didn't remember anything—taking off her clothes, climbing into bed—nothing except for the dream.

It *had* been a dream, right? Though she didn't feel sore, it had still felt so *real*.

Blushing hard, she gathered the bedspread around her naked form and peeked out of the bedroom. No one was in the apartment, and there was no way to tell whether or not someone had been there.

Except that the air in the bedroom held the heady smell of sex.

Okay. Enough. Cora jumped off the bed and ripped off all the sheets, throwing them in a pile for laundry before taking the coldest shower of her life.

EIGHT

Gods, she was beautiful. No, it went beyond simple beauty, Marcus thought as he stared at his wife sitting in one of her favorite coffee shops. She often came here to work on her laptop. Considering the state of things, Marcus had a Shade assigned to her at all times. He didn't care if she found it stifling. Her safety was a nonnegotiable.

She looked to be working through her receipts, and each of her movements was so graceful, it was like an unrehearsed dance. Her fingertips glided along the laptop keys and her arms were fluid as she moved receipts from one pile to another. Her intelligent eyes were so focused, she seemed lost to the world. It was like that with everything she did. Even when she only volunteered at an animal shelter, she gave it her all. In friendships, she never held back.

And when she loved, she loved so effusively that being on the receiving end was the most incredible and addictive thing in the world.

Marcus was just about to head her way when a young man, maybe college-aged, approached her and put his hand on the chair opposite. "Is this seat taken?" He flashed a smile that Marcus wanted to shove down his throat.

"It's mine," Marcus growled, covering the distance between them in only a few strides. The little prick turned and stiffened. He took one look up at Marcus and showed he had an ounce of brains in his head by taking off without a word.

Marcus sat down across from Cora. A deep sense of relief and rightness washed through him at being so near her again.

"What are you doing here?" she hissed. Her flashing eyes had him smiling. He loved it when she was feisty.

"We need to talk." Marcus gave a gesture with his hand. Behind him in the coffee shop, his Shades moved, escorting customers out and even going behind the counter to send the green-aproned baristas into their own storeroom.

"What the—" Cora watched his men clear the coffee shop and then snapped her gaze back to Marcus "I told you I'd call."

"This isn't a social call." His tone went grim as he remembered the not so subtle message that had been left in his bed. No one had been found in the apartment but his men also hadn't discovered how anyone had been able to break in in the first place. The lock hadn't been jimmied and nothing was broken. If they were able to get in like that, why not wait and try to assassinate him? Too many questions without answers. He didn't like it.

"It's business, not pleasure." He tossed a black phone onto her bag. "When you do call me, make sure you use this."

Cora stared at the burner phone. "Is this really necessary?"

"I'm receiving death threats. Not the usual ones I get,

either. These messages are...targeted. Serious. The kind that let me know the people sending them are knowledgeable enough to carry them out."

Her eyes went wide. "Death threats?"

"I'm handling it. But you need to be aware." He nodded towards the phone. "And take precautions."

She stared at him for a moment. Her eyes dropped in the most beautiful submission as she reached for the phone. Marcus couldn't deny the triumph roaring through his chest.

"I got it," she murmured as she slid the burner into her purse. "If I call you, I'll use this."

"When," he corrected. If she thought she could retreat now, she was out of her mind. Not after giving that little taste reminding him of how delicious it was when she submitted.

"What?"

"*When* you call me."

She glared at him and he couldn't help his smile. "After this display I may not want to call you."

He genuinely had no idea what she was talking about. "What display?"

"This." She waved her hand around.

"Neutral ground." He shrugged. "I chose a place where you'd feel comfortable."

"Normally people come in and order drinks. But you come in and get your ninjas or whatever to scare off the barista and block the door with your bodyguards to keep out all the customers."

Marcus just looked at her. She threw up her hands, her voice rising. "You did a hostile takeover of this coffee shop."

"You understand I'm here on your turf for your sake.

But I also need to feel comfortable. My enemies won't hesitate to target me."

"I got that when we got shot up at the restaurant where we were having dinner."

"We're not speaking of that here." Marcus's jaw went stiff. If he thought of that day, he'd need to break something.

"I thought you were here to speak to me. This is me talking." She threw open her arms. "I'd hate for you to clear out a coffee shop for nothing."

He bit back a smile. Gods, she was spectacular. She'd grown so much from the naïve ingénue he'd first met. Now she was a firecracker. Bold. Explosive.

He wanted to toss her laptop to the floor and lay her out over the table right here. One thing that had never changed, and Marcus hoped never would, was the fact that her every emotion played out on her face.

And like always, he felt his desire reciprocated in the crackling electricity between them. She wanted him as much as he wanted her. So why was she denying it?

He leaned in. "I have to disappear for a while." He registered the surprise on her face but kept going. "Come with me. A week of lying low. We'd be able to talk, see if we can work things out."

Emotions darted one after the other across her face and she sputtered, "What? You can't just...you're asking me to..."

"I have no reason to believe you're in danger. That's why you have a choice. But I would like us to talk. Cora, I want you back. I want us to be together."

"Marcus," she began, and sighed. "I've started a life. I know it sounds stupid. It's only been two months, but..."

She bit her lip in the way that drove him crazy. And she kept talking instead of shutting him out, which was progress. "I've started a business and I think it'll work. Perceptions is more than a model placement service. I want to be an advocate for these young women. I know what this industry can do to them."

"You know predators exist."

She nodded and leaned forward. "I help get these women legitimate jobs. Maybe not the most glamorous or highest paying jobs, yet," she admitted. "But it's starting to come together. Young women come to make it in the big city and get sucked down and destroyed. Perceptions could be a life line."

Of course she would make something like this her life's work. And this was only the beginning, he had no doubt. Her heart had no bounds.

"And now I've got clients lining up," she continued excitedly. "Armand already gave one of the guests my number; he said the man was so impressed with what I'd done and Armand told him about my business."

"I'm proud of you."

Her breath caught. She flushed, and looked away.

"Which guest?"

She paused and for a moment he thought she wouldn't tell him but she arched an eyebrow. "The big man in the white suit. Philip Waters."

What?

"Philip Waters is asking about you?" Marcus didn't try to hide his fury. That bastard knew the Code. Families were left out of business.

"Um, yeah," Cora said, sounding less sure of herself. "He met me at the party and got my number from Armand. He called me for a consultation—"

Marcus picked her phone up off the table and started scrolling. He saw Waters' number and that he'd left a voicemail. Feeling even more pissed than when he'd found the dog's heads in his bed, he pressed the button to listen to the message.

"Hey!" Cora cried as he raised the phone to his ear. Frowning, he listened to Waters' putting on a friendly voice as he asked for a consultation, as Cora said. Marcus swore.

"What are you doing?" she asked as he pressed more buttons. She made a move to reach for it and he halted her with a gesture.

"Blocked him." Marcus tossed the phone onto her bag. "If he tries to call again or finds another way, use the burner and contact the emergency number. It comes straight to me or Sharo. You remember the emergency number?"

Cora was still staring open mouthed at her phone. "I can't believe you did that. You blocked my first real client."

"Cora, run from everything I've said today but understand this—" Marcus reached forward and grasped her hand, ensuring that she was looking him in the eye. "You need to stay away from Waters. I'll talk to Armand, let him know the deal."

But Cora only looked pissed. "Oh, no," she said, shaking her head and pushing her chair back from the table. "You don't get to order me around anymore."

She was cute. He smiled. "Don't I?" But he stood up and sobered, coming around the table. This wasn't something to be taken lightly. "I mean it, Cora. I'm talking about bad shit."

Cora jerked her head back in surprise, probably at hearing him swear. He almost never did around her. His father had raised him better than to swear around women. But he had to get it through her head about Waters.

Marcus moved around the table to where she stood. "He's dangerous."

"I can handle dangerous."

Did she mean that as a challenge?

"Can you, Mrs. Ubeli?" He moved forward.

"Don't call me that."

"No, Cora? Why not?"

"We're separated right now. I don't know if I want to be Mrs. Ubeli right now."

Marcus stepped into her space, only inches between them. Her breathing grew shorter, her bosom rising and falling in response to him.

"If you don't want to be Mrs. Ubeli," he said in a voice dangerously low. "Why are you still wearing your wedding ring?"

She blinked, but before she could tear her eyes away from his gray ones, he took her left hand, and raised it slowly to his lips and kissed her cold fingers, without taking his eyes from hers. The diamonds sparkled between them, the more subtle garnets flashing red.

She tried to snatch her hand back, but he gripped it harder. Her breath caught and she swallowed hard. "I was cleaning last night...I don't remember."

A visible shiver went through her and gods, her response drove him crazy. He wanted her. He wanted her so badly that sometimes he couldn't sleep at night but for the wanting and the memory of her body beside his in the bed.

"I've decided I want a divorce," she whispered, finally taking a step back from him.

He laughed.

"It's not funny."

"All right." He shrugged. "I can grant you a divorce."

She stared, obviously not believing.

"You want a divorce, I'll give it to you."

"Just like that?"

"Whatever you want, on one condition." He held up a finger. "You talk to me, *really* talk. And we try to make it work first."

"Marcus..." She lifted a hand to her head like he was making her dizzy.

"Cora, you're still running. You wanted space, I gave it to you. You want my money? I'll give every cent and work harder for more." He closed the distance she'd put between them.

"What are you doing? Marcus." She backed up as he came forward, crowding her into the wall beside the coffee bar. All his Shades had wisely disappeared and taken up an outside perimeter. It was just the two of them in the entire shop.

He stopped her with a finger to her lips. "Whatever you want, I can get it. All I want is you."

"You can't have me." She shook her head but her eyes were full of confusion and, if he wasn't wrong, longing. "I don't want to lose myself in you. You're too...powerful."

"Is that what you want? To be powerful?" The small space between them was magnetic, drawing her closer to him. He hoped his gaze seared her the way hers did him. It was his only saving grace—that the obsession wasn't his alone. As much as she tried to deny it, he knew she felt it too.

"What you didn't understand was that you had the power. All along." He lifted her hand. "Together we could be more." He kissed her palm.

Her breaths grew even shorter and finally she whispered, "I'm afraid of you."

He quirked an eyebrow at her.

"I'm afraid of how you make me feel. I'm afraid of us.

You swallow me up." And then she leaned in as if she couldn't stop herself from breathing him in. She halted only an inch away and when she shook her head ever so slightly, their noses brushed.

"My feelings," she murmured, "my attraction to you, they overwhelm me."

He nuzzled his nose against hers. Even this simplest touch felt life-giving. "Isn't that just life? Being afraid and acting anyway?"

She closed her eyes as if to ward him off even as their foreheads touched.

"You can't manipulate me, Marcus. Not anymore. Not after everything I've proven to you. Proven to myself."

"Why do you have to prove yourself to me? Who told you that you're not enough?"

She pulled away from him, pain welling up in her eyes.

"There it is," Marcus said. "That's why you push me away, even though we have something good. Something amazing. You don't think you deserve it."

Tears spilled, sliding down her cheeks. She was hurting and hurting deeply. Why wouldn't she talk to him?

"Come with me," he tried one last time.

She shook her head and swiped at her cheeks. "I can't."

Marcus offered her his handkerchief.

"Thank you." She used the white square of fabric to dry her eyes, but didn't look at him.

As much as it killed him and as much as he wanted to throw her over his shoulder, pushing her right now wasn't going to get him anywhere. A little longer. He could give her a little longer.

But he wasn't giving up either. "This isn't over."

"So bossy," she sniffed, and laughed.

"That's right, Mrs. Ubeli." He leaned in and kissed her

temple. She closed her eyes, her entire body relaxing into him.

He slid a finger along her jaw and stepped away, breaking her trance.

"My men will be tailing you from now on. Don't try to slip away."

NINE

FOR THE NEXT couple of weeks, Cora ran around New Olympus. By day she worked in Olivia's office, keeping tabs on the brilliant but hopeless Pig (Saturday morning she found him asleep at his desk, still clutching a Sugar Juice can), wrapping up things with Armand's party and linking her model clients with gigs. By night she first packed up her stuff for the move and unpacked herself at her new apartment before falling into an exhausted sleep.

She thought constantly of Marcus. Their talk at the coffee shop had shaken her. She was alone with her thoughts, too, since all her friends were busy—Olivia had headed off to the west coast "to shake down a supplier," her words, and Anna had been offered a role in Max Mars's newest feature film, so she was never around. Armand was off the table because he was in cahoots with Marcus, and Maeve was busy opening a second shelter location downtown.

And what else was there to say, really, even if Cora did have someone to talk to?

When she'd come to the big city, she'd been running

from her abusive mother and the smallness of farmhouse life. The move had been her chance to establish herself. Instead, she'd run straight into Marcus's arms and allowed herself to be absorbed into his already perfectly ordered life. Marcus lived in a dangerous world, one that forced him to maintain a high level of control just to survive. It was natural for him to order her the way he liked, too. On some level, she'd even liked him controlling her.

But he'd never truly let her be a part of his world. He wanted to lock her up like a princess in a tower. It didn't work like that, though. Being anywhere in his sphere meant you were swallowed in the darkness too.

And when she tried to help an innocent girl escape it... She shook her head as she unpacked her last box. She'd been fighting forces she didn't understand and had only made everything worse. So much worse.

So she'd run again, to give herself a second chance to order her own life the way she pleased. To live in the light, or try to.

Even though, after the confrontation in the coffee shop, she had the feeling that her reprieve was over, and her husband was going to start taking over her life again.

She couldn't let him. She would have to prove to him how strong she was, even living on her own.

It didn't matter that being near him was the only time she'd felt alive in months. It didn't matter that even now, her hand tingled with the memory of his touch. She ran her fingers over her palm.

All I want is you.

A shutter rocked her body at the memory of the burning intensity of his eyes... Gah! She shoved the box of toiletries away from her and stood up.

What was she doing? She moved out of the bathroom

and into the living room of her new loft apartment. A low *woof* greeted her and Brutus, the huge Great Dane mix puppy she'd adopted from the shelter after getting her apartment, all but bowled her over as he rushed over to meet her.

She laughed and scratched his head, crouching down. "Who's a good boy?"

Another happy woof.

She sighed, looking around her sparsely furnished apartment. She'd gotten most of her furniture off of BuyStuff.com and filled in the rest with thrift store finds. But she needed to get some rugs before it really felt cozy and like a home.

"Wanna go for a walk?"

Woof.

Cora smiled. "Okay, give me a second. I want to check my bank balance. We'll go by an ATM and stop by the farmer's market on the way home."

She grabbed Brutus's leash and opened up her laptop on the kitchen table. "Come here, boy," she patted her leg as she sat down and logged into her bank account to make sure her most recent paycheck had hit.

Brutus trotted towards her and she was busy attaching his leash, so at first she didn't see the balance. And when she glanced over back to the screen, she was sure she'd seen it wrong. But when she choked and dragged the laptop closer, nope, she saw that the huge number *was* her balance, even though it was larger than it ought to have been. Off by two numbers and a comma... She clicked to see more details.

Reading through the deposit history, she found her paycheck, looking pathetic sandwiched between two large sums transferred directly into her account.

From her husband's account.

She shot out of her chair so suddenly that Brutus barked twice. How dare Marcus? She was going to kill him. But a reaction was exactly what he was looking for. She paced back and forth, Brutus following at her heels. Of course he was, she was holding his leash.

She cringed. "Sorry, boy. Let's go for that walk."

She was still steamed half an hour later when they got back from the park. Especially since there had been two of Marcus's men shadowing them the entire time when normally there was only one.

And when she returned to the building, she noticed two more stern-faced men in black waiting outside her apartment. One of them had no neck.

"Really?" she sighed, shoving the keys in the lock.

One of them followed her in. "Mr. Ubeli would like you to stay close to us at all times. If you need to go somewhere, a car will be available for you."

"I don't care what Mr. Ubeli told you. I don't like being tailed. I want to feel normal. And I'm fine taking the bus."

She'd slammed the door in their face.

She fed Brutus and was getting herself some rice and vegetables when her phone rang. What now? To her surprise, though, she saw it was Anna.

"Hey, what's up?

"Cora! I feel like I haven't talked to you in forever. Everything's been so crazy with the movie and Max. But tomorrow is my first official day on set—and I was hoping for some moral support. I'm allowed to have an assistant. Will you come?"

"Let me check." Cora checked tomorrow's schedule on her phone. Nothing on the agenda. "Sure thing. I can come."

"Okay, great!" Anna squealed and gave her the details of when and where to meet her in the morning.

Cora heard a man's voice in the background and Anna giggled. "Okay, I gotta go. Max is here. But we'll talk tomorrow?"

"See you then." But Cora had barely gotten the words out before Anna hung up. Cora shook her head. *Young love.*

Then she laughed at herself. When had she gotten so old and jaded? She'd only recently turned twenty.

It was chilly so she lit a fire in the fireplace. She grabbed her laptop and worked in bed, already feeling it was going to be one of those nights when sleep wouldn't come.

THE FIRE HAD BURNED DOWN, leaving only the moon's cool glow. Cora kissed down her husband's bare chest, loving how the smooth muscles clenched under her lips. Marcus drew her back up and took her mouth while his fingers fucked her, sliding easily in and out of her wetness.

She hovered over him, eyelids fluttering with ecstasy. Marcus smiled his shark's grin. And then he took his hand from her and replaced it with his cock, slamming up into her. Her breath caught as she felt herself stretch around him.

"Say my name," Marcus whispered.

There was no other choice but to obey. There never had been.

"Marcus!" she cried, and shattered.

The orgasm woke her. Cora was still panting and clenching, her hands fisting the sheets even as her eyes popped open and she came back to consciousness.

Not real. It wasn't real.

She whimpered and clenched her thighs together, feeling terribly, terribly empty. She'd come but she'd never experienced a more unsatisfying climax in her life.

The ghost of Marcus was nothing compared to the real thing, no matter how genuine it felt in the dream. She wanted to cry in frustration. Maybe she should buy a vibrator. She rolled her eyes towards the ceiling. She had a feeling that nothing would satisfy her other than the real thing, though.

Ugh! She threw her sheets off and swung her legs out of bed.

At least she had going to see Anna to look forward to today. Cora could seriously use a distraction.

She dressed in what she hoped was an appropriate backstage outfit—comfortable low-heeled boots, tights, a skirt and a nerdy tee that Olivia had given her. She took Brutus out, immediately irritated when Marcus's men shadowed them far closer than normal. And after she brought Brutus back and fed both him and herself, there was a car waiting when she exited the building.

No Neck stood waiting patiently. "We're happy to take you wherever you need to go today, Mrs. Ubeli."

Normally she would take the bus. Normal people took the bus.

Whatever. If Marcus wanted his men to tail her, at least it meant she could provide car service for her friend.

She called Anna. "Don't worry about getting to work. I'll be by to pick you up in fifteen."

They picked up Anna outside Olivia's apartment building.

"Cora, it's amazing," Anna gushed. She was glowing. "Everything's falling into place. Just like I remember it."

"You used to act?"

"Small commercials and a few indie movies. My mom wanted me to be a famous actress."

"She'd be proud."

"Yeah." Anna looked out the window, quieting, her face sad. Feeling a little guilty, Cora reached out and squeezed her knee. Anna turned, her smile springing back into place. Cora felt the familiar rush of friendship.

As they approached the movie studio, a guard station slowed them.

"Anna Flores and my friend Cora." Anna rolled her own window down to show the paperwork. "I have passes for both of us."

"And these men?" The two guards at the station frowned at the two men in black sitting in the front seat.

Anna looked at Cora, who shrugged.

"I'm sorry," the guard said. "But they'll have to remain here."

"Mrs. Ubeli—" No Neck started but Cora had already opened her door and was stepping out.

"You heard the man, you can't go further," Cora sing-songed as she pulled Anna after her. Besides, it was a closed movie set. It wasn't like anyone could get at her here. She and Anna escaped the car and trotted quickly past the gate.

The Shades both opened the door to follow, but the movie set guards started yelling at them to stop. Cora glanced back. Her bodyguards weren't following, but No Neck had a frustrated look on his face. His phone was already out, and probably speed dialing her husband.

"Still fighting with Marcus?" Anna murmured.

"Irreconcilable differences."

Anna lifted an eyebrow as they walked through one warehouse and another, passing people carrying lumber and tools.

"It's great that the set is so close to home and not on the west coast." Cora saw two men struggling to move a giant ornate staircase on wheels.

'I'll probably end up finishing the film there, but they want some outdoor action scenes with the natural background. And they got a huge tax credit for doing it here."

As they entered the next warehouse, Cora felt her purse start to vibrate angrily. Probably Marcus. No doubt that No Neck had tattled on her. She pulled out the burner phone and silenced it without answering.

People bustled all around them. The craft services table was filled with pastries, fruit trays and coffee. Cora and Anna helped themselves to hot drinks and wandered out into the activity.

"There he is." Anna nodded towards Max Mars. He was handsome, tall, and well-built, but too...well, *pretty* for Cora's tastes. He matched Anna perfectly, though. He flashed a smile and headed right for them.

"Hey," he said in his signature sexy voice.

"Hola, Papi." Anna's smile curved her red lips as she went right up to him and hugged him. Holy crap, Anna was hugging one of the biggest movie stars on the planet! He might not be Cora's type but that didn't mean she wasn't still starstruck.

Max smiled down at Anna, the suppressed desire obvious between them. Cora could almost see the sparks flying, their desire for each other was so obvious. But they didn't kiss, just wound one arm around each other's waist, as if posing for a picture of the most perfect couple ever.

"This is my friend, Cora," Anna said and Max Mars turned his mega-watt smile on her. His infamous dimple popped out, leaving Cora totally dazzled. She opened her mouth, then closed it, speechless at seeing the beautiful man up close. He had adorably tousled hair and wore a t-shirt that read, "I do all my own stunts."

Still a little dazed by being so close to a celebrity, she said the first thing that popped into her head, "Do you really?" She motioned to the shirt, "Do all your own stunts?"

She expected a facetious answer in response, but instead Max Mars puffed out his already impressive chest. "Yeah," he said his voice deepening a little. "I do all my own stunts. Like, all of them."

Tucked into Max Mar's side, Anna shook her head slightly and mouthed, "No."

Cora looked back and forth between them, not sure who to believe.

"Alright, I gotta rehearse." Max looked down at Anna and gave her a squeeze.

"Okay, baby," Anna said almost too softly for anyone else to hear. Cora looked away; the way the two looked at each other, she wanted to give them privacy. Averting her eyes, she waited until Anna cleared her throat. They both watched Max leave, a real treat considering the way his pants hugged his perfect backside.

"He's really…"

"Full of himself?" Anna finished. "Yeah. But he's a big star. And one of his upcoming films will probably get him nominated for a Golden Idol."

"I was going to say you guys look great together."

Anna beamed. "Oh we do. Should be great for the press conferences."

"So, wait, are you seeing him or is it a publicity stunt?"

"Both." Anna led her to some seats on the side of the set.

Hours later, Cora concluded that film sets were incredibly boring. Anna sat upright and totally focused on everything in front of her, as if the camera man moving for the billionth time was the most fascinating thing ever.

Cora was almost relieved when a production assistant came up to Anna. "Max Mars would like to see you in his trailer."

Cora took her cue. "You go ahead," she told her friend. "I'm going to catch a ride back to the city. I can come back to pick you up."

"I think I can catch a ride from someone." Anna's smile curved knowingly. "Don't worry about me."

Cora was walking back off set, wondering if the Shades would be parked somewhere nearby or if she really did need to catch a ride, when a voice called, "Mrs. Ubeli?"

She almost didn't turn, but a car slid up beside her and a man in a suit leaned through the driver side window, smiling. "Cora?"

Her steps slowed. Was he a Shade? He had spiky blond hair and looked vaguely familiar, but her instincts told her to be cautious.

"Do I know you?" she asked the stranger and he grinned bigger. Something was off. The windows of the car were all tinted. None of Marcus's cars were.

She noticed this at the same time the back doors opened and two thugs came at her. "If you come with us quietly, we won't hurt you."

Opening her mouth to scream, Cora tripped and lost precious seconds she could've used to escape. One of the men jabbed her neck in a gesture almost too quick for her to see, and her scream came out a painful gurgle.

She choked and they took their opportunity to wrestle her into the back seat of the car. Kicking at them, she got in a few blows before one of the men slid next to her and caught her legs. No! She couldn't let them take her. She fought harder than ever.

But the other man came around the car, got in on the other side, and the two of them together subdued her easily. The man with blond spikes watched from the front seat.

By now Cora had caught her breath, and she screamed. Please, someone hear her! The movie set had been bursting with people. But now all the car windows were closed. And they must have been soundproof as well as tinted, because her three kidnappers didn't seem upset at her screaming.

They took their time tying her arms behind her back. One wrapped his hands around her throat, cutting off her air until spots swam before her eyes. Her ears were ringing, and she didn't know if she was still screaming or not. All she knew was that she couldn't breathe. Couldn't breathe.

Was this it? Was she going to die right here? *Oh Marcus. It wasn't supposed to end this way. I never meant to...*

She kicked out again but weakly. It was no use. Spots danced before her eyes.

Dimly, she heard the driver cursing at the thugs, who growled back.

The world went black.

TEN

WHEN CORA CAME TO, her head was lying in one of the men's lap. She started struggling immediately, but her hands and feet were bound. The man hauled her up to sit properly and she looked around. Her heart sank.

They were nowhere near the studio anymore, but driving down a large boulevard lined with abandoned and decrepit shops. She didn't recognize anything. She had no idea where they were. Wherever it was, though, the area seemed largely devoid of human life. She didn't see pedestrians around or anyone who might be able to help her.

The driver's face swam into focus as she blinked and looked around.

"We don't want to hurt you," said the spiky-haired blond man who was driving. "Do as we say and you'll be fine."

Cora wanted to speak but her throat hurt. She caught a glimpse of herself in the rearview mirror. Her neck already showed bruises. Oh gods, what would these men do to her once they got where they were going? She had to get out of here.

She squirmed in her bonds, jerking her arms and trying to drive an elbow into one of the silent thugs flanking her. He caught it easily and looked down at her, face scary and blank. The pit of acid that was her stomach threatened to rebel.

"Behave, or I send men back to find that little spic hottie and make her pay," Spike Hair warned from upfront.

Cora froze. She had no idea who these men were or if they had the power to make good on that threat. But the truth was, they'd bound her too well. Even if she could manage to disable one of them, she couldn't run anywhere, not with her ankles tied together like this.

Still, she made a point to glare at the driver in defiance until he turned back to steer the car. The men on either side of her were silent, and beyond light touches on her arms to steady her, at least they kept their hands to themselves.

From the position of the sun, Cora realized they were heading south and a little east to a place below the city of New Olympus used mainly for shipping. They approached the large docks and Cora recognized the border to an area of the city called the Styx. They were close to the territory her husband controlled. She felt a surge of hope.

The car went through gates into a fenced area. Beyond the vacant dock and warehouse, Cora caught glimpses of the ocean. When they parked, she got another warning to stay silent, but now she realized the futility of struggling. They were in a wasteland of deserted commercial buildings by the docks. There would be no one to hear her scream.

Instead, she said to Spike Hair, "You know who I am, so I'm guessing you know who my husband is." Her voice was still raspy from that bastard strangling her earlier. It probably would be for a while.

One of the silent thugs took her arm as a warning, but Spike Hair nodded.

"So you know what he does to people who threaten me." Marcus might not be here at the moment but he could still be her shield.

"We're not threatening you. Our boss wants to talk." Spike Hair motioned and they cut the tape binding her ankles and propelled her forward towards a building beyond the parking lot, into a hanger large enough to fit two small planes.

Stiffening her legs, Cora resisted a little but her captors simply dragged her along. Her boots scraped across the ground. A wild thought gripped her—at least she'd worn the perfect outfit to be kidnapped, durable and comfy. She hoped their boss would approve. A laugh started to bubble out of her and caught in her dry, bruised throat. She wheezed and felt lightheaded.

They got her halfway across before she got her feet back under her, and worked up enough air in her lungs to ask, "Who's your boss?"

Spike Hair simply led the group to the stairs on the side of the building, up into a finished office, and she saw for herself who'd ordered her abduction. She gasped.

Philip Waters wore a pinstripe suit, looking equal parts dapper and intimidating, if not more so, with the sun shining through the great windows over his giant form.

"Cora Ubeli." He smiled, white teeth gleaming in his midnight skin. He came forward, greeting her like an old friend. She would have stopped in her tracks but the thugs prodded her forward. As the giant man came closer his gaze dropped to her collar bone and he sighed. "I said no force."

"She fought." Spike Hair held up her burner phone. "Her link to Ubeli."

"Which can be traced, you fool," Waters rumbled. Cora trembled and felt the fear really start to sink in, even though his anger wasn't directed at her. This man was extremely dangerous. What would he do to her? His bald head jerked as he ordered, "Get rid of it."

She wasn't sure if she felt terror or satisfaction as she watched Spike Hair scurry off. She was alone with the two thugs and her terrifying 'host.'

"Apologies, Mrs. Ubeli. I promise, no more harm will come to you." Said the spider to the fly.

Licking her lips, she found her throat was too dry to answer him. She nodded instead.

"Can I offer you a drink?" Philip asked. He walked back to the windows where a few modern looking couches were arranged around a bar area. The ocean spread out behind him. "Something to soothe your throat, perhaps?"

"How about a ride home to my apartment?"

He glanced up at her from the bottle he was pouring, and her heart seized. A grin spread across his face and he laughed. "In due time, my lady."

So that meant he didn't mean to murder her where she stood? He and Marcus had looked at each other with such hatred at that party... But if this was a game, her best bet was to start playing along. She couldn't run or fight anyway. If he liked her enough to laugh, maybe he wouldn't kill her. Either way, she shouldn't show fear. A predator would sense that weakness. Marcus had taught her that much.

She held her head high as she walked forward and took one of the seats at the bar.

Waters poured different things into a glass and handed to her. She sipped politely, glad to taste something like a hot toddy.

"Are you turning this into a restaurant?" She looked

around the large empty space with the one corner developed.

"Not a bad concept."

"The view is nice." She stared out at the ocean, wondering if she stood in the far corner and looked to the left, she'd see a way to escape down the built-up shore to the docks near the Styx.

"Ah, yes, my favorite. I was born on a ship, you know. I'm the son of illegal immigrants, who were smuggling themselves into the country. I received dual citizenship because of it. My first lucky break."

He offered his own drink and after a second, she clinked it. A kidnapper and kidnappee, hanging out, drinking like two old friends.

"It's a little late, but I want you to know I was intending to return your calls," she offered. "Your voicemail got deleted from my phone."

The white teeth were back with his grin. He reminded her of a shark. "I understand, lovely lady. I was happy to wait, but forces beyond my control moved up my timeline."

She stared at her drink, willing her hands not to shake. "So, you want a consult?"

"That won't be necessary at this juncture. For now, I simply wish the pleasure of your company. In a few hours, we'll be meeting with your husband, who is eager to trade for your release." His voice was smooth as silk

Aha. So that's why she was here. She'd been used like this before. AJ had used her as a hostage to force Marcus to reveal the location of the shipping container. And look how that had turned out.

She'd tried to escape the dark but it kept pulling her back under. Maybe this was her penance.

Now she stared at Philip Waters, taking in his calm,

controlled demeanor. She wanted to ask what was going on, but didn't want to anger him. Did he know what was coming for him? Marcus didn't look kindly on people who took what he considered his.

Deciding to keep with her plan to be the best hostage ever, she asked instead, "A few more hours?" She looked out at the sun, biting her lip and thinking of Brutus whining, all alone in her apartment and wondering where she was.

"Our meeting is at dusk. Is there something you need?"

"My dog is in my apartment all alone...he'll need to be walked. He's a puppy."

"We'll send word that someone needs to take care of him." Waters assured her.

Cora blinked at him, her eyebrows furrowing. "Thank you."

He chuckled. "Your concern is for your dog and not your own life?"

"I can do something about my dog. I can't stop you from doing anything to me." She squeezed her hands between her legs to stop her tremors.

"Practical as well as lovely," Waters toasted her and she looked up, surprised, into his dark brown eyes. "Marcus is a very lucky man."

Continuing the most surreal conversation she'd had in her life, she blurted, "We're separated. I asked for a divorce."

Waters cocked his beautiful head. "Interesting. He made no mention of that in our last conversation."

"I told him I wanted a divorce. I've moved into my own apartment and started a business and everything." She didn't know why she was telling him this.

The door opened and they both watched Spike Hair

walk back in. "Meet at six thirty. They agreed to every demand."

Water looked at Cora smugly. "Despite everything, your husband still cares for you deeply. Two months trying to schedule a meet and no success. Two hours after picking you up and he gives me everything I want."

She sagged in her seat; she couldn't help it. She was Marcus's weakness; everyone knew it. She needed to separate from him for his good as well as hers. But now that the criminal world associated them together, would it be too late?

Waters had come out from behind the bar to give orders to his men. Cora turned when she heard her name. "Cora's dog will need to be walked." He looked back at Cora and she forced a small smile.

"Why do you want to meet with my husband?" she asked when the men had gone. Maybe this man could give her the answers that Marcus never would.

Waters gave her a puzzled frown.

"Some parts of his business he keeps from me."

"Ah," he chuckled. "Perhaps this is the reason for your marital dispute?"

That hit a little too close to home, so she said nothing. Philip Waters seemed tickled by this, and Cora was glad, because it made him only too happy to share.

"He owes me money. Quite a lot of it actually. We had an agreement. Now we have a... disagreement. I'm confident it can be settled without too much bloodshed." Cora cringed. *Too much?*

"It would help, actually, if you encouraged him to talk with me." He said the last part eagerly, as if recruiting her as an ally would make her forget all the trouble he'd caused.

Still, Cora pondered it. "Is my husband in danger?"

"Not from me. Not if I get what I want." A smile played around his lips. "For someone who wants to divorce your husband, you seem to care for him an awful lot."

She didn't answer.

ELEVEN

Marcus would kill Philip Waters for this. The man had no excuse. He knew the Code. Women and children were left out of their business.

But there was no honor left in the world and Marcus should have known it. He shouldn't have given Cora a choice in that damn coffee shop. He should have thrown her over his shoulder and dragged her to the safe house with him. How many times would he make the same mistake? He'd never have the chance to win her over if she was dead.

His hands fisted and he wanted to break something, preferably Philip Waters' face. But not yet. Not until he saw Cora safe and sound. Marcus strode behind Waters along the docks, Sharo at his back.

"If only you'd been reasonable and taken my request for a meeting," Waters said, "it would never have come to this. Why don't we discussed terms and then I'll take you to her?"

"You're not getting jack shit until I see her," Marcus growled, hands flexing.

Waters sighed. "This way." He led them into a large

warehouse. "Here she is," rumbled Waters. "Safe and unharmed."

Safe?

One of Waters' thugs was holding a gun to her temple and she was pale, her eyes wide with fear.

"I want to speak to her." Marcus kept his voice tight and controlled. If that idiot holding the gun had even the tiniest slip of his finger... Marcus's chest went cold with rage and a terror he didn't want to examine too closely.

"Be my guest," Waters said. "Let's sit, shall we?" He gestured towards a long table.

Marcus didn't take his eyes off Cora. The bastard with the gun to her head shoved her forward until she sat at one end of the table and Waters gestured for Marcus to sit at the other end. Sharo stood behind Marcus, along with two more Shades.

Waters himself took a seat right beside Cora. Another man bent down to chain her ankle to the table. Marcus's fingers itched to riddle them all with bullets.

"Are you okay?" he asked Cora, ignoring everyone else in the room.

She nodded shakily, attempting a smile and failing. "Mr. Waters just wants to talk. He's assured me that once you hear him out, he'll let me go."

Were those bruises around her neck? Marcus clenched his teeth so hard he thought they might crack.

Don't think about it right now. Just get her out of here. Get her to safety. You weren't too late this time. You can still save her.

Marcus fought down the rage bubbling inside him and set the large briefcase he'd brought with him on the table.

"Let's do this," he told Waters, not taking his eyes off Cora.

Waters didn't beat around the bush. "This is a hostile meeting and you know why we're here. And yet, my hopes were for us to continue to do business with one another."

"Negotiation ends when you snatch one of ours. We leave family out of it."

"Ah yes, your Code. Well, I haven't harmed her, she's spent a quiet afternoon and is returning to you safe and sound." Philip smiled at Cora as if she was sitting down at a meal, not a tense business negotiation with a gun to her head. "Like you, I merely want what's mine."

"The bruises on her neck say different," Marcus couldn't help growling.

Waters frowned. "An unfortunate miscommunication with my men. It was never my intention for any harm to come to her as long as our business concludes on good terms."

Every word coming out of Waters' mouth only made Marcus feel more murderous. He shoved the briefcase and it slid down the long shiny table. It stopped only inches from Waters' hand. Marcus watched Cora stare as the man opened it and checked the multiple stacks of large bills. The tension in the room heightened as Waters closed the briefcase, locked it and handed it off to one of his men.

"You've delivered, I've delivered," Philip waved a hand at Cora. "Now, we talk. We will be nothing less than civil; you have my word."

Marcus barely stopped himself from scoffing out loud. "That held weight up until the moment you took my wife. Now, your word means nothing to me."

"It meant something to your father." Waters folded his hands in front of him, his expression respectful.

"That cash is for Cora's safe return. It has nothing to do with our business arrangement."

"And yet I don't think of it as a ransom, but as you settling up the debt you owe me." The temperature in the room plunged to subzero as Waters continued. "The original terms of our agreement was that we'd deliver the first shipment and receive payment. Instead, in return for our delivery, we received nothing but a formal governmental inquiry into our behavior in international waters."

"Terms changed when the police seized the shipment. You agreed to the change."

Cora sat up straighter, obviously realizing Waters was referring to the night with AJ on the docks. The last time Marcus had failed her and put her life in danger.

"Yes, and then we reviewed things more carefully. We planned that meeting for months. You assured me there would be no trouble. I can only assume you or your silent partner didn't do your job." Philip Waters paused and took a deep breath. Cora's bowed head and her shoulders hunched as Waters grew angry beside her. Marcus had to de-escalate this and fast. He didn't want Cora any more traumatized than she already was.

"The events of that night were...regrettable," Marcus said, keeping his voice calm and taking back control of the conversation.

"And your responsibility," Waters insisted.

"I am willing to accept the blame." Marcus inclined his head, allowing Waters the point if only to drain the tension level in the room. Still, he couldn't help a caveat. "At least, until I know more about what really went down that night."

"That's all well and good," Waters said, his impatience rising to the surface again, "but we're receiving new reports that worry us. There's evidence that the shipment in question has already been distributed, without us getting a cut."

What? What was he talking about?

"There's been no distribution—not by my men."

"Someone is selling it, because people are buying a drug that sounds a lot like ours. If anything, this advance release proves how popular the drug will be."

Marcus narrowed his eyes. "What do you want, Waters?"

"You have one week to prove the drugs are in your custody and you're back in control of distribution. If not, I will be forced to find other investors and distribution channels. I'm sure you agree it's in our best interest to find the best partner who can deliver."

"There's only one player who can deliver in the New Olympus market. You're looking at him." Marcus stared Waters down, but the big man shrugged. His large fingers, bare but for his onyx ring, drummed the table.

"I'm being courted by a few others, and one group is especially eager. I'm notifying you out of courtesy, because if we choose to use them, the money they make off this deal may fund an incursion into your territory."

Sharo spoke for the first time, but not to Waters. "He talking about who I think he's talking about?" he asked the room in general, his deep voice echoing.

"I am, in fact," Waters said. "If you can't provide me with what I want, I must seek other partners. And they very well maybe your sworn enemies, the Titans."

Cora's eyes widened just a fraction but otherwise she stayed still.

Marcus kept his face bored. Few knew of his wife's connection to the Titans—that she was Demi Titan's daughter—and he preferred it stay that way. "The Titans haven't been in this market for over a decade. I should know. I drove them out."

"And they're anxious to use their prior knowledge to

rebuild." Philip spread his large hands as if to say, *What can I do?*

"You don't want to deal with them any more than we want to," Sharo said.

"On the contrary, they don't hold a grudge against me." Waters was playing with his onyx ring again, twisting it.

"Give them time," Sharo said, his voice heated.

Marcus took over. "They won't be satisfied with letting you rule the water. They want it all." Back in the day, the Titans (secretly led by Demi) had been ravenous for power and territory at any cost. Now that she was back in charge, she would suffer no challengers if she had her way. "And they don't operate by a Code. One day you'll want out, and you'll regret ever doing business with them."

"Given that you've been negotiating in bad faith, I'm not sure that I can trust a word you say." Waters looked at Marcus. "Your father was honest. I'd hoped more of his son."

Marcus glared the man down. "This meeting is over. You have your money. Give me my wife."

Waters nodded, rising. The men down the table did too. Cora remained sitting, the gun still on her. "I'm sure you have enough courage to take on me and the Titans. But think of the price you might pay." He looked pointedly at Cora.

He dared threaten Cora to Marcus's face? On top of all he'd already done? He was a dead man walking.

"Let her go," Marcus ordered darkly.

Waters tossed a key on the table. "Free for the taking."

Marcus was moving forward even as Waters left with his crew. Swiping the key, he knelt beside Cora to unlock the shackle.

"You alright? We gotta go." He helped her up and

hustled her to the far door. She trembled on his arm but he didn't dare stop. Waters definitely had eyes and guns on them still. Once they exited the warehouse, they were immediately surrounded by Shades, but Marcus didn't breathe easy until they were in a black SUV headed out of the parking lot.

More than anything, Marcus wanted to immediately send his men after Waters for daring to touch what was his, for making her tremble in fear. He wrapped his arm around Cora and pulled her close to his side. She didn't resist at all, that was how fucking scared she was. Fury beat like an ugly creature with wings in his rib cage

Sharo turned in the passenger seat and looked back at him. "You gonna order the hit?"

Marcus glared at him. He knew better than to talk about business like that in front of Cora. Sharo nodded and turned back around front.

Marcus put two hands on Cora's shoulders and bent his head to hers. "He touch you?"

She curled her hands around his and looked into his eyes. Gods, it was everything to touch her. To be this close again.

"No. He was polite, actually."

She dropped her hands as he cupped her head, tilting it gently to study the marks those fuckers had made on her neck. His hand hovered over her pulse but he didn't dare brush the bruises marring her skin. The beast in his chest roared.

"They'll pay," he growled. "I'll make them pay for every bruise."

"I'm okay."

"They had a gun to your head."

Cora bit her lip. "I think...I think he wanted this

meeting to go well."

Marcus's mouth tightened but he didn't say anything. He didn't trust himself at the moment and he didn't want to scare her any further. His family and Waters had long been allies but after today, they could be nothing but enemies.

Cora frowned and grabbed his hand. "It's my fault."

What was she going on about now?

She clutched his hand tighter. "I slipped my guard at the movie set." Swallowing hard, she went on. "If I hadn't, they'd never have been able to take me."

Fuck but she was sweet. Too good for him, but he'd known that a long time now. She was looking down so he nudged her face up with a finger under her chin. When she still kept her eyes averted, he moved closer to her, pulling her legs over his lap. She resisted only a moment.

"Waters and me have been dancin' a long time." He shifted, lifting her into his lap. Maybe he was a bastard to use this to steal a moment of intimacy with her, but after getting Waters' call and hearing she'd been snatched, he needed her close. Apparently she needed it too because she leaned into him.

He kept his voice soft as he murmured into her hair. "Taking you was his way of getting my attention. Now that he has it, we'll see what he does."

"So you're not mad at me?" she whispered, so soft like she was aware of everyone else in the car and wanted only him to hear.

"Mad? No. But every time you run," his arms squeezed her, "I get tempted to kidnap you myself and tie you to the bed."

She swallowed hard and her breath hitched. Maybe because underneath her, he was getting hard. He couldn't help it. Having her so close, her soft, delectable body finally in contact with his. Plus after the showdown with Waters and the relief of finally having her back safe in his arms—he was only a man.

She obviously felt it but she didn't pull away. Sighing, she tucked herself under his chin, relaxing only when his arms slowly came back around to hold her. It was the most peaceful Marcus had felt in months. This was right. This was as things should be. Together, they watched New Olympus's skyline loom closer.

When the car entered the city limits, she stirred. "Where are you taking me?"

"Somewhere safe—" Marcus started, and her body suddenly went stiff as she yanked away from him. "No, I want to go home."

"We need to—"

"Don't take me to the Estate." She gripped the fabric of his shirt. "I don't care where else you take me, just don't make me go back there."

Was this a clue as to what had happened *that night*? Had AJ actually dared to steal her off of Marcus's own fucking family estate? But how? Marcus had interviewed the guards on watch that night a dozen times over. He gazed at Cora, waiting for her to give more away.

But she suddenly looked around as if realizing how still and silent the entire car had gone. She let go of Marcus's shirt and looked out the window, shutting him out.

He wanted to press her. He wanted to know what had happened that night. But she'd been through another trauma and it would have to wait.

"Alright." He ordered the driver to head toward The Chariot Club instead.

Cora looked back at him. "Okay. But once we get there, we're going to talk."

TWELVE

Once there, Marcus guided Cora to a private room in the back. Usually he came here for weekly poker nights with his associates and key lieutenants. A spread of food lay on the long table, reminiscent of the one they'd left.

Marcus and Sharo left her for a moment to speak with Shades in low voices. They came back in and sat down.

Cora sat and waited. It felt like old times—Marcus off doing business while she waited for him.

She took a deep breath and decided she wasn't going to wait anymore. When Marcus turned from speaking to his men, she was standing in the door, arms folded.

His eyes warmed as he approached her, but her next words stopped him cold. "What's my mother up to? What's happening with the Titans?"

She watched, fascinated, as the mask slammed down over his features. She was so used to seeing him unguarded with her that watching him face her like she was one of his enemies was novel. Fascinating, even.

He moved into her, herding her back into the room with

his body. She let him, even sitting in the seat he pulled out for her.

"Have you eaten?" He didn't wait for an answer before filling a plate from the family style dishes on the table. "You need to eat." He set the plate in front of her, full of chicken verdicchio. Her mouth watered; it did smell good.

Instead, she picked up her fork and pointed it at him. "You wanted me to talk to you. I'm here, listening. So talk. Tell me what I'm up against."

She couldn't be the girl who stuck her head in the sand anymore. She still wanted nothing to do with Marcus's world. But it didn't look like his world was going to let go of her so easily. If she was going to live in the light, she had to be aware of the shadows and how to avoid them.

Taking his own plate, Marcus sat next to her right, between her and the door. A slight smile quirked his lips. "And to think you were once a meek, country mouse."

He started eating, arching an eyebrow and nodding toward her own plate. She wouldn't get anything more out of him until he got his way, so she crammed food in her mouth. The second she did, flavor exploded on her tongue.

A moan of pleasure must have escaped her lips, because Marcus bumped her elbow intentionally, and she turned into the full on blaze of his smile. Her mouth nearly dropped open at the sight of it. Instead, she gulped down her food and mumbled, "It's really good."

"Two months without Gio's cooking. You were due." He rested his hand on her knee, which sent electric little tingles straight to her core. Her body fell into old habits whenever she was around him. Her eyes fell closed. She should move her leg away. And she would. In another minute. Or five.

Gah, what was wrong with her?

She pulled her knee away from Marcus's touch. "Tell me about my mother."

He let out a long-suffering sigh.

"I was gonna shield you from this—"

"Wake up, Marcus, it's not working," she said, a little surprised at her own forthrightness. Olivia's bluntness was rubbing off on her. Marcus went still, a sign he was surprised, too. Cora put her hand over his, damning herself for the action because the electricity was back. Still, she didn't let go.

"You're not one hundred percent to blame. I've been trying to keep my head in the sand. But it's not working for me anymore and I need to stop. What's going on? I'm tired of being in the dark."

"Waters put you in the middle of this," Marcus growled. "He's a dead man."

Cora felt a chill; she knew all too well that he would make good on that promise. The image of AJ's limp and disfigured body flashed through her head. And the sound of the wet saw as they prepared to cut him into pieces to send back to the Titans as a 'message'. She'd never forget the sound of the wet saw cutting through the night air.

The food didn't seem so appetizing anymore. She pushed her plate away, and taking a deep breath, she looked up and met Marcus's gaze.

"I'm involved no matter what. Being married to you comes with a price. Not just late nights and hanging around men with guns, or the chance that I might get shot at while eating in a restaurant. I have to be a player too, and you're keeping information from me."

"It's not your fight."

"Marcus, what I don't know *will* hurt me. I don't know

what to look for, I don't know who the threat is. I don't know who your enemies are."

"You shouldn't have to worry about those things." The vein in his forehead was visible, a sure sign that he didn't like what she was saying.

Too bad. It was the truth. He thought he could control everything but as much as he might like to pretend otherwise, he wasn't a god. He couldn't see everything at once, be everywhere at once.

"You treat me like a child, but I'm not a child. I'm a grown woman. You married a *woman* and I need to know what we are facing."

"She's right," Sharo put in. Cora turned to him, blinking. She never expected support from his corner. Marcus glared at him but the large man could take the heat. "She's not reckless because she's stupid. She's just ignorant."

"Thank you," Cora told him and frowned. "I think."

Marcus glared at them both. "Another reason I don't want you involved. You get picked up by the cops, you can deny everything."

She scoffed and tossed her hands in the air. "Marcus, I know Santonio has a stable of women. I know the DePetri brother's run shipments of contraband up and down the coast. I don't know what Rosco's men sell on the streets, but my guess is they'd sell anything you want."

He looked like he wanted to interrupt so she continued before he could, "We have dinner with them; they talk, and so do their girls. I'm not an idiot. I can put the pieces together."

Marcus pushed his chair forward, getting right in her face.

"You don't get my business. It doesn't *touch* you," he slammed a pointed finger on the table. "You stay clean."

Maybe before, she would've felt intimidated. But not now. Not after all they'd been through together, the good and the bad and the ugly.

"No," she shook her head vehemently. "You don't get to make this decision for me anymore. I want to know. If you don't tell me, then I never want to see you again."

But he shook his head, too. Stubborn as ever. "You stay clean. My father always kept my mother out of it. When things got deeper, she had his back, but she only knew the surface."

"And look how well that turned out for her!"

Marcus shot back in his chair as if she'd slapped him. She might as well have.

She cringed and ran a tired hand down her face. She was a horrible person to throw his mother's death in his face like that. "Marcus, I— I'm sorry. I should never have—" She shook her head. "I can't do this."

She stood up, her chair shoving back, and ran for the staff bathroom. She couldn't handle being in the same room as him anymore. It was too hard. This was all too fucking hard.

Burying one's head in the sand had a bad rap. It was a great plan, really. Coming up for air, now that was the stupidest idea she'd had in a long time.

She slammed the bathroom door shut behind her and let out a deep breath. She walked to the sink and turned the faucets on full blast. She leaned over and splashed her face. Again and again and again.

But she couldn't get clean. She could never get fucking clean. No matter how many times she scrubbed her body top to bottom. Sometimes she took showers so hot her skin blistered, but still it didn't come off. Iris's blood had seeped through Cora's pores down to her bones. She'd never be clean of it.

She didn't hear the door open at first, not until it slammed into the wall.

Her eyes lifted to the grimy mirror and there was Marcus, shoving the door shut with as much force as he'd opened it with. "Wha—?"

But she didn't have time to finish her half-formed question or anything else, because before she could even turn off the water faucets, Marcus had crossed the space between him and had her in his arms.

He pushed her up against the wall and cradled her face roughly in his hands.

"I will never let what happened to my mother happen to you. Never." His hands shook, and in the raw pain in his face she could see it.

Holy gods. He'd been right.

She really *had* held the power all along.

Oh Marcus.

How was he breaking her heart when she didn't have any left to break? She wanted to wrap her arms around him. He looked so lost.

"I wanted you to be clean," he whispered.

"Then you don't want me!" She tried to shove him away but he didn't let her.

And the next moment, his lips were crashing down on hers. She grabbed his shoulders, not sure if she was trying to tug him closer or shove him away. But by the next moment, she was surging up to tiptoe, moaning into his mouth, and giving as good as she got.

Her hips pushed frantically at his, her right leg hooking around his hips so she could press her pelvis closer. She wanted, needed to be close to him as if he was her second half. When he was inside her, she became whole.

This, finally, wasn't a dream and she'd never needed it more.

"Cora," Marcus's groan was deep and feral, ripped from the depths of his heart. He palmed her head, fingers tangled in her wild hair. "I need..."

His eyes were wide, pupils blown. His chest rose and fell, the bellows of his lungs pumping as he teetered on the edge of control. Cora nodded frantically, helping him claw up her skirt. She needed, too.

With a jerk, Marcus's large hand tore her stockings to shreds. Somehow she undid the button on his pants and unzipped them enough for Marcus to shove them down. And she was up, feet leaving the ground, legs twining around Marcus's lean hips as he drove into her, bracing them both against the wall.

She writhed, adjusting to his great girth, scrabbling at his broad shoulders to pull him closer. He propped her higher, letting gravity slide her further onto his thick length, and she cried out as his cock his spots inside her she'd forgotten existed.

He filled her beyond limit, invading more than her body. She felt him in every corner of herself, in her very soul.

Her eyes watered with the intimacy. It felt so right. She hated to love this powerful, infuriating man, but she'd never stopped needing him.

"Cora," Marcus's brow wrinkled at the sight of her tears.

"More," she ordered. "I need more."

With a groan, he thrust hard enough to bang her head on the wall. A shelf above them shuddered. A vase fell and shattered on the floor. Cora didn't care. Neither apparently did Marcus. Shards of glass crunching under his shoes, Marcus's only reaction was to carry her to the opposite wall. He gripped her bottom, angling her body to slam his cock deeper.

It was coming, oh, *oh!* It was coming. Every muscle in Cora's body spasmed as her orgasm shot through her. Her hand flung out, smacking the hand towel dispenser. With a whirring sound, the dispenser started spitting paper wipes in a long line.

"Fuck, Cora, fuck," Marcus shouted over the dispenser's whine. She was moaning, her body drawn taut as a bow. Before she snapped she buried her hands in his dark, silky hair, hanging on for dear life as her orgasm crashed around her.

More paper towels poured out of the dispenser in a white flood, filling the sink. They triggered the soap dispenser, which squirted into the sink, causing the water faucet to start pouring.

Marcus slapped his hand on the wall beside Cora's head, growling through his climax. "Fuck me. That was—"

"Yeah," Cora panted. Her body trembled in the wake of pleasure. The world was spinning too fast.

Her husband rested his head beside hers, his eyes closed. Beyond him, water gushed into the sink, soaking the paper towels, threatening to overflow onto the floor. The dispenser was still whirring. Soap squirted again and again, coating the glass shards with scented bubbles.

Marcus and Cora raised their heads at the same time to take in the destruction of the small room.

"Fuck," Marcus swore again, resigned. He carried her to the far corner, away from the broken glass.

"Typical," Cora muttered, wriggling away as soon as her

feet touched the floor. She wrenched down her skirt. The stockings were a lost cause. She tore the remains off. She sighed. Being with him like this again... It felt good, she couldn't deny it. Great even. And after everything that had happened with Waters...she'd been so afraid when those gangsters had kidnapped her. She'd needed the reassurance of Marcus's touch.

But it didn't change anything. She looked around them and shook her head. "This is why we shouldn't be together. We're like...fire and dynamite. We destroy everything we touch."

"We're certainly explosive," Marcus said mildly. He tore off a clean sheet of paper, offering it to her. "But Cora, we belong together. I'd lock you in this room, if I could."

Couldn't he see? "That's not going to work for me, Marcus. If I have your back, I need to know who I'm backing. And I need to know what monsters are out in the darkness, so I can help defend us. So I can help fight."

His deep eyes stared into hers, pulling her into unfathomable darkness.

"You think that when your enemies come for me they're going to spare me because you never told me about them? I'm the weak link, Marcus. I don't want to be anymore."

"Fine." He sighed. "You want to know my enemies. I'll give you the list."

Her eyes widened; he was actually going to share?

"I don't need to know everything, Marcus. Maybe start with the major players and work down from there," she suggested.

His mouth twitched, and for a moment he looked like he would laugh. "Gods, I forgot," he said.

"What?"

"How cute you are."

"Marcus. The list."

"You know Philip Waters. Started in shipping, now owns the largest privately held fleet in the world. Ships oil and goods all over the world. My father helped him get his start, financed some of his first shipments, back when New Olympus was a major port."

"So what's the shipment?" She already knew what it was, but she wanted to know if Marcus would tell her the truth finally.

"Drugs. Something new. Supposed to be more benign than coke."

"Didn't they say that about heroin?" She pushed out of the bathroom, needing to be out of the small space.

The back room was as empty as they'd left it, their food untouched.

Marcus watched her pace. "You see why I didn't want to tell you."

"I know the business you're in. Better I find out from you than someone else, or worse, just catch a stray bullet."

He came after her, caught her in his arms. "Never, ever joke about that." He gave her a little shake.

She put her hands on his arms. "You made your bed. I married you. We both lie in it."

"I live by a Code. And if I didn't control the drug market, someone else would. We sell to adults, not kids. The Shades are disciplined; if anyone else moves in, things would get worse. It'd be war."

"The Titans," she said, searching his face. "My mother and uncles. They want to move in."

Marcus swore. He let her go, but she cupped his face with both hands. "Tell me."

"If we don't deliver Waters' shipment and his cut of our take, he'll bring his business to the Titans."

"Can you stop them?"

"Not if they ally with Waters. If that happens, things get ugly."

"What's ugly?" Cora asked, even though she could guess.

"War," Marcus confirmed.

Cora blew out a long breath. The Titans aligning with someone like Philip Waters would give them enough power to make a move on New Olympus.

"We've been preparing. I wanted to make peace with Waters, but the missing shipment is a sticking point. This drug is his baby, and he wants it back."

For a moment they sat in silence while Marcus poured a glass of wine and tasted it. He offered it to Cora but didn't release it. Instead, he tipped the glass until the red liquid washed her lips.

"What about the death threats?" Cora asked.

"What about them?"

"You said you were getting them, going to go into hiding."

"I'm certain that either the Titans or Waters are behind them. I can't retreat now, not with things heating up." He reached out and tucked a strand of hair behind her ear. "At some point this shit is going to blow over, and we're going to talk about *us*."

She let out a sigh and leaned her head against his chest. She liked hearing his heartbeat and it meant she didn't have to look him in the face. "Maybe once the death threats let up."

He ran his fingers through her hair. "You going to have nightmares after all this." He muttered, sounding unhappy.

"I already do," she said before she thought it through, and wanted to kick herself when his entire body tensed.

"When we work things out, I'll help you get over them."

His words let loose a flood of desire. She couldn't stop the shiver that started at the core of her and radiated out into the rest of her body. Marcus's face got intense and she knew he saw it.

"Come on." She smoothed down her hair. "They'll be missing us."

"Later," he promised. "Soon."

At his words, she felt another shiver, but fortunately he didn't see this one. He was busy pulling open the door, no doubt to signal Sharo it was safe to return. Soon after, Sharo reappeared.

"We good?" Sharo rumbled.

Marcus raised his eyebrows at her.

"For now," Cora didn't take her eyes off her husband.

"Good. Because we got a situation."

Marcus straightened, waved a hand to Sharo to continue talking in front of Cora. She sat quietly, feeling oddly pleased.

"Got word from my contacts inside the force. The shipment was large so they put it in a warehouse for confiscated evidence. One box was opened in his sight, dusted for prints."

"No way only one box was opened."

Sharo confirmed. "They opened the rest of them after checking them. Only AJ's prints on them; our guys wore gloves. But now the boxes are empty. Contents removed. My guy checked."

"How'd he miss it before?"

"Because he's fucking stupid. Checked one box, didn't think to check the others."

Marcus cocked his head, and Cora could tell he was

supremely annoyed. "So someone got to the boxes when they were in evidence."

"Not unlike what we were planning."

"Who would do that?" Cora asked. "Who had access?"

Marcus leaned back in his chair thoughtfully. "I think it's time we revisited our friend the Mayor."

Cora bit her lip. She'd been there the night the mayor's man had promised that the shipment would be returned to Marcus within the week. Obviously that hadn't happened.

"You won't get anywhere near him." Sharo said. "He hasn't returned our messages for two months—what makes you think you can do it now?"

Marcus glanced at Cora. "A little persistence will wear anyone down."

Cora resisted the urge to roll her eyes. Marcus was already counting himself the victor.

"Send Cora," Sharo said. "I bet we can get a meet with the mayor, if she's the front."

Cora's body tightened.

"Absolutely not," Marcus lost his cool and growled at his second in command.

"What choice do we have?" Sharo shot back. "We've tried every channel. She could walk right in, no problem."

"I don't want her involved," Marcus said.

"Like it or not, Waters made the right play," Sharo said and the room turned arctic.

"What?" Marcus breathed, facing his underboss with enough rancor that Cora put her hand on his arm.

"Don't like that he took her, but it got you to sit down and chat. Maybe we've been going around the wrong way. Someone like her can walk right in—no one sees her as a threat."

"She's not—" Marcus started.

"Is it safe?" Cora interrupted.

The two men stared at her.

"You'd be covered. It's the mayor's office. No one will touch you," Sharo said, but her husband spun his chair around and pulled hers closer.

"No, babe," Marcus cupped her face. "You don't have to do this."

It was her fault the cops grabbed the shipment in the first place. Maybe if she could make it right, Marcus would forgive her once he found out what she'd done.

"I want to. I want to help." She looked into his deep brown eyes, drawing strength from them. "What do I have to do?"

THIRTEEN

"Is this really necessary?" Cora asked right before Marcus grabbed her from behind and wrapped an arm around her throat.

"I'm not letting you walk into an unknown situation," he growled in her ear, "I don't care how public it is, until I'm confident you have some basic skills to take care of yourself. That's twice you've been kidnapped so you'll forgive me if I'm a tad overprotective of what's mine. Now. Again." His arm around her neck cinched tighter.

Just for his comment about her being *his*, she jabbed especially hard with her elbow into his gut, like he'd spent the last few hours teaching her. She went to stomp on his instep, too, but he maneuvered out of the way. She growled in frustration and he only tightened his arm more.

The bastard had the audacity to laugh. He was fucking *laughing* at her?

She tried to scream her fury but it was muffled by his giant stupid arm restricting her airflow. Not completely, but enough to be uncomfortable.

The next thing she knew, he'd swept her legs and had her on the mat, his big body crouched over hers.

"How many times do I have to tell you to turn your head to the side to free your airway? You get too excited about jabbing me but you'd be passed out before you had the chance to do any real damage or escape if you don't remember the basics."

She bit the inside of her bottom lip. *Don't scream in his face. Don't scream in his face. It'll only make him more smug.*

They'd been at this for hours and she swore they spent far more time down on the mat, him pinning her and droning on *about* defensive moves than actually *practicing* them. She'd told him that yesterday in the bathroom had been a one time slip up and she meant it. They were *not* back together.

"Turn your head to the right so your windpipe isn't obstructed, then attack only long enough to get free."

For once she'd like to get the jump on *him*.

"All right." She raised her arms above her head, giving a little stretch that made her breasts jiggle. A thrill of satisfaction went through her when Marcus's gaze dropped to her form-fitting t-shirt.

"I'm sooo tired," she mock-yawned. "You're so big and strong. Fighting you is hard work."

Marcus's brows knitted together. Oops, she overdid it. Rubbing a hand over her upper chest to distract him, she offered an innocent smile. "Grab me again?"

This time when his arms closed around her, she turned her head. Her hand went to his groin, but instead of striking, she cupped the hard ridge and gave it a good rub with her palm. Marcus stilled, holding his breath as if wondering what she'd do next.

She lifted her legs, creating unexpected dead weight. When he lurched forward, off balance, she twisted out of his grip and scurried away. Marcus landed on the floor.

"Ha!" She did a victory dance. Her would-be attacker lay face down on the ground, unmoving. Oh crap. "Marcus? Marcus? Did I hurt you?"

She worried her lip, tip-toeing closer. He'd hit the floor pretty hard. Had she hurt him somehow?

Her foot nudged his side and he snapped into action, grabbing her ankle, pulling her leg out from under her. She shrieked but he caught her and cushioned her landing.

Cora found herself once again on her back with a large, aroused male rearing over her. With a stone expression, Marcus grabbed her hand and brought it back to the front of his workout shorts, using her palm to stroke himself, harder than she would've done. His eyes were steel. "You think this is funny? A game?"

She shook her head, wide-eyed. Her hair spilled over the floor. "Marcus, I was just—"

"You touch anyone else like that, I'll kill them."

She flinched at the vow. He smiled, the corners of his mouth turning sharp. "Other than that, well done." He raised her palm and kissed it.

She gave a tentative smile. "Thank you?" Her voice went breathless as he licked up her lifeline, a tongue stroke she felt in her groin.

"Marcus," she wriggled. "Let me go."

He shook his head. "You made a mistake, angel." Slowly he lowered himself over her, keeping her pinned. He shook his dark hair from his face. "You should've run while you had the chance."

With a hard hand gripping her right breast, he lowered his head to nip and suck at the vulnerable junction of her throat. And everything in her rose up—all the longing and bone-aching need—a dizzying rush of arousal. Yesterday hadn't been enough. It would never be enough.

She was almost too far gone when Marcus slid his hand up to lightly collar her throat.

"Cora," he growled. "My own." His hand flexed, lightly squeezing the way she used to love, used to beg for, when she was old Cora and willing to succumb, to let him subsume her until she was completely under—

"Mine," he said, and it was enough to jar her back to reality.

She jerked her knee up—he twisted to block it, but she rammed his inner thigh until he rolled off of her.

She rose, tugging her clothes back into place, willing herself not to face her husband. She could see him in the wall mirror, though. He sat, face carefully blank, watching her from the floor. Part of her longed to comfort him, but to what end? There was a chasm between them, filled with secrets and lies. She couldn't breach it, not even for a moment. Not even for him.

It was better this way. She would leave and shower and change, and stick to the plan.

"I told you earlier. Yesterday was a mistake. I'm not yours." She headed for the door. "Not anymore."

FOURTEEN

WHEN CORA LEFT the locker room, Marcus was already waiting for her, his tall form devastating in one of his tailored suits. His wet hair slicked back from his face was the only sign he'd spent the last hour exerting himself. Proud of the cool nod she gave him, Cora strode past him, only to have her heart and limbs quiver when he fell into step beside her.

"What are you doing?" she snapped when he opened the door for her and followed her out as if he had a right to be there. As if she'd invited him along when he knew that wasn't the case. When he knew—despite the longing in her chest—that he wasn't wanted.

"Seeing you home." The corners of his mouth turned up as if she amused him.

"You said your driver would take me." She hated the petulant sound of her voice. Especially since *he* was the unreasonable one. "You said it was safe, that you swept my apartment and it was clear."

"We did," he shrugged. "But I'm going the same way.

Why waste gas?" He opened the car door for her, looking so sensible and innocent she wanted to kick him.

She spent the entire trip with her arms crossed over her chest, refusing to look at his handsome profile. Her cold shower hadn't helped. She was so aroused, so aware of him, it physically hurt not to turn and throw herself into his arms.

"One more block," she whispered to herself, and when the car pulled up to the curb, she threw open the door and leapt onto the sidewalk. Only to find Marcus opening his door and following her again.

"No," she almost shouted, enraged. "Marcus, you can't be here. This is my apartment—"

"It's not, actually," he murmured, walking right up to the keypad and entering a code. Her mouth almost fell open when the gate unlocked and he opened it for her. "You don't own the place, you're only renting." With a sweep of his palm, he indicated she should precede him. "After you."

She was inside before she realized she'd obeyed his subtle command. Once he shut the door, she whirled to confront him in the inner courtyard. "Marcus, what are you doing?"

"Seeing you home." In the dark garden, his body seemed to grow larger, his shadow swallowing her whole.

"Where did you get the keycode?" If he'd had one of his Shades watching over her shoulder while she or one of the other residents entered the building, she swore she'd—

"I got it when I bought the building." A dimple flashed in his cheek as he gave her a panty-drenching smile.

Cora forgot about how hot he looked as her brain processed this. "You...what?"

"I own the whole building."

"You own the building." She put a hand to her temples; she could feel a headache coming on.

"I bought it." He moved closer and she watched him warily, wishing he didn't fill out his suits so well. His hair was a little long, brushing the edges of his collar. It made his professional garb look somehow...a little bad boy, a little dangerous, as if he knew the line of decorum and chose to step over it.

"You bought the building." Even in the dim light of early evening, she could see his eyes crinkling in his almost smile. She mentally shook herself for parroting everything he said. "So...the new upgrades the landlord's been doing lately..."

A new security system had been installed, including the call box up to the apartments. Along with a second entryway door and a doorman. The guy didn't wear all black, but yeah, thinking back now, it was so obvious that he was a Shade. How had she not seen it before?

"My requirements." Marcus inclined his head, shadows falling over the planes of his face, making his features look sharper. "When I heard you were touring the place, I made inquiries. The owner has some debt he needed clearing. Gambling is such an unfortunate vice." Marcus shrugged. "He was really very grateful."

Cora made a noise and inadvertently took a step back towards the front door. She wondered why, whenever her husband said something that scared her, she had the burning desire to go to him and rip his clothes off.

"No wonder Olivia thought I was getting a steal on rent. You fixed this whole thing, didn't you?" She held up a hand. "Never mind, I don't want to know."

She pulled out her keys, but just her luck, fumbled and dropped them.

"Here let me help you," Marcus said in his sexy, gravelly voice. His hands were graceful as he reached down and swept up her keys. Her heart stilled, remembering his long fingers moving with a different task.

She wouldn't jump him, she wouldn't. *No, no, no, no.* She crossed her arms over her chest.

He held open the door for her and, deciding it would be petulant to keep standing out here in the courtyard, she went through and smiled at Dennis, the doorman, before remembering that he was working for Marcus. Thinking about it now, he rarely even opened the door for people. Well, other than Cora. He sat at the desk, ignoring the computer on it and staring stoically at the outer door.

Seeing Marcus, though, Dennis hopped to his feet and opened the second door that led up to the apartments. Cora rolled her eyes and continued up the stairs.

Loud feet sounded on the stairs behind her. She spun around to face Marcus when she got to her door. "I don't care if you own the building, you aren't coming in here, buddy."

He arched an eyebrow as if to say, *buddy?*

"I thought nothing of the sort," he said. "I'm merely heading home to my own apartment after a long, exhausting day."

He pulled out his keys, turned to the apartment across the hallway from hers and turned the lock. "Sleep tight, *neighbor*." He didn't turn around but she heard the grin in his voice.

Her hands squeezed into fists and she wanted to hit something really, really badly. Instead she let out a very unladylike frustrated grunt, unlocked her own door, and slammed it shut behind her.

She went straight for the wine.

"The nerve of him," she muttered, pacing back and forth two hours later. She'd tried everything to distract herself. Watching reruns of her favorite TV shows. Trying to get into a new TV show on her favorite streaming service. Picking up the book that had her captivated only the night before.

Nothing worked.

After a few minutes, inevitably her mind would wander to the apartment across the hallway. What was Marcus doing? Was he thinking about her? Was he working? Was he watching porn and jerking off?

She took another swig of wine. It was only her second glass. She never allowed herself more when she was home alone, and usually not even that.

She glared at the clock on the wall. 9:30. That was a perfectly acceptable time to go to bed right? Responsible grown-ups went to bed at 9:30. She went to the bathroom and spent longer than usual on her nighttime routine, but when she climbed in bed, still only fifteen minutes had passed.

She sighed and flopped her head down onto her pillow. *Fates be kind, please, for once, let me* sleep.

Two hours later, she was laying on her stomach and banging her forehead repeatedly into her pillow.

Sleep deprivation was a form of torture. They had rules against this under the Genoa Convention.

So finally she gave up and went to the bathroom to seek out the little baggie with Armand's pills. Tomorrow was important. A text had come through an hour ago from Marcus letting her know they'd arranged a meeting with the mayor. He and Sharo would be by early in the morning to prep her.

She couldn't be a zombie with only an hour of sleep, if

that, and dark circles under her eyes. She frowned at the little baggie. The pills were almost gone. She bit her lip. Every time she took one, it was a little easier for her to justify.

Oh, screw it. She popped one in her mouth and swallowed it down with a cup of water. There. Now to lie in bed and drift off. And who knew? Maybe she'd have a nice dream like the one before, imagining Marcus coming to her...

No, no, no. She did *not* want to dream about her husband. *Ex.* Wus-band.

Cora rolled over and punched her pillow. She'd picked the softest sheets and mattress when she moved in, so why did her bed feel so hard? And why was it so damn hot? She clawed her clothes off and flopped one way and the other.

She wasn't falling asleep. Shit. She'd swear she almost felt...like, *more* energetic, a little frenetic almost. What if the pill didn't work tonight? Hadn't she heard you started getting immune to sleep medication if you took it too often?

She had to sleep tonight. *Had* to. After another few minutes tossing and turning, she went back into the bathroom and took out the second to last pill in the baggie. And before she could think better of it, she threw it in her mouth, swallowed it, and drank another half glass of water.

She went back to bed and waited.

Her room wasn't large, but the darkness made it seem endless, cavern-like. The shadows on the wall made weird shapes. The one in the door looked like Marcus's profile—

"Can't sleep?"

Cora let out a little scream, slamming back into the headboard. "Marcus?"

His shadow stretched over her as he moved into the depths of her bedroom.

"Gods, you scared me."

"I can't sleep either." Marcus looked down at his hands and Cora sensed his frustration. He would hate anything he considered weakness or a lack of control. *Oh, Marcus.*

"You shouldn't be in here," she forced herself to say. Even though what she really wanted was to invite him in for the night and wrap her arms and body around him. Sleep would come, cool and delicious. She'd rest peacefully knowing the monster was in her bed.

He paused at the end of her bed. "You lied to me."

Her heart plummeted to the floor. *He knew.* Her breath came in short gasps. *How did he guess? What would he do now that he'd figured out her betrayal?*

"What?" she managed to squeak.

"Earlier." His hands were at his tie, unknotting it. "Back at the gym."

"The gym?" she repeated, mind blank with relief. He hadn't guessed her part in the bust at the docks.

"You remember." His hand closed over her ankle, and before she knew it, she was on her back under him. He straddled her hips, loosely binding her wrists with his tie before securing them to the headboard. Her pulse pounded in her pussy, the throbbing beat so loud she was sure he could hear it.

This was it. He'd broken into her bedroom and now he was going to claim her.

He smiled down at her, gray eyes flashing. "You said you didn't belong to me." His voice deepened, roughened. "You lied."

He shifted off her and her moan caught in her throat. She wanted him back, his weight, his heat. He stood looking down at her as if he owned her. She felt his gaze like a touch but it wasn't enough.

He ran a finger down the middle of her collarbone, between her breasts. Of course she would be naked when he decided to invade her bedroom.

"I wasn't lying." Her breath caught as his finger traced down, down.

"No?" An arrogant brow arched. "What's this then?"

His finger trespassed between her soft folds. Cora's body curled in on itself, dying for more. "You're wet for what, no reason?"

"No..."

"Then why, angel?" His finger twisted, probed, not quite filling her. She bit her tongue so she wouldn't ask for more. "Is it for me?" A second finger. Her toes curled into the bed.

"Marcus, please—"

"Please, what?" His cheek curved in the darkness. A devil's smile. "'Please stop'?" His fingers stilled and her hips pressed upwards, seeking. "Or 'please more'?"

This was a bad idea. There were so many reasons she should stop this. Kick him out. Never let him touch her again.

His fingers stroked the wet grooves on either side of her clit. So many reasons to tell him 'no', but she couldn't think of a single one.

"More," she begged, breathless. "Don't stop."

"Sweetheart," that devastating curl of his lip. "I'm never gonna stop."

His fingers hit her sweet spot, setting off white hot electric flashes in her brain. He stretched over her, lips close, his scent washing over her. She sucked in lungfuls, growing dizzy drunk on him.

His fingers rubbed along her sensitive furrows, finding

her orgasm, drawing it out as he whispered against her mouth.

"You're mine. You've always been mine. 'Til the day we die and beyond. 'Til stars fall and this world is forgotten. Forever."

"Marcus," she cried as her orgasm blew up, a storm, a supernova. Sparks shot through her, her torso tensing, her limbs trembling, mouth opening to his as the climax consumed her. Transformed her atoms, turned her cells into shining suns. If she hadn't been tied to her bed she'd have floated.

In the corner of her eye, Marcus reared up, wearing a shark's smile as he undid his shirt cuffs.

The biggest orgasm of her life and he wasn't done with her. He'd never be done.

She wrenched free of the tie and ran to the door. The knob wouldn't turn. Locked.

She pounded on the door, begging, "Let me out, let me out."

The darkness danced behind her, gathering into a potent form, a monster made of all her deepest desires. Her fist uncurled and she slapped the door, sobbing as it opened—

"Cora?" The shadows dissolved and Cora blinked in the light. Staggered backwards.

She was in the hall of her apartment building, standing in front of Marcus, who'd opened his door. The door she'd been pounding on—*in her dream.*

Sleepwalking? Oh shit. Well, this was new.

Marcus's eyes dropped to her body and flared with heat. "Cora, you're *naked.*" Her head jerked down to look at herself. Double shit. He was right, she was naked, well, underneath the sheet she had loosely drawn around herself.

"Get in here." Marcus backed up to let her in.

She went forward on his command. When her legs wobbled, she balanced herself on the wall. Marcus pushed the door closed and came to help her. She stopped him with a raised hand.

"What happened? Are you okay?" He stopped at her outstretched hand, respecting her request for space.

"I'm sorry. I wanted to sleep. I must have had a dream." She averted her eyes. She couldn't look at him. Her skin still crackled with sensitivity, dying to have her husband close the last few inches and put his hands on her.

A dream, it was only a dream. Except her pussy throbbed and she felt the wrung-out weakness of an incredible orgasm. *Don't think about that—*

"Sweetheart, you don't look well." His fingers brushed her forehead lightly. The single touch sent runners of heat through her. She gasped.

Marcus's forehead furrowed. "What's going on?"

"I wanted to sleep," her words came slurred and heavy. "I can never sleep."

"Your pupils are dilated—"

"Marcus." She couldn't think with him touching her. She grabbed his hand and he stilled. Her body convulsed. Not in climax, not quite. But close. She'd almost cum from his touch alone.

Marcus's eyes widened, wild. He knew. He was always so attuned to her. "What the—"

"Marcus," she moaned. "Touch me, *please.*"

And she pressed his hand to her breast.

He stared a moment. His hair was tousled, wild, as if he'd been running a hand through it. She imagined him sitting on his couch, drinking scotch and debating whether to knock on her door. Never knowing he'd already invaded her dreams.

With a groan, a helpless sound, he bowed his head, shoved her sheet to the floor, and took her nipple into his mouth. Lightning sizzled through her. She arched upwards.

"Marcus, *Marcus*." Her hands dug into his silky raven dark hair, mussing it further. He was always so buttoned up, so in control. Except when he was with her. With her the beast broke free.

FIFTEEN

MARCUS'S TONGUE circled his wife's nipple and she hissed, clawing him closer. With a growl, he raised his head, grabbed her wrists and trapped them above her head, against the door. Something wasn't right. This wasn't the same woman who'd been so cold to him only earlier today.

I'm not yours. Not anymore.

But here she was, her body stretched before him, legs thrashing, trying to hook his hips and pull him to her. He fixed her with a glare.

He wanted what she was so freely offering. By the gods, he wanted it. It was all he'd been able to think about from the second he'd pulled out of her yesterday in that damned bathroom. He wanted to impale her for about a month until she forgot everything else in the world but his name.

"Marcus, please," she panted, struggling. Her flesh was so hot, rosy with lust. "I need—"

He thrust his fingers into her cunt. He would always give her what she needed. Her head flew back, slamming the wood. Marcus watched her, jaw rigid, as one orgasm rocked through her, and another.

What the hell was going on? His woman was sensitive, it was true, but not usually *this* hair-trigger. He twisted his fingers in a way that would have been painful if she wasn't so wet, and her convulsions only increased. She went absolutely wild on his hand. He'd never seen anything like it. He frowned even as his cock stiffened past the point of painful.

"Easy," he crooned when she kept thrusting against his hand even though she'd come a handful of times. "You can have all you want. There's no rush." But he slid his fingers out. He needed to figure out what the hell was going on.

Cora blinked, her features turning devastated. "You just said—"

"You want more?"

"Yes." She nodded furiously. "Yes, I need more." She licked her lips and his eyes followed. "I need you."

"Are you sure? After what you said today—"

"I was wrong."

Marcus's whole body jerked. Did she really mean that? Or was she—

"I was wrong," she said louder, cutting into his thoughts. "I belong to you. In every way. And I need you." Her voice edged on a whine. "Now. I'll die if you don't take me." He couldn't remember the last time he'd heard anyone so desperate.

The breath left his chest in a harsh rush. He wrenched her around, making her face the wall. She sobbed, obviously thinking he meant to deny her.

Didn't she know? He could never do anything that would hurt her. No matter how much it might kill him to touch her now and have her deny him tomorrow.

But he didn't know what this was. Her inhibitions were obviously lowered. He didn't smell any alcohol on her breath, though, and he couldn't imagine her taking any kind of drug— He shook his head even at the thought. Was she on some sort of medication?

He wasn't the sort of man to take advantage of a woman in a vulnerable state.

"Marcus," Cora begged, almost sounding in pain. His fingers returned to her pussy, probing as he tried to think. But she was driving him fucking insane. Pushing him away only to show up like this?

"So wet." His voice was edged with cruelty. "So desperate. Are you always this wet?"

"Only when you're near."

"You lied to me earlier?" He worked his fingers more roughly. "What does that make you?"

"A liar," she cried out.

"Do good girls lie?"

"No." She twitched her hips to invite his touch. "I'm a bad girl."

Her words made Marcus's cock pulse painfully. "You are a bad girl. You gonna cum again?"

Her escalating whimpers said yes. She arched her back, pressing her nipples to the hard wall. "Yes. Please, I need it."

"Not so fast." Marcus spun her around and tossed her over his shoulder. She shrieked and grabbed onto him. The floorboards creaked as he carried her down the hall and dropped her on his bed. She landed on her back and when he didn't immediately follow her, her whines immediately started up again.

"Please, Marcus. Please. Fuck me. Fuck me now."

She reached for him and when he backed out of her grasp, her hands went to her own pussy. She started rubbing herself frantically, her face pinched with frustration as she sought release. "It's not enough. I need your cock. I need your big, fat cock stuffed in my pussy. Right now. Please fuck me. Fuck me, Marcus!"

"That's enough," he barked, putting a knee on the bed and grabbing her wrists, wrenching them above her head and slamming them into the bed. "Stop this right now."

"That's right," she breathed out, big, innocent blue eyes blinking up at him. "Punish me, Daddy. Punish your bad girl."

For fuck's sake.

"I'll tie you to this bed if that's what it takes," he growled, "but you *will* tell me what the fuck is going on."

"I need you. Fuck me. Fuck my cunt. Fuck my ass. I need it all. Fuck all my holes. Marcus, *please*—" Her body writhed under his, her knee rubbing against his rock-hard cock. Like yesterday, but this time, he knew she had every intention of seeing her promise through.

He wanted to give in, to plunder her depths, to fuck her so hard she wouldn't be able to walk for a week, to mark her as *his*—

But then her eyes flashed with a different fire. "If you don't give it to me, I swear I will walk out this door, naked, and jump the first guy I see. But I will get a cock, any cock, in this cunt, within the hour."

Raw fury and terror scrambled over one another in his guts. It was not something he'd ever felt before.

Marcus forced himself to let go of her and step back from the bed. She scrambled up as well, eyes flicking to the door like she might make good on her threat.

He casually moved in front of it as he slowly began unbuttoning his shirt. She tried to dart around him but his hand shot out, slamming the door shut.

"No, sweetheart." He gave her a cruel smile. "You came to me. We do this my way."

He grabbed her by the waist and felt her body melt into his touch. Which only pissed him the fuck off. Would she melt the same way if he was any other man? Would she squeal so good for a fucking stranger?

He forced her face-down on the bed and smacked her ass. She pushed her bottom up higher, inviting his touch.

"You're a bad girl? You need discipline."

"Yes, yes, please, Marcus—"

"Enough. I think you've said quite enough. Now keep your hands on the bed." Marcus yanked his belt out of his slacks and doubled it up. He slid the leather across his palm.

Cora took a peek over her shoulder and he watched her eyes widen in excitement. *I'll die without it*, she'd said. For whatever reason, she needed this. So much so, she'd take any fucking cock and lie to him about wanting him, trying to manipulate him into—

Leather cracked against her ass. He'd teach her a lesson, that was for sure. He'd teach her a lesson and they'd be done with this. But as soon as the blow landed, her back arched, followed by a little mewl of pleasure.

She sobbed out a sigh and snarled when Marcus paused too long. "Again! Give it to me again."

Marcus paused. He'd been careful with his force, no matter how angry he was. But he hadn't taken it easy on her, either. He swung again. The belt bit her bottom once, twice, a third time.

Cora tensed and melted into the bed with each strike momentarily before rising back up on her haunches and waving that lovely, now bright pink ass at him again.

When she next turned to look over her shoulder at him, tear tracks marked her cheeks and her brows were furrowed in need. "Please. Marcus. Can't you see how much I need you?"

She looked helpless. Desperate. His beautiful wife. Literally on her knees.

Whatever was happening to her, she'd come to *him*. She'd been in need and come to her husband for help. As it should be.

A thud sounded as Marcus threw away the belt, dropped to his knees behind her and buried his face in her pussy.

"Fuck, you're so wet." He sounded awestruck because he was. He gripped her wriggling hips, forcing her to remain still as he dived in and began making a meal of her.

He'd never in all their time together seen her so drenched. Her wetness was sloppy on his five o'clock shadow. He could barely slurp down one mouthful before more of her juice spurted forth.

Cora raked the sheets, sobbing his name, "Marcus, *Marcus*," her legs shaking on either side of his head as if an earthquake had struck, it's epicenter at her pussy.

"No, no, it's too much," she moaned, writhing and thrusting against his mouth in contradiction of her words. "I can't."

"You will," he growled. "You belong to me. You said so. You admitted it." He didn't care about the circumstances, he was fucking holding her to her admission. "So when I say cum, you cum. Now do it. *Cum*."

She writhed, her climax hitting again and again, an unstoppable tide. It was fucking incredible to witness. Each crest seemed to bring her higher and higher. Her cries became higher and higher pitched until finally she was gasping out little high-pitched whimpers.

And Marcus's cock had never been harder in his entire fucking life.

Marcus flipped her over and she grabbed his shoulders. He withdrew her hands and pinned her to the bed.

"You don't touch me, not without permission." At this point he wanted, no, *needed* her, with an insane vehemence that might even match her own. But he *would* remain in control. No matter the fact that his thighs shook with the need to thrust inside her.

More tears slipped down her cheeks.

"Marcus, please."

Shifting forward, he thumbed away her tears. He couldn't stop himself from tasting them. Her breasts arched outward as if that was the most erotic thing she'd ever seen.

"*Bellissima,*" he whispered, body tense with restraint. "If this is what you want..."

"It is. I need it. I need you. Now, Marcus, you have to—"

"Shh, Cora, *cara,* calm down. Let me be gentle—"

"I don't want you to be gentle," she shrieked. "I need it now, please, gods, please, Marcus. I need you now."

His hand shot out and collared her neck. At the same time he shifted, angled his hips and slammed into her.

Cora's eyes lit with ecstasy, her body seizing around him in orgasm.

"Is this what you want?" Marcus snapped his hips, forcing his cock deeper. She was tight, so fucking tight, but so wet that he slid right in. Made so perfectly for him. He hitched her legs up over his shoulders and bent her in half, hammering savagely.

"Marcus, yes. Fuck me harder." She closed her eyes. Her cunt milked him, sucking him deeper as he groaned above her. "*Harder*, Marcus."

It was good she kept saying his name. The thought that she might have gone and shared this with some other man—

He pulled out and thrust in again, hard. But as soon as he was rooted deep in her, his heart calmed.

"Cora. *Mi amore. Ho bisogno di te.*" *My love. I need you.* Could she not see what she did to him? How the two months apart had been hell on him?

"Marcus," she whispered as shockwaves flowed through her. Gods, the way her pussy kept clamping on his cock—she was cumming non-stop, her legs shaking uncontrollably. Her hands scrabbled against the hard wall of his chest, fighting to bring him closer.

He let himself lay flush against her, coarse hair scratching her oversensitive nipples. "I'm here. I'm here. *Baciami. Abbraciami.*" *Kiss me. Hold me.*

His cock nudged deeper, sliding against her sensitive walls, and as his lips touched hers, the largest climax yet detonated. Her eyes rolled back in her head.

"Cora? Cora?"

After a moment of silence, she blinked again, mouth open and eyes wide like she'd seen a holy fucking vision or something.

"Cora," he called again, cupping her cheek, smoothing her hair, almost frantic. "Cora?"

"I'm here," she panted. Her gaze connected with his and she giggled. "I think I came so hard I passed out for a second."

She reached up and dragged his head down, nuzzling his forehead against hers. She sounded a little more like herself. He was still inside her, filling her, and she clenched around him with a low groan.

He didn't know whether to laugh, cum, or spank her ass again. This woman would be the death of him. But he didn't fucking care. He buried his hands in the back of her hair and kissed her hard. Their tongues tangled, Cora clawing at him.

"Will you take my ass now? Please, Marcus? I need to feel you everywhere."

Marcus shook his head. Cumming so hard she passed out wasn't fucking enough? "You were unconscious." He sat up and pulled out of her.

She reached for him but he grabbed her wrists again to stop her. "Please, Marcus. Please fuck my ass."

"And if I don't, you'll go get any random bastard off the street to assfuck you, is that right?" He'd never been so horny and so angry at the same time before.

She winced. "I'm sorry. I'm sorry. I took some sleeping medication and I think it's making me act weird— But please, Marcus. I'm so *empty*."

Sleeping medication? Marcus supposed he'd heard of people sleepwalking on sleep meds and maybe getting up in the middle of the night to eat a pint of ice cream. But this?

"I know it's a lot to ask." Cora looked pained. "But please, will you fuck my ass? Fill me up?"

Tears poured down her face. She was more herself but her need wasn't any less. Her nipples were beaded so tight they looked like they could cut glass. She was the most beautiful thing he'd ever seen in his life. He knew the merest brush would set her off.

And she wanted him in her ass. His beautiful wife was begging for him to claim her *completely*.

He'd vowed he'd always see to her every need. He inhaled deeply. Her scent was thick in the air and his cock twitched, still wet with her juices.

In one swift movement, Marcus tumbled her over his hard thighs.

"You will never," he punctuated his words with sharp

smacks to her already pink rear, "ever, *ever*, touch another man ever again."

He shoved his fingers into her pussy, making her buck. Her spine seized with another jaw-breaking climax before he slid his hand out and spread her ample slick over her asshole. He probed her ass, invading the tight ring of muscle with one, two, three fingers.

"You want my cock in your ass?" he demanded.

"Yes." Her reply was muffled by the bed. Not good enough. He spanked her so hard she gasped.

"Tell me."

"Yes," she shouted. "I want your cock in my ass. Fuck my ass, Marcus, please. Fuck my ass!"

For all his rough discipline, when he lined his cock up and started to invade her ass, he was exceedingly gentle.

His cock breached her tight hole in stages as she moaned into the comforter. This time Marcus was afraid *his* eyes would roll back in his head.

So. Tight.

So fucking tight. They'd done this only once before, the night before she'd left and he'd lived off those memories for so many lonely nights—

She flexed, clenching on him and he lost his damn breath. He was trying to keep in control, he really was. But gods, she was testing him. Having his perfect, innocent little wife whimpering and thrusting her hips against the bed, searching for friction while he fucked her all-but-virgin ass —he almost came right there on the spot.

But no. Fuck no. He was gonna draw this out. She might have demanded it, but he was gonna make sure they squeezed every pleasurable drop out of this claiming.

Once he was fully seated, the hair on his chest brushed her back and he wrapped a strong arm around her middle.

"Is this what you wanted?" he asked, barely managing to keep his voice measured.

"This is what I wanted." She reached down and caressed his thigh, and looked back at him over her shoulder. "You're so strong. All that power, sometimes I can feel it, you know? How you're barely keeping it inside. Barely keeping it on a leash." She squeezed his thigh, a line appearing between her brows. "But you don't have to. Not with me."

"I'm yours, Marcus." Her blue eyes were crystal clear as she admitted the truth. "I always will be. You know it and I know it. So claim what's yours and don't hold back."

Her words flipped a switch. She was his. She was his and she trusted him completely. He propped himself up with his fists on either side of her hips. With a roar, he did as she asked. He stopped holding back.

He thrust his hips forward, pounding her into the sheets, filling her. When her knees buckled, he wrapped an arm around her waist, fingers seeking her clit. She screamed and bucked back against him, mouth slack as her entire body—including her ass—clenched and spasmed with her orgasm.

Oh gods, so tight. His wife. His. Fucking *his*. Forever. Electricity rolled down his spine, but still he drove into her, his thrusts growing harder and wilder. His weight drove her hips into the bed, her raw pussy stuttering orgasm after orgasm until she was sobbing and writhing on the bed.

"*Mia moglie. Sono pazzo di te.*" *My wife. I'm crazy for you.* Gentle words as his body was anything but.

He'd never known passion like this in his life. Never knew it could exist. Never knew he could love anyone or anything so much. So fucking much.

He held her body cemented to his as his hips thrust

more violently than ever, her sweat and his and her slick all mixed up together and soaking the bed.

"Cum," he shouted. "One last time. Cum with me."

His huge palm massaged her swollen pussy, fingers sawing in and out of her as he filled her up from behind. She screamed out as Marcus's orgasm tore through him.

His cum filled her, dripping from her ass as he pulled out, joining the already wet sheets.

His gorgeous wife had never been more perfect than when she smiled up at him, a blissful grin on her face, finally satiated.

"Thank you," she rolled to her side, reaching blindly for him. He collapsed beside her.

Her fingers traced his face, his jaw, the blade of his nose, his eyebrows, up to his forehead. She smoothed the lines there. He sighed and let his cheek rest in her palm.

"I've missed this." She stole the words right out of his mouth.

But before he could ask her why she left or demand any answers, her eyes had fallen closed and she was gently snoring.

SIXTEEN

CORA WOKE up to a splitting headache. Ugh. She clutched her head with both hands and moaned.

Gods, what was that racket? She fumbled around on the nightstand and frowned, really opening her eyes this time.

What the—? She wasn't in her apartment.

She knifed up into a sitting position. Ow! She grabbed her head again. Okay, okay, no sharp movements. Got it. But what the hell? She'd never gotten migraines before.

She looked around. Where the hell was she?

Then it all came rushing back. The dream.

Because that's all it had been, right? That's all it ever was. Dreams. She shifted and winced at the soreness in her...in her *bum*.

Shit! *Not* a dream.

That meant— Cora swiveled, looking this way and that. She was in a bedroom, decorated in cool, masculine tones.

No, no, no.

She got to her feet, wincing again, and walked slightly bowlegged to the door. She pushed it open and peeked her head out.

"Hello?" she called.

No response but the noise that had woken her up sounded again. Her cell phone ringing. She all but jumped out of her skin at the noise. "Crap!" She shrieked, hand to her chest as she made her way back towards the nightstand by the bed.

She frowned as she picked up her phone. According to her muddy recollection, she'd shown up at Marcus's door in nothing more than a sheet. So how did her cell phone get here?

She touched the button to answer the call. "Hello?"

"You up, sleeping beauty?"

Marcus's voice. He sounded like he was smiling. Cora sank back down onto the bed. She missed the sound of Marcus when he was happy.

"Yeah," she said tentatively.

"Good," he said. "You feeling okay?"

Cora blinked, a thousand thoughts shooting through her head. *No, I have a headache from hell and for some reason I can't explain, I think I sorta came by your place last night accidently and screwed your brains out, had about a gazillion orgasms and begged you to fuck my backside, but ya know, apart from that...*

"Yeah," she said instead. "Feeling good. A little tired."

Marcus chuckled and her toes curled hearing the noise. Why did he always have to sound so damn sexy?

"I bet."

Cora felt her cheeks heat to about a thousand degrees. "Is there a reason you're calling?"

"As a matter-of-fact, there is," he said, continuing to sound amused. But then he sobered. "The mayor's schedule has been reshuffled due to a ribbon-cutting of some sort, but he can still see you. The meeting has been moved to 9:30 instead of 11:00."

Cora's eyes shot to the clock on the nightstand. "It's already a quarter after eight!" she shrieked, jumping to her feet. She had no idea what she looked like, but considering last night's activities, she didn't even want to imagine.

"That's why I'm calling. I had to step out to deal with some unresolved business—" he definitely sounded less than pleased about the fact "—but I'll be by in half an hour to pick you up. We'll debrief in the car on the way."

"Half an hour?" she squeaked. "But I have to go shower. I have to do my hair. And makeup. And— Shit!"

"Calm down, baby. We got this. Now hop to it, see you in 30."

"Right." She reminded herself that she'd offered to help, convinced him to accept her help. She couldn't start bitching about it now.

"Oh, and put on some clothes before you leave the bedroom." With that he hung up the phone.

And Cora commenced freaking out about how in the world she would be able to get ready in time. She was meeting with the mayor. The *mayor*. He was in Marcus's pocket, or at least he used to be, but still, he was one of the most powerful men in the city.

Cora threw on one of Marcus's shirts and hurried out of his apartment. Rushing, she threw open the door to hers, and stopped short with a scream when she saw a man in all black sitting on her couch.

"Easy, Mrs. Ubeli, I'm here on your husband's orders." The man courteously averted his eyes towards the wall. He was identical to every other Shade—black slacks, black shirt and dark shades, sitting right in her living room. Meanwhile her hair was a mess and she was wearing nothing but one of Marcus's oversized undershirts.

"I thought you guys were supposed to wait outside." A thought hit her and she asked with not a little bit of horror, "How long have you been in here?"

"Since about sunrise."

Was that when Marcus had left the apartment? Gods, so obviously these guys knew she'd been sleeping over at his place. Biting her lip, she warred over whether to turn and shower, or go make coffee. She didn't have time, like *really* didn't have time.

But in the end, she couldn't imagine facing the day without caffeine. Maybe it would help with this damn headache. Ignoring the man, she crossed the room and started a pot, feeding Brutus while it brewed.

"I'll take him out, if you want," the Shade offered. "I like dogs."

"Uh, thanks. If it's not too much trouble."

"My partner Fats will be in to wait in the living room while you get ready," he warned her. "You're to have a man with you at all times."

"Ok," she mumbled, rolling her eyes. At least they hadn't been ordered to wait in the bedroom.

The man waited until Brutus was done eating, clipped his leash on and walked him outside. A tall, gangly man walked in.

"Fats?" she asked, eyebrows going up.

The man grinned. Grabbing a mug of coffee, she went to hide in the bedroom.

She showered and dressed in record time, putting on only a light dusting of makeup. When she was ready, the Shades were waiting to walk her to Marcus's car.

Marcus himself got out to hold the door for her. Cora's

breath caught at the sight of his handsome figure, broad shoulders and narrow waist with a suit tailored to show them off perfectly.

And every moment from last night came back in vivid, high-res detail. Shamelessly grinding against him right in the doorway. Begging him to fuck her. Cumming around his fingers. His cock. Begging for him in her ass—

"You need a robe," Marcus said after they'd slid into the back seat.

"I know," she said, blushing. The Shade must have turned in a report.

"Come here," he demanded.

Shit. Because the other thing she remembered from last night?

Other than orgasm after orgasm after *orgasm*?

I'm yours, Marcus. I always will be. You know it and I know it.

What. The. Hell. Was. Wrong. With. Her?

More like, what was wrong with those pills? She was never taking another one again, that was for damn sure. She should never have taken two, she got that, but damn—couldn't Armand have warned her about possible side effects? And what the hell kind of side effects were those anyway??

And now here Marcus was, gray eyes expectant. And she had to go face the mayor and try to get him to give up information about the shipment—

She scooted a little closer to Marcus but not too close, pulling her dress down as she did so. Her outfit was professional, yet flirty, the dress a coral color with a scoop neck that skimmed the top of her cleavage. It showed off her figure perfectly and the color made her skin glow. Marcus's eyes swept over her and they narrowed, but he didn't say anything.

"You sure you're ok this morning?"

Now her face was really red. "Coffee's helping the headache." She held up the travel mug she'd brought from home, crossing her legs, reversing the movement once she realized what she'd done.

Marcus mistook her unease as nervousness. "You don't have to do this if you don't want to."

"You got a meeting with the mayor in less than twelve hours. I think it's too late for me to back out now. How did you manage that, by the way?"

"Called in favors. Armand helped."

"Armand?" Cora wanted to ask how her friend had an in with the mayor, but of course, Armand was a Merche. His last name carried all sorts of weight with the highest echelon, disowned son or not.

Marcus started drilling her again on what to say. They spent the next fifteen minutes as they crept through morning traffic going over it.

"The mayor will toy with you. And he's good at reading people—it's probably his number one skill. But you, more than anyone of us, have nothing to hide."

Cora nodded, thinking of the phone call she made to the detective before she ran from the Estate and set all this mess in motion. Right. Nothing to hide...

Her husband was still talking. "...and relax. Stick to the script and remember, you have an advantage."

"What advantage?" Cora asked, worry starting to gnaw at her.

"Your legs look fucking great in that dress."

"Marcus," she protested, and tugged at her hem.

His dark head darted close to hers. "As soon as this business is done, we're settling things between us once and for all."

If she looked at him anymore, she'd drown. She stared out the window for the rest of the ride, running over the script in her head.

"MRS. UBELI? THIS WAY PLEASE." A young man in a navy suit motioned Cora to go into the office.

Inside Zeke Sturm stood, the leader of the most powerful city in the world, with his short blond curls, bouncing with boyish energy.

"Please call me Zeke." He took Cora's hand and kissed it, guiding her into a seat as his gaze raked up and down her body.

"Thanks for meeting me on such short notice." She flashed him a smile.

"No trouble at all," he said smoothly, even though Cora knew it must have been a lot of trouble. Between nine and noon was prime time for a politician, and they'd arranged the meet twelve hours prior. If he was annoyed, though, he didn't show it.

"Please, help yourself." Zeke gestured to the silver coffee and tea service on the desk. She waited, but instead of going back to sit in his chair, he leaned against the desk and looked down at her.

His position offered him a perfect view of her cleavage, she realized, but his smile was mild and nothing more than friendly.

"So," he started, "you're here to talk me into being the guest of honor at the fundraiser for the animal shelters?"

"A fashion show." Cora leaned forward in her seat. She

and Maeve had come up with the idea ages ago, and last night Marcus and Sharo decided it was a good enough cover for her to meet with Zeke. "Models and pooches. And Armand and his team at Fortune are in charge of the designs."

Zeke grinned. "Fashion is going to the dogs," he quipped and she laughed.

"Exactly. Just show up to cut the ribbon for the new dog park, and a quick photo op. Your constituents will love it."

"Never hurts to support a good cause. Alright," he said, slapping the side of the desk. "I'll do it."

"Really? That's great...Thank you."

Zeke's face also held a smile, but it looked wrong somehow. "Is that it? Your husband pulled every string to get you in front of me and that's all you want?"

She flushed under his piercing gaze and he spread his hands apologetically. "I'm a busy man, Mrs. Ubeli. No sense beating around the bush."

She cleared her throat. "He did have a question for you. Some property was collected from the docks a while ago. He'd like his personal effects returned to him."

Now Zeke looked amused but he stayed quiet as she went on.

"He thinks the boxes have been tampered with and the contents removed." Before continuing, she glanced into the corner, where a mounted camera fixed her with its glossy eye. Under its impassive watch, she tried to remember everything Marcus and Sharo had drilled her on this morning.

"She's walking into a lion's den," Marcus had said, almost calling the whole thing off right before she'd gotten out of the car.

"In the daylight, the lion's muzzled." Sharo had

responded, looking for all the world like he was at ease. Cora knew better.

"Ezekiel Sturm does not do business in the daylight, never forget that. Most of his shit is buried deep, like an iceberg. But it's there," Marcus said, and answered her question before she asked. "I've known him a long time."

Now, staring into the mayor's cutting blue eyes, she told herself to breathe. "Can you help us?"

Zeke paused, letting his gaze drift over her. "They were smart, sending you," he said finally. "I like a new sweet little thing in a sundress, every spring." He picked up a pen off his desk and pretended to study it. "How far did your husband tell you to go to soften me up?"

Cora stiffened and, gripping the hem of her dress, drew it down.

He laughed at her. "Relax. I don't want you."

Lion's den, she reminded herself.

"Good, because you can't have me," she bit out.

Zeke tossed the pen he'd been toying with on his desk. "Tell Ubeli that I can't do anything to return his personal effects. They're part of a police investigation. If he submits a claim I'm sure it will be filled in...a few years."

She stood. The conversation was obviously over. He wasn't going to give them anything. "See you at the fundraiser."

He inclined his head, his blond curls falling attractively into his face. "I hear you and Ubeli were separated. Are you working something out?"

Cora wanted to tell him it was none of his business. "We're talking."

He studied her with quick, cutting blue eyes. "If you want to divorce him, I can protect you."

"Thank you," she said politely. "I'll let you know." She

didn't tell him that she'd been with her husband long enough to know that protection came with a price.

"Practicing your husband's poker face?" Zeke seemed amused and she'd had it.

"Thank you for your time. I also appreciate you giving us the use of your penthouse suite at the Crown Hotel. We do *so* enjoy it."

Anger flashed on his face; she turned on her heel and hurried out, frightened and elated to have scored at least one hit.

SEVENTEEN

Marcus sat, tense and on edge inside the back of the SUV outside the mayor's office waiting for Cora. He glared up at the building.

"She's been in there too long," he growled.

Sharo glanced back at him in the rearview mirror. "Only been 45 minutes. And you know Sturm. He probably had her wait outside an extra half hour because he could."

"I've had about enough of Mayor Zeke Sturm flexing his muscles. It's time to remind him of who is really in charge of this city."

Sharo raised a brow. "Maybe don't declare war on the mayor's office until you heard what he's gotta say. And maybe when you don't got a target on your own forehead."

Marcus grumbled under his breath and glared back out the window.

Finally. There she was. Cora was pushing through the exit. Marcus took a deep breath, the first it felt like he'd taken in 45 minutes.

He should never have let her go in there alone. Never

again. He didn't care what sort of sense it made. It was his job to be her shield and he couldn't do that if he was outside waiting in the Fucking car.

She hurried down the steps, looking as beautiful as ever in her sharp, knee-length pencil skirt and tailored vest that was buttoned to accentuate her narrow waist and womanly curves. She'd been wearing a coat on the way in. Probably a good thing because if he'd seen that outfit, no way would he have even let her out of the car.

Sharo jumped out and moved around swiftly to open the door for her.

She slid gracefully into the car, staying near the door as Sharo closed it. As if she thought Marcus would allow her to put distance between them. After last night? He didn't think so.

He quickly disabused her of the notion by grabbing her around her tiny waist and sliding her across the seat until she was flush by his side.

She let out a little squeak but that was her only protest.

"How'd it go?" asked Sharo.

Cora frowned, still wiggling to put distance between herself and Marcus. "Not well. He won't help us."

Marcus was far from surprised. There was a reason Zeke had been ducking meeting with him. Something was wrong. Either Zeke had double-crossed him and sold the shipment to someone else—a fatal mistake, Zeke would soon find if Marcus discovered it was true—or something else had happened that Zeke was trying to hide. Either way, Marcus would get to the bottom of it. With or without the mayor's help.

"Tell me what he said. Don't leave out a single detail."

So Cora did, replaying the conversation blow-by-blow. She looked nervous as she came to the end of her story, like she expected Marcus to lose his shit. She ought to know him better by now. He valued control far too much to lose it over someone like Zeke Sturm

"It's okay, babe." Marcus patted her thigh. "We'll get the shipment back; we have other ways."

She didn't look convinced. "What if you don't by the end of the week? What will Waters do?"

"Worried about me?" Marcus grinned.

She sniffed and looked away. "Making sure that I get alimony."

Marcus laughed and, hooking her close, kissed the top of her head. He cupped her cheek and slowly turned her face back toward his. "But things are getting serious now. I need to go back to the safe house. And you need to come with me."

Her head immediately started shaking no.

Not this again.

He lifted his other hand so that now he cupped both cheeks, holding her face still as he dropped his forehead to hers. "Stop denying what we have. Who you are. You are my wife and you belong by my side. Last night proved that. You said it yourself."

She pulled back from him, quick enough that he lost hold of her. "Last night didn't change anything. It was..." She shook her head and threw her hands up in the air. "Okay, well, I don't know exactly what last night was. A timeout from the real world. Two adults blowing off steam, I guess."

What. The. Fuck?

A timeout? "Blowing off steam?" He got right in her face. "You saying that you're mine forever and begging me to claim your pussy and your ass was blowing off fucking steam?"

Her cheeks went pink and she tried to look away but he cupped her face, forcing her to look at him. "Why did I know you were gonna try to pull this shit?"

"Marcus, I wasn't myself. I'd taken some sleeping medication and—"

"What the hell are you taking sleeping medication for? And who prescribed it? Because they should lose their license. It was irresponsible and—"

"Stop it. Stop it!" She jerked away from him. "You don't get to control every little thing in my life anymore. I'm my own person. I can go to whatever doctor I want to. You don't own me. I can do what I want, when I want—"

Marcus glared at her, his chest in a vice, her words from the night before ringing in his ears about how any cock would do. "You better not be blowing off steam with any other adults."

"Of course I'm not!" She looked appalled and his stomach unclenched, but only a little.

"Then come with me."

"No. How many times do I have to tell you that it's over?"

He got right in her face again. "As many times as it takes for you to get it through your head that it'll *never* be over between us. And deep down, you know it too. Otherwise, you wouldn't have ended up on my doorstep at two in the morning begging me to fuck you."

Her head jerked quickly back and forth in the negative. "I— I wasn't— That wasn't like me. I couldn't sleep and I was in bed and I got to thinking about you—"

"Please, do go on."

Her cheeks flushed and she stopped, her lips hardening into a thin line. "You know why I'll never go with you? Never be with you again? Because you're an ass!"

"You certainly seemed to like my ass last night," he leaned in and hissed in her ear, "the way you were grabbing it and demanding, 'harder, Marcus, fuck me *harder*.' I have the fingernail scratches to prove it."

If he thought her cheeks were bright pink before, they were nothing to the cherry red they went now.

"I did not."

"I'll turn around and drop my drawers right here, right now. It's nothing Sharo hasn't seen before." It was true, since Sharo had once helped to dig fragments from a ricochet bullet out of Marcus's ass. Marcus would be proud to add Cora's marks to his other scars.

"Don't you dare," Cora bit out, her tiny hand batting at his bicep.

He grinned at her. "So it's settled. You're coming to the safe house with me."

"Sharo?" Cora knocked on the glass partition Sharo had raised once they'd gotten on the road. "Sharo!" Cora yelled when he didn't respond at first.

Marcus could imagine the wary sigh as Sharo finally pushed a button and the partition began to retract. "Thanks Sharo. Could you drop me off at my apartment?"

Okay, now she was really pissing him off.

"This isn't a game, Cora." Marcus gripped her thigh. "People have died."

Her head spun his direction. "You think I don't know that?" She said it so forcefully, almost like she was accusing him of something.

It felt like being doused with ice. Was she thinking of his mother? Of Chiara? Was she thinking of how women in his family had a habit of dying, because of their proximity to Ubeli men?

My father always kept my mother out of it.

And look how well that turned out for her!

Marcus sat back hard in his seat. Was she right? Was the safest place for her far away from him?

"You heard her," Marcus barked to Sharo. "Take her to her apartment."

He ignored her surprise. Sharo merely said, "You got it, boss," and turned the SUV to go uptown instead of toward the south side.

Cora didn't say a thing for the ten-minute drive it took to get there and neither did Marcus. He did feel her eyes on him occasionally. He wanted to growl at her to keep her eyes to herself because he was three seconds away from changing his mind, dragging her to the safe house with him, and chaining her to a bed again. Every mile they drove it sounded like a better and better idea.

Finally the SUV stopped in front of her apartment building. She paused before opening the door and Marcus clenched his fists to stop himself from reaching for her.

"Marcus—"

"Don't," he cut her off. The only way he was making it out of here at all was if he left right this second. "Stay safe. Don't go anywhere without the Shades."

He didn't wait for her acknowledgment. The second she'd stepped from the car, he ordered Sharo, "Drive."

EIGHTEEN

MARCUS HAD DEFINITELY BEEN PISSED at her when he dropped her at her apartment two days ago. And Cora understood. She really did. After their night together, for her to turn so cold and bitchy...ugh, she didn't want to think about it anymore.

But thinking about it was all she'd been doing nonstop ever since she'd last seen him. She felt horrible. To raise his hopes like that was cruel.

She hadn't been completely in control of her faculties when she'd sleepwalked to his door, though! Okay, so she remembered almost everything that happened that night. In far too great of detail. She didn't even know how to describe the overwhelming, all-consuming need and desperation she'd felt.

And when Marcus had finally given in... Cora's eyes fell closed, a shiver running through her at the memory.

It was like her deepest and filthiest desires had bubbled up and she had to have them fulfilled, no matter what. No matter what she had to say, how she had to manipulate or... She wished she could say, no matter how she had to *lie*.

But that was the thing. Other than the one off comment about going out and looking for another man if Marcus didn't satisfy her, she was afraid that everything else she'd said had been the truth.

It was like some damn truth serum had been poured down her throat. Things she'd never even admitted to herself had popped right out of her mouth. Thank the Fates but she'd been too concerned with servicing her libido to make any other confessions...

And when Marcus had cornered her in the car after the meeting with the mayor, what was she supposed to do? Go hole up with him at a safe house? The two of them, alone?

No. The night before had been a temporary madness.

It was unfair to keep sending Marcus such mixed messages, she knew that. Jumping him one moment and telling him to stay away the next—first in the back of the club and then again the next night? Gods, sometimes she didn't even know her own mind.

Because she couldn't want him. She wanted the light. She wanted nothing to do with the darkness Marcus's life was drenched in.

So she couldn't let herself be swallowed back up by him, by his world. No matter how tempting. No matter that some pills had mixed up her head for a little while. No matter that she couldn't stop thinking about his strong hands on her body, the commanding bass of his voice, the taste of his lips on hers...

All of it kept her awake at night. And after the sleep-walking incident, she didn't dare take the last sleeping pill. She flushed it down the toilet. Wednesday rolled into Thursday rolled into Friday with her imagining more and more horrible things. What would happen on Monday when Waters' countdown clock wound down?

If she came clean and told them all everything—both Marcus and Waters—would it help? Or was it too late for it to make a difference?

A stronger woman would have come clean, no matter the consequences. A stronger woman would have *tried*.

The couple of hours she actually managed to sleep at night were always filled with nightmares. She woke each morning feeling heavy and sluggish, like her body was full of concrete. Even walking Brutus didn't limber her up much; her torso ached and she had a headache that wouldn't quit.

With no end to the tension in sight, and no word from Marcus, she took some painkillers and puttered around her house trying to focus on getting back to normal. Maybe if she settled into her normal routine and relaxed with her friends like she used to, she'd think of a solution.

Which was how she found herself wearing a little black dress, her hair teased around her face with smoky makeup, walking into a large row house on Park Avenue. Two Shades tailed her, looking unhappy.

Armand met her at the door, in his signature rock star look—tousled hair, Fortune jeans, black band tee, and bare feet. He looked effortlessly sexy, and not for the first time Cora wondered if she would've dated him if she hadn't met her husband first.

"Darling, you look fabulous," he said. "This little get together isn't as elegant as the party Perceptions put on, but the canapés are to die for and the booze is free."

"Sounds perfect," she mumbled. She was *so* tired. She'd slept maybe a total of three hours in the last three days. But Armand had called and enticed her, saying Anna would be attending.

"You okay?"

"I'm tired." She didn't quite know how to describe the achy, horny malaise that had settled in her bones, but she was chalking it up to worry and missing Marcus.

"You sleeping?"

"Sometimes." Right now probably wasn't the time to ask him what the hell was in those pills. She was likely in the minority who had extreme side effects, anyway.

"Who are the suits?" Armand looked over her shoulder.

"My bodyguards. Fats and Slim."

"Nice to meet you." Armand grinned big at them.

"No fraternizing with the muscle," Cora ordered, taking Armand's arm and steering him into the house.

"Darling, I wasn't going to stop at fraternizing..." Armand craned his neck to watch the two men follow them in before hurrying along as she swatted him. The back of his t-shirt was ripped a little so the tops of his angel wing's tattoo peeked out.

As Armand rounded the corner, a demanding female voice boomed his name. "Armand, there you are. The caterers ran out of ice, and I can't find Buddy. Without him they're too stupid to know what to do."

Cora peeked around Armand to see the tall woman who'd stopped him. She wore a long white and gold caftan that swirled around her arms and legs, allowing a peek of light brown skin. She stopped short once Cora rounded the corner. "Hello, I didn't know we had new company."

She didn't smile, though, as her eyes swept over Cora. Her dark hair was pulled back taut from her face and only made her look more severe.

Shrinking a little under the woman's frowning perusal, Cora felt like a child playing dress up in her mother's clothes: weighed in the balance and found wanting.

"I'll find Buddy," Armand promised, putting his arm

around Cora. "Olympia, meet my friend Cora. Cora, this is Olympia Leone, the lady of the house."

"Cora? As in Cora Ubeli?" Olympia fixed Cora with a hawk-like stare and Cora's greeting died in her throat. "I've know all about your husband." The look on her face told Cora that she didn't approve of Marcus Ubeli at all.

"We're separated," Cora blurted out, quailing under the woman's glare, and giving thanks that it was technically true. Olivia always told her she couldn't lie "for beans."

Armand, however, seemed impervious. "Come on, Cora belle, let's round up the head caterer and I'll introduce you to the people here."

"Wait," Olympia said. "Who are they?" She pointed to the Shades. "Ubeli's men aren't welcome in my home. Not now, not ever."

"Relax, they're Cora's bodyguards. I have my eye on them." Armand grinned impishly. He pulled Cora past Olympia, slipping in a quick cheek kiss that seemed to soften Olivia's harsh countenance a hair.

"Right, let's check on the ice situation," Armand said, leading the way through the long, open living room/dining room into the back kitchen. A few guests already milled around the table laden with food.

"Is Anna here yet?" Cora asked. It was so weird, going from living with Anna and Olivia, seeing them every day, to now having little idea what was going on with her good friends. She missed both of them, badly.

"Supposed to be arriving soon. With Max Mars. Are they a thing?"

"I saw them together at the studio where they are filming their movie. They are most definitely a thing." Cora smiled as she gave this piece of juicy gossip, watching Armand's eyes flash happily as he devoured it.

It felt good to be here, talking about frivolous things, forgetting her heavy reality for a moment. It made her feel young, like she could reverse the hands on the clock and go back, back to before...

"Let's hope they ditch the paparazzi before coming here," Armand said. "The rest of us would rather not be so famous."

Cora shook off her melancholic thoughts and threw herself fully into the moment. "Who else here is famous?"

"Olympia used to be the DA of the city. She's thinking of running for mayor now."

"Against Zeke Sturm?"

"Yep.

Cora remembered that her meeting with the mayor the day before had been Armand's doing. "Wait, how do you know Zeke so well?"

"I met him through Olympia."

Cora's head went back a beat before she put two and two together. "Ok, right, she was the DA."

Armand shrugged. "That, and she used to be married to him."

Cora put a hand to her head, rubbing it. "I need a drink. It's been a long week and New Olympus is one big incestuous pool."

Armand barked a laugh. "You got that right. Incestuous pit of sin." He slid up to the drinks table, getting her a white wine. He took a cocktail, raising it to salute someone across the room.

"Olympia is cool. She took me in when I was homeless, and made it clear that I'd always have a home here."

"Ok." Cora felt a little better about the stern-faced matron. "She didn't seem to like me or Marcus very much."

"Oh, she hates Marcus. With a passion. District attorney, remember?" Armand swigged his drink. "Of course, don't take it personally. Olympia hates everyone at first. By the way, how did the meet with our fair Mayor go?"

"Not great. Like I said, it's been a *loooong* week." She looked around at all the people laughing and having a good time. She felt envious.

It would be so lovely to get away from it all, even for one night. She wished she could be young and silly and get drunk off of neon colored drinks with umbrellas in them. But after her experience with the sleeping pills, she was not in the mood for anything even slightly mind-altering. "I don't suppose there's any coffee?"

"Coffee?" Armand barked out a laugh. He tossed back the rest of his drink. "Girl, you have got to learn how to party."

Two hours later, Cora wandered into the backyard, feeling so tired she was edging on delirious. The grass felt nice under her feet. If she lay down, would she finally be able to sleep? She twirled around, her arms out. She'd never realized before that you could reach a point of exhaustion where your limbs were so heavy they felt light again. A little like she was floating.

Anna and Armand stood on the patio, and Armand started clapping. "Ladies and gentlemen, I give you: our friend plus a single glass of wine." Armand flung out an arm towards Cora.

Anna giggled. "That's it? I guess she really isn't used to drinking. It's not even midnight and she's wasted."

What they didn't know: she hadn't even drunk that single glass of wine. She'd been sticking to bottled water all night. Her exhaustion was just finally catching up with her.

Fats and Slim stood on either side of the small garden space, looking even less happy than they had a few hours ago, but Cora didn't care. She didn't care about anything. She was so damn tired. Tired didn't even begin to cover it. She was exhausted. Worn out. Pooped. Obliterated. Smashed. There weren't enough words in the thesaurus for how tired she felt.

Cora teetered to the edge of the garden and leaned against a tree.

Anna stepped off the edge of the stone patio and her five-inch spike heels sank right into the grass. She came towards Cora anyway.

"Hey, are you okay, babe?" Anna's brow furrowed with concern. "You've barely said two words tonight. You look tired."

Cora started giggling as Anna's thumbs ghosted over the bags that were undoubtedly underneath her eyes.

"I'm so exhausted," she confessed.

"Oh, honey," Anna said, pulling her into a hug. "It's gonna be okay. Let's get you somewhere you can sit down. Maybe lay down."

"No, I don't want to leave," Cora protested. "I never get to see you guys." And going back to her empty apartment was the last thing she wanted.

"How about a nap?" Armand said, joining them. "There are rooms upstairs. Take a little power nap."

Cora nodded. A power nap. Perfect.

"We can take care of her," the two Shades moved forward. Cora stepped to follow them but stumbled and almost face planted.

"Whoa, I've got ya," Slim said, and the next thing Cora knew, Slim had her over his shoulder and the whole world went topsy-turvy.

She went limp over his back. It actually felt nice not to

have to hold herself upright anymore. She really, really needed that nap.

"Marcus is going to kill me," Armand muttered. Anna patted his shoulder.

"I'll be back soon," Cora mumbled, her eyelids already falling shut.

"We should take her home." Fats stepped forward, light from the tiki torches glinting off his shades.

"You're wearing sunglasses, at night." Cora giggled, pointing. It all suddenly seemed so absurd.

"What did you give her?" Fats demanded, getting up in Armand's face.

Cora eyes watered and she felt dizzy as she looked between Fats and Armand. Armand was taller, but skinny compared to Fat's shorter, compact form. She didn't want them fighting over her. Thankfully Armand backed down from Fat's challenging stance.

"Nothing but a glass of wine, I swear. And she only sipped at it. She didn't eat but it still shouldn't have affected her this badly."

"I'm just really tired, guys," Cora tried to explain.

"Get her upstairs." Olympia appeared in the doorway to the kitchen, in her regal looking robe. "Now. You—" She pointed to Fats, "Out. You've overstayed your welcome."

"Go take care of Brutus," Armand muttered. "Cora will be safe, we'll all be here to watch her."

Olympia kept giving orders. "Get her upstairs, put her to bed in the peacock room. There's a private bathroom in that one. You—" She pointed to Slim with a look on her face like she'd seen a cockroach. "Can stay. But don't cause trouble."

Olympia shook her head, obviously frustrated. "Andrea Doria just arrived and she brought a bunch of security with her, too. There are more bodyguards than guests." Olympia turned away, still muttering.

Slim nodded to Fats and carried Cora down the hall with Armand leading the way.

She dropped her head against Slim's chest, suddenly feeling more exhausted than she ever had before in her life. The good news was that she was pretty sure she'd be able to sleep the second she laid her head down on any kind of pillow.

In the upstairs hallway, she caught a glimpse of another tall black woman standing in a bedroom doorway, a giant blonde wig on her head and fabulous makeup highlighting her midnight skin. She stared in surprise down at Cora in Slim's arms.

"So sorry, Andrea." Armand sidled up to the woman as Cora was carried on by. "Novice drinker."

"No problem, we've all been there," the tall woman laughed. Cora craned her neck to stare at Andrea's heavily made up face under the outrageous blonde wig. She looked vaguely familiar, and Cora almost had figured out why, but the thought escaped her when Slim put her in bed.

"I don't think coming out tonight was the best idea," Cora murmured to him before the darkness of the room closed in on her and, exhausted, she finally slept.

NINETEEN

In the Mayor's mansion, Zeke Sturm strode back from his study, tossing his cell phone to an aide. With his usual exuberance, he threw open the doors to the dining room and looked down the long table at the assembled guests.

Every night the same, like a boring joke, Zeke thought as he viewed their expectant faces. *A visiting dignitary, a decorated war hero, and a kiss-ass aide walk into a bar...* Out loud he said, "Apologies for my tardiness. I hope the first course was to your liking."

Polite murmurs came from up and down the table. Zeke made sure to share his smile all around. People could be so petty if they felt not enough attention had been directed their way.

"I'm told the chef received a gift from one of the ships docking in our ports," Zeke said as he sat down. "So tonight we dine on fresh sea bass. It was imported specifically for a particular shipping tycoon's meals, now graciously gifted to us."

The guests all expressed their appreciation.

"Please, enjoy." Zeke smiled and gestured, and took his

first bite as everyone would wait on him. "Mmm," he said. "Much better than the way my ex-wife used to char it."

The guests around the table laughed, right on cue.

"What we call a sea bass is actually two species of tooth-fish, renamed to sound more palatable," said a man from midway down the table in a heavily accented voice. He had a neatly trimmed salt and pepper beard, and piercing blue eyes. He was a professor, if Zeke recalled correctly. Professor Wagner or Ziegler? Something like that.

"A fish by any other name...is still delicious." Zeke savored a forkful and motioned to the servers, calling for more wine around the table.

A round, bald headed man bustled up to the table. "My apologies for being so late."

"Commissioner," Zeke greeted the newcomer, and only the very astute would pick up the slight twitch of his lips, a micro-expression of annoyance. Zeke thought the bearded professor had noticed, though. Observant, that one.

"Sorry, boss," the heavy man breathed, tucking his napkin into his collar and grabbing a dinner roll. The man was the opposite of refinement and it was his position alone that afforded him a seat at the table. "This new drug has got us all scrambling."

Zeke wished he was sitting closer so he could kick the man under the table.

"New drug?" The dignitary from Metropolis, Claudius, perked up before Zeke could change the subject.

"Just hit the streets," the commissioner said, oblivious to Zeke's glare. But Bill wasn't the cleverest man and had always been slow at picking up on social cues.

"Limited quantity, but we think that will change. Couple of rich kids got picked up for indecent exposure, said they had taken something. Their parents went to swinger parties and came home with a couple pills. The kids know their stash; they try everything their parents do. We questioned them in the hospital and it all came out."

The commissioner finally paused in buttering his roll and realized that every eye around the table was trained on him in fascination.

"Are the kids ok?" a woman asked, Zeke forgot her name in his budding fury at his commissioner. Zeke had gotten re-elected, it was true, so he wasn't immediately worried about campaigning again. But a mayor was only as strong as the confidence he inspired. If his guests left with the impression that he couldn't control the drug traffic on his own streets—

"Oh yeah, effects wore off hours ago," Bill continued. "Just a little groggy, dehydrated. One of them still had a high, and he had an erection the size of—" Bill finally saw Zeke's face and bit off the rest of the sentence. Cheeks ruddy, he continued, "We rushed the labs to figure out what was going on."

"Interesting," Zeke said, his tone frosty.

The commissioner winced, having obviously caught onto Zeke's disapproval. Finally. But it was too late. The rest of the guests leaned in as one.

"What is the effect of the drug?" the professor asked in a scholarly tone.

"An extreme high, leading to almost uncontrollable arousal. Sets off...uh, climaxes that are...uh, off the charts, as it were."

"Again, nothing like my ex-wife," Zeke said, going for laughs and hoping to steer the conversation away from talk of drugs.

"Detrimental side effects?" the professor's fork was frozen halfway to his bearded mouth.

"Too soon to tell. But for some it seems to cause aggression. In all cases the high is followed by a crash. Sweating, shakes, a little dehydration, withdrawal headaches, that kind of thing." The commissioner, sweat beading on his forehead and obviously as desperate as Zeke was to end the conversation, shoved the entire roll into his mouth.

TWENTY

Cora woke up in the dark, with a slight headache and screaming thirst. Her body was soaked with sweat. Ugh, gross. A glass of water waited on a side bed table; she downed it and staggered to the adjoining bathroom to drink some more.

Her shoes were gone, and gods, where was her purse?

She should never have come out when she was so tired. How long had she slept for? She looked around but she didn't see a clock. She searched for her purse so she could look at her phone, again, no luck.

She stumbled around the dark bedroom but still couldn't find her purse. She must have dropped it downstairs somewhere. Crap.

After looking around the bedroom one last time in vain, she slid into the dark hall. Pulling a shaky hand through her hair, she leaned on the wall to rest a moment. Where was Fats? Or Slim? The upstairs was one long hallway with rooms off of it.

Which direction led downstairs? Well, she wasn't getting anywhere just standing here, so she turned left and started walking. As she got closer to what she suspected was the front of the house, she heard a man talking. He sounded a little like Armand.

It wasn't until she'd opened the door and was halfway inside that she realized she'd entered another bedroom.

And it was occupied.

In the low lamp light, she could clearly see the couple on the bed. She recognized Armand immediately, he was the one on top, the angel wings tattooed on his back moving as his shoulder muscles worked. A woman's long legs wrapped around his body, as his rather beautiful backside pumped to the rhythm of the music.

Oh shit. She did not need to be seeing this. Cora backed away in horror, fumbling for the door handle, but not fast enough.

A new partner entered from another side door, coming from the master bath, Cora guessed. The newcomer was the blond, stunningly beautiful Andrea Doria. She put her hand up to straighten her wig, and Cora saw the large onyx ring she wore. Andrea's robe fell open to reveal a very masculine chest and, lower down, male parts. Impressive, very aroused male parts.

"You all ready for me?" the drag queen drawled to the panting couple on the bed.

Armand reared back and Cora caught sight of the woman's face who was beneath him—it was Olympia. Her dark skin was slick with sweat, but her head was propped on the pillows and she looked as a regal as ever.

She saw Cora, too, and glared daggers at her as she addressed Andrea, "He's ready. Climb on." Her toned arms pulled Armand back down over her and Andrea leaned forward, climbing on the bed. Armand hadn't seen Cora and she'd rather it stayed that way.

Cora backed into the hall before Olympia could alert anyone to her presence. Andrea noticed the movement by the door, though, and called to her, squinting through the darkness. "Come on in, honey, plenty of space on the bed."

Reversing hard, Cora turned and hustled down the hall the other direction, hoping the tall drag queen didn't decide to chase her down and insist she join in.

Cora passed a second door that had drifted open, but she didn't look. The noise of moans and cries made it sound like an entryway to hell, but she was sure the occupants were having a blast.

She hurried by. The hall turned and finally, stairs!

Cora ended up in the kitchen, so it must have been a service stairwell. She looked around. Where was everybody? Her eyes moved to the digital clock on the stove. 1:30 a.m. Seriously, where was everyone?

More importantly, where were her bodyguards, shoes, cell phone and purse? Cora was ready to get the hell out of here and curl up on her bed back in her apartment. Maybe she'd break her own rule and let Brutus sleep up beside her on the mattress tonight. She could use a little comfort cuddling, even if it was only with her Great Dane.

Continuing her search, she walked out of the kitchen. The lights were low and all Cora could hear was some sexy, throbbing music. Without thinking, she flipped on an overhead light, and gasped, her hand flying to her mouth.

Olympia's living and dining room was filled with naked people.

A few looked over at Cora briefly when the lights turned on, but the rest were too caught up in the throes of lust to pay attention. For her part, Cora couldn't move. Even her hand was frozen on the light switch.

The food had been cleared off the table, making way for

the long, sexy body of a naked woman, who lay shuddering in pleasure as the mouths of three men traveled over her pale skin. One of the men briefly turned away, grabbed a spoonful of thick whipped cream, and dabbed it on her perky breasts before licking it off.

Beyond them, several couples were in a clinch, making out while leaning against the wall. Right before Cora's eyes, one of the couples embraced as the man lifted the woman and started thrusting into her, pressing her against the wall. His partner moaned and wrapped her legs around his naked body, digging her nails into his muscular shoulders and urging him to go faster.

Above all of this, Anna stood on the arm of a large armchair, naked but for her signature red lipstick, watching the goings on with a satisfied smile. Seated below her was Max Mars, his own legs spread with a woman kneeling between them.

As Cora watched, the movie star reached up to Anna, and Anna stepped down so she was standing on the chair cushion with one leg cocked up on the armrest, straddling Max's face. Gripping his blond hair, she thrust her pelvis forward, her head falling back as his mouth moved between her legs.

Cora was blushing so hard, she was sure her face would explode. Marcus had always teased her that she was naïve and sheltered. But even after two years living in the city watching Armand flirt with every hot thing that moved and Olivia delighting in saying the most graphic things to embarrass her...Cora still wasn't prepared for this.

"Come on, babe," the man with the whipped cream beckoned to Cora. When she still stood frozen, he grinned. "Oh, I get it. Here, there's a few left." He set down the whipped cream bowl onto the side board and reached for a little bag filled with white pills. "One of these will loosen you right up."

Cora couldn't find air to speak. The man shook the bag impatiently. "Olympia won't mind. She scored them for all of us." He came towards her, a lanky Adonis, smiling as she stared at him, wide eyed. His own green eyes were long lashed and mesmerizing.

"Here, beautiful," he took a pill out of the baggie, and proffered it to her. "Down the rabbit hole."

A squeak may have escaped from her throat. She backed away even as she stared at the pill that looked identical in shape and color to the pills Armand had given her.

"Cora," she heard someone call, and she looked across the room, grateful for the interruption.

At first, her eyes flew to Anna and Max Mars. Anna had fallen to the couch, her body arched backwards over the arm of the chair as Max's gorgeous muscular torso reared over her. The woman who'd been between his legs before now was kneeling behind him, still doing her best to lick him as he pounded Anna aggressively.

Cora reluctantly tore her eyes away from the threesome, looking past them to see the man who'd called her name. A man in an olive-green suit, dapper except for his hair, tufted unusually in blond spikes.

Oh shit. It was Spike Hair. Philip Waters' thug, the one who'd been there when she was kidnapped.

Cora didn't even stop to question what he was doing here. Her hand shot out and she hit the lights. As the entire room went dark, she jerked backwards, away from the man offering her the pill, back into the kitchen, escaping the man who'd called her name.

TWENTY-ONE

Around the Mayor's dinner table, conversation was stilted as all the guests waited for the poor commissioner to finish his mouthful.

"So this new drug, what's it called?" Claudius, the diplomat, piped up as soon as it looked like the man might be close to swallowing. Claudius took another bite of fish as he waited to hear the answer. He'd finished almost half his plate, not as put off his meal as the rest of the crowd by the conversation.

Glancing nervously at Zeke, the commissioner answered, "On the streets, it's now being called A, or Bro, or Brew. Short for Ambrosia."

"Sounds lovely," Claudius's wife said with a smile to her husband. "Causes extreme arousal? If the only cost is a little headache, might be something I'd want to try." She finished with a mischievous glance toward Zeke. "If it weren't illegal, of course."

"The libido is a powerful drive," said the professor. "Unexpressed emotions never die, but are merely buried alive to appear later in uglier ways. We suppress our desires to fit into society but when we suppress them too long, society may collapse."

"That's Freud, isn't it?" Zeke recognized the quote.

The professor nodded, looking pleased that someone had caught the reference, and raised his glass to Claudius's wife. "So you see, a woman such as yourself, keeping your libido under wraps could be dangerous to all."

She laughed delightedly, and the rest of the table looked impressed with the professor's musings. Zeke barely kept himself from rolling his eyes. The professor slipped down a few rungs in his estimation. He'd met academics like him before—old, self-important windbags who were relevant only to the campus bubble they lived in.

This was the last thought he had before he gasped involuntarily and hunched over a little. Fuck, his *stomach*. A cramping pain tore through his stomach and radiated outward to the rest of his body.

"Honey, what's wrong?" he heard Claudius's wife say. Looking up through watering eyes, Zeke saw Claudius collapse forward, face down into his meal, gagging.

Help. He needed *help.*

But when Zeke opened his mouth to shout for help, all he managed was another desperate, choking gurgle. The pain. Zeke had never felt anything so intense. Gods, he was going to die. He was going to die!

Zeke thrashed and plates and cutlery flew. His dinner partners jumped up as his hand went rigid, gripping the tablecloth as he slowly sank to the floor.

"Mr. Mayor?" The commissioner's voice was a distant shout.

Zeke's vision went blurry and he prayed to pass out because the pain, oh *fuck*. His eyes went wide as another spasm tore through his stomach.

The professor crouched beside him. "Get an ambulance!" he shouted in his thick accent.

"Is he choking?" someone cried out.

The professor stared down at Zeke and Zeke wanted to beg him for help, to do something, dammit. But all the man said was, "I do not think so." He looked down the table. "Two choking at the same time? It cannot be a coincidence."

A woman was screaming and Zeke peripherally registered that it was Claudius's wife, that her husband had collapsed, too.

"Madam!" The professor bellowed at her from the floor beside Zeke. "Does your husband have a food allergy?"

Zeke didn't hear her reply. All he knew was that the next moment, the professor was cradling his head and ordering someone, "Take his feet, now! We must carry him to the car."

"But, the ambulance—"

"It will be too late. We must go. *Now*."

"What about Signore Claudius?"

"He's already dead. Now hurry or we'll lose the mayor, too!"

TWENTY-TWO

Spike Hair? Here? Cora could wonder why and how later, though. She wasn't about to let herself be a victim again. She rushed onto the patio. As she rounded the house, she tripped on a man's outstretched legs.

"Oh!" she screeched and slammed a hand over her mouth. Because it was Slim. Laid out and unconscious. Was he— Was he—?

She dropped down and put her fingers to his throat. But even before she felt his heart beat, she felt his chest moving up and down. He was breathing. But in the light from the back patio lamps, she could see a tiny trickle of blood marking the spot where he'd taken a blow to the head. Whimpering, she checked his pockets, but whoever had knocked him out and tied him up must've taken his weapon and his phone. Dammit!

It was only now is she looked closer that she realized that his hands and feet were tied together. But even if she could untie him, there was no way she could carry him. Her options were either: go back inside and interrupt her friends who were...otherwise engaged, or possibly get kidnapped by Spike Hair again.

Shit.

Or she could run and hope whoever had knocked her bodyguard out wouldn't come back and finish the job.

"I'm getting help," she whispered to Slim as if it would make a difference. "We'll come back for you."

Crap, how long had she been crouching here exposed? Time to get moving again. Barefoot, she escaped across the grass and ran straight into the foliage beside the back fence, oblivious to the briars scraping her.

A childhood in the country had taught her how to climb a tree. Which she did now, grabbing onto a low branch and swinging herself up until her legs got purchase. She climbed higher and higher, all the while waiting for one of Waters' soldiers to yank her down at any moment.

She was quick enough, though, to get up high and drop to the other side of the fence that divided Olympia's house from her neighbor. Scraped up and limping a little from the shock of landing on her bare feet, Cora dashed around their house and slipped out to the street beyond.

After a few blocks running on the pavement, she slowed and reality set in. Shit. She had no money, scraped palms, no shoes, and no phone. Her bodyguard was hurt, maybe even dead if Spike Hair decided to come back and finish the job...all because of her frivolous desire to go to a party.

She kept trying to pretend that if she just closed her eyes and wished it all away, the reality of who she was would disappear. But it didn't work like that. She'd been foolish and childish and now people might get hurt because of her.

Holding back tears, Cora tried to think and take stock of her surroundings. Self-flagellation wouldn't do anyone any good right now. Armand, Anna, Olympia, Waters' man—she put them all out of her head so she could figure out what to do next. She was on Park Avenue, not the best place to be in New Olympus after midnight, but not the worst.

There was a place close by that she knew well—the Crown Hotel, where Marcus had his penthouse.

Gathering her bearings, she slipped down back alleyways, moving as quickly as she could while still watching for broken glass that might cut her feet.

When the brilliant gold facade of the grand hotel appeared, she nearly sobbed. Even in the late hour, the door was busy with returning guests.

The senior doorman, Alphonse, recognized her. "Mrs, Ubeli, what—" His eyes widened at the sight of her bare feet and scraped arms. "Come," he said, wrapping her in his coat and ushering her quickly inside.

Wincing as the fabric brushed her raw arms, Cora padded to the elevator, her head down, grateful for his help.

"I don't have my keycard on me," she said, feeling desperate.

"It's no trouble, Mrs. Ubeli. Your husband will want to see you right away."

"He's here?" Cora asked. "I lost my cell phone. I was at a party and...it got wild."

"Ah," the doorman said in a kind tone. "No matter. You're home safe now." He used his own keycard to get her to the penthouse floor, and dropped her off, only leaving when she insisted she was fine. The penthouse lights blinked on as soon as she entered.

She hadn't been here since... She shook her head, taking it all in. The place was clean and perfect, but with maids that came through daily, that was no surprise. It looked the same, and nostalgia hit her hard.

Using the hotel phone, Cora called the number she knew—Marcus's cell. It went to voicemail; she left a message in a quavering voice. "Hey, it's me. Something went wrong at the party where I was tonight. I should never have gone. It was stupid, but I didn't think... Anyway, one of Waters' men was there. Slim is hurt...I didn't know how to help him, so I left him and ran and now I'm at the penthouse. I lost my cellphone," she ended awkwardly. "Call me."

After going to the bathroom and washing her dirty feet, she pulled off the little black dress and looked in the mirror. The sexy makeup she'd put on earlier seemed like a joke now. She wiped it off and threw her dress in the trash. She stared at herself in the mirror, cataloging her week so far.

Kidnapped, drugged, betrayed. She'd moved into a new apartment and gotten a bodyguard almost killed.

She glared at herself. "You wanted your own life, huh?"

She closed her eyes and breathed out a long breath through her teeth. It was time to stop running and grow up. For real this time.

She needed to talk to Marcus and sort things out. He deserved to know everything. She didn't know what that meant for their relationship or what she even wanted it to mean... And she needed to confront Armand.

Those pills he'd given her... What was happening to those people at the party looked an awful lot like what had happened to her the night she'd sleepwalked. Armand had lied to her. Told her they were sleeping pills when they were actually... How could he have done that to her? And then on top of it all, invited her to a party like that? He had to have known what it would turn into, with them passing out the pills like candy. And he'd certainly been enthusiastically participating.

Cora scrubbed at her eyes and headed for the closet. Her clothes lay just as she'd left them. Marcus hadn't moved a thing. She opened one of his drawers and drew out one of his undershirts, lifting it to her face and inhaling. The familiar smell of his detergent made her feel calm and desperate at the same time.

She stepped further into the closet and ran her hands over his suit jackets. He was always so strong. She could use some strong right now.

Finally she pulled on a pair of her jeans, wincing slightly at the scrapes on her legs. She tugged a simple plain white tee over her head and went out to check the clock again.

Almost 2:00 a.m. No calls.

Waiting, she watched the clock until she was convinced she saw the second hand hesitate. Surely Marcus would have gotten her message by now? Or wherever he was hiding out, did he not even have a cell phone? What about Sharo? Where was he?

But Alphonse said Marcus was here. Or had she just assumed? A big part of her had secretly hoped that this was his safe house—that he put out the word that he was going into hiding but he'd snuck back to the hotel to wait it out here.

She frowned, looking around. During their marriage Marcus *did* like to work out before bed, usually opting for the private penthouse pool. Maybe he *was* here and had gone upstairs for a quick swim?

Okay, so maybe she was grasping at straws now, but she had to check. Anything was better than sitting here doing nothing.

Walking gingerly on bare, scraped feet, she left the penthouse and took the stairs to the top floor.

The top floor of the Crown Hotel had a spa and gym dedicated to the more elite guests, plus an open-air patio and a few small, shallow sunning pools outside, along with the Olympic sized indoor one. Cora padded through the workout area, completely dark at this time of night, and through the women's dressing room. The lights turned on as she passed through.

She played out the conversation she would have with Marcus in her head. He'd be angry, she knew. Two narrow misses was enough for her for one week. Her insistence that she be left alone to live her own life sounded stupid now.

Plus, would it *really* be so bad to be holed up alone with him? All week she'd been so lost and lonely without him.

The pool lay under a huge glass canopy, a dark pit that drew her eyes. One moment she was staring at its tar-like depths and then the lights blinked on and—

"Marcus!" she screamed. "No!

A man floated face down in the blue water, fully clothed in a dark suit like the ones hanging in her husband's closet.

Cora ran to the edge of the pool. "Marcus!" His dark hair waved gently around his submerged head and his limbs were spread wide, completely limp.

Cora didn't stop to think. She leapt into the water and swam towards her husband with everything she had.

It was only as she drew close that she saw the blood clouding the water around him.

"Marcus!" she screamed as she grabbed him and flipped him over in the water. She let out another shriek, jerking backwards.

The man was dead. His head was bashed in.

But it wasn't her husband. It wasn't Marcus.

"Cora," Sharo called and she spun around in the water. "Get out of there," he said. "Come on. Hurry."

Cora swam towards the shallow end, tears clogging her vision. "Where's Marcus? Is he safe?"

Sharo met her at the edge of the pool, grabbing her elbow and all but dragging her out of the water. "I just got off the phone with Mr. Ubeli. He's safe. But that man is dead. And you can't be found here." Sharo's voice was so deep she had trouble deciphering what he said.

Cora shook her head as she stared into his black eyes, uncomprehending. Marcus was safe. But a man was dead. Everything was happening too fast. "Who is he?"

"I don't know." Sharo made an impatient sound as he bent and swept one arm under her knees, scooping her up. "We gotta get out of here."

The gory sight at the pool receded until Cora saw it only in her mind's eye. She pressed her face into Sharo's warm shoulder. She was getting him all wet, ruining his suit, but she couldn't care.

Back in the penthouse, Sharo swung her down. She winced when her damaged feet hit the floor, but didn't sit when Sharo motioned she should. She was drenched and dripping all over the carpet.

Sharo already had a burner phone to his ear. "I got her," he said without greeting.

"Is that Marcus? I want to talk to him." Cora could feel her brain sizzling, the events of the night burned so deeply into her memory.

Sharo answered her with a shake of his head.

Cora went to stand in front of him, her body shadowed by his bulk. He hung up and glared down at her, imposing in black slacks and a black shirt stretched tight across his awesome muscular form.

"You don't move from my sight until Marcus gets here."

"What about the body?" Her voice came out almost an octave higher than normal, but she felt near the edge of her rope. "What are we going to do?"

"Nothing."

"We can't just do nothing. We have to call the cops."

"And get fingered for murder? Not today." Sharo ran his hand over his bald head, looking down at her. "What were you even doing up there?"

"Looking for Marcus." She wrinkled her forehead, staring up at him. He was two hundred and fifty pounds of black muscle, and so scary most people wouldn't even look at him. Cora wanted to smack him. "I didn't know it was going to be dangerous."

"Bet the body in the pool helped wake you up to that fact," he said sarcastically and she saw red.

"It's not funny!"

"Course it's not fucking funny." Sharo loomed closer into her space. "You could've surprised the killer, taken a bullet. You're lucky to be alive."

"That man—who is he?"

"Don't know, probably some poor suit who got drunk downstairs tonight."

Cora sucked in her breath.

"Our enemies don't care about the body count." He saw her pale face and paused, weighing his next statement. "It's a message to Marcus from his enemies. They can't find him, so they get a guy with build and hair color that looks like Ubeli. We find the body; we get the message."

Biting her bottom lip so she wouldn't scream, Cora barely dared to ask, "What message?"

"Death threat. Target: Ubeli. Now, go change outta

those wet clothes before you catch your death and the boss kills me for not taking care of you right."

Cora nodded, swaying on her feet.

"Gods, woman, sit." He took her shoulders and guided her down onto a leather settee. She should protest. The chlorinated water might mess up the leather—

But before Cora could say anything, Sharo left the room. He came back carrying another of Marcus's undershirts and a pair of his boxers.

With the gentleness of a mother, Sharo turned Cora's back to him and peeled off her shirt, replacing it with Marcus's. Next, he braced her while she stood and tugged off her jeans. He looked away while she kicked them off and tugged on the pair of black boxers.

He pulled her elbow so she sat back down. He sat next to her and, without a word, swung her feet into his lap to inspect them. After a second he grunted in annoyance and stood again, gathering her into his arms.

"What—?" She caught sight of his grim face and shut up.

He set her on the sink in the bathroom, and fished around for first aid supplies. He found the first aid kit and lifted her foot to start treating her cuts.

Halfway through, his phone beeped and he checked the message. "Fats broke up the party."

"He did? Is Slim okay?"

Sharo blinked at her. "You mean Jorge?"

"Fat's partner? I call him Slim," she said.

Shaking his head, Sharo went back to cleaning her cuts. "You're lucky you're cute."

"What's that supposed to mean?" she bit her lip to keep from crying out as the antiseptic he applied started to sting.

"It means you're a fucking pain in the ass, but we'll put

up with it." Sharo finished with a soothing ointment and started bandaging. He went to work on the angry red marks she got from climbing that tree in a panic.

"Gods, woman." he muttered, turning her calves this way and that before treating the scratches. Cora sat still, trying not to wince.

"I didn't know it was going to be an orgy," she said in a small voice.

"Right."

"I didn't," she insisted. "And obviously I didn't know Waters' man was going to be there, either. I wouldn't have gone if I'd knew it would be dangerous!" She started to push up from the counter and Sharo grabbed her waist to hold her in place, keeping her from standing up as he got in her face.

"Like you didn't go to the enemy's strip club for kicks?"

Not fair. That was completely different. "A girl was missing! I wanted to help!" she shouted back, not caring that his large, angry face was only a few inches away.

"You need to pull your head outta your ass. You put yourself in danger, and left to keep doing it. For all you know AJ is still out there, waiting for his chance."

"Oh please, I know AJ's dead," she said before she could stop herself. "I mean, I hears..." her voice trailed off at the blank, scary look on Sharo's face.

"What do you know?" he asked quietly. No anger, no intimidation. Just scary quiet.

Cora's heart was racing, finally realizing the danger. "I watched Marcus kill him. I was hiding, I saw the whole thing. Marcus beat him to death."

"That's why you ran." Sharo looked almost satisfied. "Couldn't take it."

"He killed a man in cold blood." She gripped the edge of the countertop.

Sharo's black eyes studied her face. "Fucker deserved it."

"I grew up in a world where people call the cops. Where they let them handle things."

"Yeah, for what? Scum like AJ gets a fair trial, parole? Back on the streets."

"Yes, if that's the way the system works."

"Yeah, the system works sometimes. But when it doesn't, we fix it."

"You can't play god, Sharo."

"We can't walk away. Not now."

"Oh, yes, because you're better than the Titans," Cora said scornfully. "Because you follow some stupid Code—"

Sharo's hand moved so quickly she only caught it out of the corner of her eye.

She flinched, but he didn't strike her. Instead, he stuck a thick finger in her face.

"Don't ever disrespect the Code," he said, and her stomach dropped at his tone. She could feel the angry tension in his body, but when he lifted her again in his arms and carried her, his arms were gentle.

He set her down on the bed. "Get some rest."

"Sharo, where's Marcus? When can I see him?"

"He's in hiding. Not even I know where he is. Total blackout until we flush Waters out."

"He didn't leave me a message?"

"He won't send anything to a phone that can be traced. But if you want a message, I'll give it to you—stay here, stay quiet." Sharo looked her over, obviously noting the dark circles under her eyes. "And get some sleep."

"Great, orders. Definitely Marcus." The penthouse was

silent besides the two of them. "You don't have to babysit me, personally. I'm sure you have better things to do. Or did you draw the unlucky straw?"

"No," Sharo said. "The lucky one. And your safety is top priority right now."

Cora's head went back a beat. "Me?"

Sharo chuckled, shocking her again. She'd expect the floor to open up at her feet before she'd ever witness Sharo laughing.

The big man sensed her confusion. "Family always takes priority. Old Man Ubeli thought the same way. Protect the core." He walked closer slowly, until he towered over her. She still hadn't moved. "The world can tilt on its axis but when you're home, you're upright again."

Cora waited, perfectly still, for the giant to finish what had to be the longest speech of his life.

"Marcus and I made our choice long ago, when we lost all the family we'd ever had. Someone threatens you, we'll fight, bleed and die before we see it carried out."

He gripped her chin gently. "You've got nothing to be afraid of, Cora. Marcus and I are tough because we have to be. We were made for this moment."

His finger slid under her jaw, tipping it up until she met his eyes. "Trust me."

TWENTY-THREE

CORA LAY in her and Marcus's bed, cheek to the pillow, body curled in the blankets.

She didn't sleep, just lay staring at the ceiling, where the smooth paint turned into a pool with a body floating in it.

What would she have done if it had been Marcus? Her chest clenched even at the thought. Reliving those moments in her head when she'd been so certain it was him, that she'd lost him, that it was all over...

Her breath hitched. She couldn't— How could she live in this world without him?

She raised her head when she heard voices outside. And barking. Brutus!

She jumped out of bed, not caring that she was only wearing Marcus's oversized undershirt and boxers.

She scurried into the living room and dropped to her knees when she saw Brutus. She threw her arms around his neck and he barked happily, licking her face all over. Stupid tears sprouted as she hugged her dog, laughing and petting him on his tummy while he jumped and did little excited leaps at seeing her again.

The reunion was so sweet it took Cora a second to realize that sitting opposite Sharo in the living area was Fats.

He looked older, tired. The night had taken its toll.

Cora's lower lip trembled as she looked at him. It was her fault his partner had been hurt, and now possibly—"You find Slim?"

"Slim's gone," Sharo said succinctly. "Disappeared. Waters must have taken him."

Cora willed herself not to spill more tears.

"We'll get him back," Fats told her. He didn't look like he blamed her at all. "You alright?"

"Just tired," she said. "I'm sorry about Slim. I should've gone to ground with Marcus."

"Cops are swarming this place," Fats said. "They found the body in the pool."

"Took 'em long enough." Sharo looked unimpressed.

"I'd say pretty quick, considering everyone's preoccupied with the situation with the mayor," Fats said.

"What situation with the mayor?" Cora asked.

Fats glanced at Sharo first and the underboss nodded permission. Cora gritted her teeth but listened to the report.

"Mayor Sturm was taken to the hospital last night. They think it was poison. He had a late-night dinner party—one of his midnight specials. He's in critical condition, and another guest died."

"Cora," Sharo said and she fixed her eyes on the big man. "They think that Waters did it."

"Philip Waters?"

"They're giving him credit for the body upstairs, too. At least, unofficially."

Cora wanted to ask how Sharo knew this, but she remembered his ties to the police and shut her mouth.

Fats agreed, "Two hits, one night. Trying to take out a major player and threaten the other. Gotta be Waters."

"You're sure it's not my—" Cora swallowed. "You're sure it's not the Titans?"

Sharo shook his head. "Doesn't make sense. They don't have any motive to hit the mayor. Doesn't do anything to forward their agenda."

"So why was Waters' man at the party last night?" Cora asked, suspecting she already knew the answer.

"Looking for you," Sharo confirmed, and, try as she might, she couldn't read his penetrating gaze.

She swallowed. "What do we do now?

Fats got to his feet. "We let this guy out." He nodded to Brutus. "I'll go with you. I need to stretch my legs for a bit."

Cora looked to Sharo for permission, and the bald head nodded. "Take the couple extra Shades downstairs to shadow you."

Fats nodded.

After a brief walk in the park across from the hotel, they waited for Brutus to do his business while watching the lights from the cop cars wash over the golden facade.

"Will they come to question me?"

"Probably not. If they do, though, we'll brief you." Fats handed over her cellphone. "I found that winged fellow and got your purse."

Cora took her phone, avoiding his eyes. "Thanks. You didn't have to do that."

"I had backup. Actually, it was my pleasure," he grinned.

"Sharo said you broke up the party."

"Naw. Just flipped on the lights. Everyone had mostly finished."

Cheeks heating, Cora hesitated. "I didn't know that was

what the party was about." It was important to her that Fats understand. "And I didn't want to leave Slim behind."

"I know," the Shade said, so softly that she dared to look at his face. What she saw there was scarier than any rancor. Devotion. Loyalty.

She swallowed hard. "I'm going to follow orders from now on."

"Aww, don't say that." Fats winked at her. "It's more fun when you don't."

TWENTY-FOUR

CORA WOKE, her mouth dry and heart racing. Her hand was vibrating; her phone. She answered it before she realized it was an unknown number.

"Hello?" she held her breath, hoping it was Marcus.

"Cora?"

It took her a moment to recognize her friend's dulcet tone. "Anna? Is that you?"

Anna's voice sounded strained, weak. "I'm at the hospital."

"Oh my gods," Cora swung out of bed. Brutus's ears pricked up and he raised his head. "What happened?"

"Max got in a fight." Anna choked out. "I thought it was all fine. At the party, everyone took those pills and then it was, I don't know—it was just like, free love, ya know? Everyone kissing and hooking up with everybody else."

"A group of us went back to Max's place and I thought it would be more of the same. Max was fine with it at the party. I mean, we all were. But this one guy started kissing me and Max went ballistic. He punched the guy and they got in this big fight, and a couple other guys joined in—"

She paused and Cora could hear her crying. "And one of them started getting rough with me, slapping and hitting me. Max didn't even notice, he was so busy beating the shit out of that other guy."

"Anna, you're going to be ok," Cora said, her heart breaking as she went to her closet to find shoes. "Tell me what hospital; I'm coming." Cradling the phone between shoulder and ear, she stuffed her bandaged feet into her sneakers.

"I don't want you to see me like this." Anna's whisper was broken.

"Anna, please. Let me come be with you." Cora was already grabbing a large purse and shoving some essentials into it.

Anna told her the name of the hospital. "Don't tell anyone yet, please."

"I won't."

A Shade sat in a chair by the door, not Fats or anyone else she knew. His head snapped up as Cora came rushing out of her bedroom, her designer bag over her shoulder, heading to the kitchen to put out food and water for Brutus.

"Good boy," she told the dog before racing to the door.

The Shade stood, his jaw set as if ready to stop her from leaving. She'd learned her lesson, though. She wasn't going anywhere without protection.

"I need to get to Main Hospital, right away," she said, and he blinked. Grabbing a jacket from the coat closet, she started out the door. "Come on."

A hand caught her arm before she was half gone. She looked back to see the Shade frowning at her. "Sharo said you need to stay here."

"It's an emergency," she told him and watched orders war on his face.

"I drive," he said finally and she nodded.

Her phone rang again when they were almost at the hospital. This time a blocked number. Marcus, or Sharo, calling to scold her. In the second of hesitation, a car darted out suddenly and Cora slid forward in her seat. The Shade cursed, reaching over to keep her still.

"Buckle up," he ordered.

Cora clicked her seatbelt on, one hand on the dashboard. She silenced her phone with a swipe. As soon as they pulled into the emergency room parking lot a couple minutes later, she opened the door. "I'll be right inside, you can find me in there."

She ran for the building. The Shade wouldn't be far behind and Cora couldn't stop replaying in her head how Anna, strong, fearless Anna, had sounded near broken on the phone earlier. Cora had to see her. Now.

"She's in room 210," a nurse told Cora. "We're not supposed to let people back here, but she asked for you specifically. You're her sister, right?"

"Right," Cora lied straight-faced. "Her sister."

When the woman looked at her skeptically, Cora straightened her shoulders and glared. "We have different fathers."

The nurse nodded and Cora hurried down the hall to Anna's room. She tried to brace herself mentally for what she might be walking into. What had happened to the man who hit Anna? Who'd gotten her to the hospital? And what the hell was wrong with her supposed boyfriend that he would let a thing like that happen in front of him and not stop it?

The lights were out in the hospital room, but Cora could still see the bruises blooming on her friend's face, looking dark and angry.

Anna's lower lip trembled as Cora approached. "Hey," Cora said gently.

"It was my idea to move the party back to Max's house. This is all my fault. I ruined everything."

"Shhh," Cora shook her head. "No, honey, it's not your fault. You have to know it wasn't your fault."

Tears rolled down Anna's face; Cora held out a tissue. Anna took it and mopped at her injured skin, wincing.

"It doesn't look that bad," Cora said, studying the black half circle over the orbital bone.

Anna laughed half-heartedly. "Thank you. You're a bad liar." She sniffed. "The doctors want to keep me overnight, to make sure I don't have a head injury."

"From the blow?"

"The guy also pushed me down. I hit my head. I don't know, I came to and was seeing stars."

"I'm so sorry, Anna. You don't have to talk about it if you don't want to."

"I have to tell someone or else I'll go crazy, but I don't want everyone to know." Anna leaned back into the pillow, turning her head to hide the marred side of her face. Against the white pillow, her profile was perfection.

"After the party we went to his place... We were all having fun, drinking. Max drank a lot. A few guys took some more of those pills we'd all had at the party. It seemed natural when our friend Nathan started kissing me. Like earlier. But Max got pissed and started hitting Nathan. And one of Nathan's friends decided it was my fault." She shrugged, winced at the movement.

"And he just hit you?"

"I may have screamed that him and all his friends had tiny, limp little dicks. Then he just came at me."

"Max didn't stop him?"

Anna's eyes went distant. "I don't even think he could see me. He was consumed in this rage. There was no getting through to him. I thought he was going to kill the other guy he was busy pounding on. Someone called the cops. They showed up and pulled him off Nathan. It was only then he saw me and tried to get to me."

Anna slumped into the pillows. "It took two officers to drag him away, he was fighting so hard to get to me. But I was glad they were taking him away. I hate violence. I could never be with someone like that. It's over between us."

Cora bit her lip. Marcus was violent. She'd witnessed him beating someone to death and there hadn't been any cops to pull him off AJ at the last minute.

"I'm so sorry," Cora whispered, almost too low for her friend to hear. Pulling up a chair, she smiled at Anna until Anna finally reciprocated with a wan smile of her own.

"Thanks for coming. I feel better already. The doctors are going to do a CAT scan and keep me for the night."

"That sounds really serious, Anna."

"Oh, it's just my doctor being fussy." Anna raised her head a little and confided, "He's a former client."

"Ah. So you're in good hands." Cora smiled and pulled her purse into her lap. "In that case, it's good I brought you something to feel more normal."

She pulled out a small camisole and pajama shorts, a toothbrush still in its case, and a book. "And I barely use this makeup." Cora waved a small case of eyeshadow and lip gloss.

When she looked up Anna's eyes were shimmering with unshed tears. "Thank you. For everything. It's nice to have someone who cares."

"A lot of people care about you, Anna. Olivia, Armand, pretty much everyone who meets you loves you."

"Not Max." Her voice wavered. "He never said he loved me."

"Max is a twisted, fucked up asshole." Cora surprised herself with her own vehemence.

"Wow. I've never heard you use curse words. I didn't realize you knew any."

"Come on, I lived with Olivia for a month and a half." Cora grinned. "I'm a quick study. And seriously, Max Mars isn't worthy of you. If there was any justice, someone would kick his ass and teach him how to treat a lady."

Anna nodded and sighed.

"Or tie him up and make him watch his own movies over and over," Cora said with a wicked smile.

Anna laughed, and this time, it sounded hearty. "Now that would be truly cruel."

TWENTY-FIVE

Marcus burst into the hospital hallway. He'd been running for the past forty-five minutes, ever since he got the message that Cora had gone to the hospital for an 'emergency'. That was all his man could tell him. And that she'd been walking upright when she dashed into the hospital, but that was it.

The nurse at the desk wouldn't give his man any more information, declaring he wasn't family and saying she'd call security on him if he didn't back off.

She'd continued stonewalling until Marcus himself arrived. He'd called the hospital Chief of Staff, a man who owed him more than one favor, so by the time Marcus got there everyone was falling over themselves to guide him where he needed to go.

And now, at the end of the long hallway, sitting on the floor with her head in her hands, was his wife.

"Cora."

Her head jerked up as Marcus jogged down the hall towards her. He crouched down in front of her as she swiped at her eyes.

"You're okay?" he asked, heart in his throat even though he could see with his own eyes that she was all in one piece. "My man said you needed to come to the hospital."

She winced. "Not me. Anna. A man beat her up. I should have explained."

What man had fucking dared lay a hand on his wife's friend? He would find out and make them pay. "She alright?"

"No." Cora's eyes filled but she tilted her head back to keep in the tears. "She hit her head pretty bad when he knocked her to the ground. That's why they're keeping her overnight. The bruises will fade in a while. But her arm was wrenched out of its socket and she's got a concussion."

Cora shrugged once, twice, and then her face crumpled. "I'm sorry," she sobbed lightly, putting her hand over her face. "It's hard seeing her like this."

Marcus could relate, if it was anything like what he was feeling, seeing Cora so torn up. His chest felt tight and all he wanted do was make it better. She was trembling and the thought of her sitting here all alone on this cold, anti-septic floor was enough to drive him nuts.

He pulled off his suit coat jacket and settled it over her shoulders. Her fingers grasped onto it like a lifeline as she pulled it around herself and leaned into his chest as she cried.

Marcus waited. He exhaled, the tension he'd been carrying all week since he'd last seen her finally easing. It had been hell, sitting in that safe house, not being able to communicate with anyone, not knowing where she was or how she was or if she was safe.

He was done being Mr. Nice Guy. Cora was going back with him. The only place she was safe was by his side. He was the only person he trusted with her safety. With her life.

When her tears finally subsided, Marcus took his handkerchief and wiped her face. He watched her carefully.

"What did the doctors say?"

"They want her to talk to a cop. She's pressing charges. And breaking up with her boyfriend who was too involved in a brawl to realize what was happening and to stop it. Max Mars."

"Pretty boy. His movies suck," Marcus said.

Cora couldn't help herself, she laughed sadly. "Yeah, he sucks a lot."

Marcus took her hand and brought it to his lips. He wanted to yank her into his arms or better yet, throw her over his shoulder and drag her to a basement somewhere he was sure she would be safe. Instead, he forced himself to let her hand go after pressing the briefest kiss.

He didn't know quite what to do with the two voices raging inside him, one screaming at him to go with his barbarian impulses and the other whispering to fight for his better nature. Things in his life used to be simple. So cut and dry.

But after knowing Cora, he could never go back to simple. She was beautifully and wonderfully complex. She blazed with the light of the noonday sun and cast a prism of colors over his previously colorless life. He couldn't go back to black and white after living in glorious color.

But how did he let her be free and also make her do what he wanted her to do? What he *needed* her to do so that he knew she was safe?

Every day since she'd left him, he'd only grown more and more impatient treading that thin line. Yet still he knew, somewhere deep down, that the only way it would ever work was for her to *choose* him. She had to *choose* their life together.

Her puffy, tear-stained eyes met his, suddenly crinkling with concern. "Shouldn't you be in hiding?"

"I needed to make sure you were all right."

"Oh." She frowned. "Guess I'm still in the running for worst wife ever." Her lower lip trembled.

Marcus blew out a breath in an almost laugh. "Come here." He stood and drew her up. He held out his arms. Offering comfort.

Cora slid into his arms and his entire body relaxed at how right it felt. How natural. His arms closed around her and his eyes sank shut. He needed to memorize how she felt in his arms. She might pull away soon and he needed this to fuel him until she was in his arms again.

"Thank you," she said.

"Of course."

She stayed there for long minutes. "I can hear your heartbeat," she whispered into his shirt.

His arms tightened around her. He wanted to feel her heartbeat in the place he loved best, her pulse throbbing while he sucked her clit.

He wanted her back in his bed, underneath him, screaming his name, acknowledging she was his wife, that she was his, only *his*—not in the throes of one night's passion but in the morning and every morning for the rest of their lives.

She pulled back, and he forced himself to merely stroke the hair back from her face. For her, he could and would hold back. "What do you want me to do?"

Cora bit her lip like she was actually considering his offer when a woman in a white coat cleared her throat.

Cora swung around. "Yes? How is she?"

The doctor took them in with a dispassionate gaze. "She has a concussion, but no brain swelling we're worried about. Normally we'd discharge her but we want to monitor her through the night."

Marcus nodded. "Thank you, doctor. Can you keep our numbers in case there's any change?"

"Of course, Mr. Ubeli."

Cora looked startled, probably wondering how the doctor knew his name.

"She can bring this to the cops. Assault," the doctor said.

"We'll talk to her." Marcus glanced at Cora.

"She's sleeping now," the doctor put in. "I'd recommend letting her rest and visiting her in the morning."

Cora nodded, blank like she was numb. Marcus needed to get her out of here. He pulled the doctor aside for a moment and spoke to her for a few minutes about Anna's continuing care, all the while watching Cora. He came back to her as soon as he was done with the doctor.

"Cora?"

She looked up blearily.

"You ok?" Stupid fucking question. Obviously she wasn't okay.

"I'm ok." She stared blankly at his shirt buttons. She looked so lost, it killed him.

He held out his hand. "Come on, goddess," he said. "Let's go home."

Without pause, she slid her small hand in his and followed him out.

TWENTY-SIX

AFTER THE HOSPITAL, Marcus brought her home to her apartment. Brutus greeted them; one of his Shades had brought him. Cora relaxed as soon as they stepped foot into the apartment with its warm, welcoming design.

Marcus stood in his trench coat, attending to messages on his phone as she got Brutus's food, but really he watched her. Brutus's bowl was already half full, so she only poured a little more in.

"When was the last time *you* ate?" he asked.

Closing her eyes, she shook her head.

She wasn't taking care of herself. There were dark circles underneath her eyes. She needed him. She needed to be taken in hand and—

Marcus forced that line of thought quiet and breathed out through his nose. "I'll send a man with some food." He couldn't help following up with, "Go lie down."

He braced himself for her to snap back at him that he didn't own her and she could do as she liked in her own apartment, but instead she blinked wide, vulnerable blue eyes up at him.

"Can you...can you stay with me?" she asked.

His breath caught and he nodded, not trusting himself to speak because if he spoke, he might fuck it up.

He followed her as she moved toward the bedroom, taking off the coat he'd offered her earlier as she went.

She didn't turn any lights on, just went to the bed and lay down on her side, cheek to the pillow, staring at the wall.

There was a chair by her vanity and Marcus sat down, still not daring to speak. Just being here was enough. Just the fact that she *wanted* him here... Was this the beginning of the way back? Or was this only for tonight because she'd been so affected by seeing her friend hurt?

Everything in him wanted to close the space between them and claim his wife in a way she'd never forget and could never again deny.

She was fragile like a flower right now, though. If he squeezed too tight, her bruised petals would never flourish again.

So he remained still. Gods help him, he remained still.

His beautiful wife turned her head towards him. The pain in her gaze cut straight through his gut.

He opened his mouth to say her name, to try to say something comforting, but she beat him to it.

"Will...could you hold me?"

She didn't have to ask twice. He was up off the chair and sliding onto the bed beside her in the blink of an eye.

And finally he did what he'd been longing to do all night. He wrapped his arms around her and slid his body into hers from behind, one leg tangling with hers.

It was a familiar position, one they usually settled into after sex, not before. Marcus knew tonight wasn't about sex, though. It was about comfort and letting Cora know she wasn't alone.

She never had to be alone again or to face anymore nightmares without him at her side. He'd fight all her battles, slay all her beasts. Things were bad now but they'd be good again. She'd see. He'd give her the most beautiful life anyone ever had.

He tucked her close to him and covered them with a blanket. He watched over her as she quickly fell into what he hoped was a dreamless sleep.

They stayed like that, her asleep in his arms and him memorizing the feel and smell and sight of her for over an hour. She only stirred when there was a knock at the door. A text pinged on his phone, letting him know that his Shade had left their food at the door.

Cora lifted her head but Marcus urged her to lay back on his chest.

"It's just the food," he said. "You hungry?"

"Not really." She wormed so that she was lying beside him, facing him.

"Why haven't you been able to sleep?" He lifted a gentle finger to caress the shadows underneath her eyes.

She didn't pull away. "I get these dreams. Nightmares really."

"Tell me."

"Mostly about AJ."

Marcus felt his entire body tighten but he forced himself to relax. He'd almost blown his lid when Sharo told him that Cora had seen him put AJ down like the dog that he was. Somehow she'd been there and he couldn't imagine what it must have looked like to an innocent like her.

"That fucker doesn't deserve to take up any space in your head."

She hesitated. "I watched you kill him."

"Sharo told me."

"It scared me." Marcus thought of the violence of those last, brutal moments. Of course she'd been scared. Scared of *him*. Shit.

"He would've hurt more people. It was my responsibility to make it stop." He paused and took a breath. Justifying it wouldn't help anything. He wasn't sorry that he'd killed AJ, but he was sorry that she'd seen it. She'd been an innocent when she married him. All he'd done since was corrupt her.

"I understand why you ran." He reached forward to sift his fingers through her light hair, but he couldn't quite meet her eyes. "You married a killer. It's a part of my life you were never meant to see. But if this is going to work, there can't be anymore lies between us. This is who I am. It's who I have to be."

"That's not what scared me."

He lifted his gaze to hers and she was the one reaching out this time, laying her hand on his chest. Her brows were scrunched together, upset. "I watched you smash his head in, and I was...I was *glad*. AJ killed Iris like she was nothing. I wanted him to die. I *wanted* it to be brutal." Cora's tortured gaze met his. "I hated him. I watched you kill a man in cold blood and I was glad."

She started to take her hand away, but Marcus captured it and held it to his chest. Could she feel his heart beating?

Their gazes caught again. "I was glad," she repeated, gripping his shirt. "I wanted you to hurt him. All these months I've been telling myself that I had to get away from you because you were the darkness and I wanted to live in the light."

"But the darkness..." Fat tears trembled at the edges of her eyes. "The darkness was inside *me* all along."

Marcus dragged her close to him and kissed her forehead before tucking her head under his chin. "You wanted justice."

They lay like that for a few moments. Her body shook and he held her tighter. His stomach tied in knots at seeing her suffering. She was in so much pain, he could feel it. And it was wrong, so wrong.

She was supposed to be kept separate from all of it. She was supposed to live up on a pedestal where only light shined. The darkness was never meant to touch her. But he had failed her, time and time again.

"I'm sorry I ran," she finally murmured.

He moved his head back so he could look at her. "Don't be sorry. You were frightened."

"I didn't leave because you killed him. I mean, I thought I did. It was what I told myself. I wanted to go back to a simpler time. A simpler life."

She frowned and shook her head. "But I think that was an illusion. Life's never been simple. The darkness has always been there. In the loneliness of my childhood. When my mom got mad and hit me. Even the whole reason we were hiding out on the farm—"

Her features scrunched with pain. "What my family did to your sister... You said to me once that the sins of the father would be visited upon the children."

"Gods, no, Cora, I didn't mean—" Fuck. He had meant it at the time but that was before he'd gotten to know her, to love her. "That was a long time ago—"

"No, you were right. That's the legacy they left me." She sat up in bed and swung her legs off the side, pulling away from him. "I can't ignore it or pretend I'm not a part of it. The darkness is inside me."

"Cora," Marcus started, moving to sit beside her, but she cut him off, eyes distant.

"I wanted vengeance for what AJ had done to my friends. I wanted it bloody and I wanted it brutal. With every blow you landed I wanted the next one to be twice as hard. I was disgusted with myself but I still couldn't look away."

She was killing him, didn't she know that? All Marcus had wanted to do was protect her and yet here she was, the strongest, most resilient woman he'd ever met...and she was so close to breaking. Because of him. Because of his world.

Finally, finally, she looked at him, eyes wide and lost. "What does that make me? I was glad you got rid of him. He got what he deserved, but the more I thought about it, the more scared I got. Because, I mean, where is the line? How far is too far?"

"I draw the line," Marcus said firmly, reaching down and grabbing her hand. If she felt lost, he'd be her anchor. He'd fix this, he swore he would.

"That's an awfully big responsibility, Marcus."

"Yes. I take it seriously. And you're wrong. You aren't the darkness. Baby, I've looked into the face of the dark and depraved." He cupped both of her cheeks gently. "You are the light."

She started to shake her head but he held her still. "Okay, so you've seen some things. You were glad when a bad man died. You had a shit upbringing and fell into the clutches of a bastard with bad intentions."

Her eyebrows furrowed but he continued. "But *you changed* that man. A man most said was bound for hell, and good riddance. *You loved* me. And if you gotta have a little bit of darkness in you to love a man like me, then damn it, I'm glad you do. But goddess, otherwise, you shine so bright, you blind me most times."

Twin tears fell down her cheeks at the same time she

leaned in and kissed him. Kissed him so sweet he thought he might die. The lightest press of her mouth, but she let her tongue stroke his lips lightly, asking, inviting.

His cock almost tore a hole through his suit pants, he went so hard so quick. But still he didn't press. He let her take the lead. He didn't dare scare her off, not now that it looked like she might finally be coming back to him. For real. Not for some frantic romp in a bathroom after getting kidnapped or a lusty madness in the middle of the night where any cock would do.

No, he'd take things slow, careful, making sure she was with him every step of the way. So he stayed perfectly still.

Cora's eyes were closed and after a moment, she let her hands drop and moved back. Her brow furrowed and she looked at him uncertainly. Like she was afraid he didn't want her anymore.

Okay, fuck careful.

He stepped forward, his broad shoulders and body dominating the space between them as his arms closed around her.

And he kissed her back. He kissed her with everything he'd been withholding. He kissed her with his fury and with his longing and with his love because *fuck*, he loved her so fucking much.

He dragged her leg over his, positioning her on his lap and she kissed him back hungrily. Not with the sloppy insanity of that one strange night, but with the hunger of a woman who knew what she wanted. And what she wanted was *him*. Her arms wrapped around him and her fingers drove into his hair.

She shifted in his lap, gyrating her hips against his steel rod of a cock in a way that drove him absolutely fucking nuts.

Enough. He grabbed her tiny waist and flipped her so that she was beneath him on the bed. The next second, he hovered over her, grinding his body along the whole length of hers. Fuck. Yes. This was what he'd been dreaming about, ever since he'd let her out of his sight.

She was finally, finally, back where she belonged.

Apparently she felt the same way, because her small hands were at his waist, tugging impatiently at his belt buckle and button.

"That's right, baby," he growled. "You want this?" He ground hard against her sweetness, imagining the liquid honey pooling inside her panties. He needed to taste her, but no, he needed inside her more.

He needed to reclaim what was his. This time wouldn't be sex. He was done with fucking his wife in a one-off here and there.

He'd given her space and they'd finally cleared the air between them. Now it was time for them to be man and wife again. It was time to make love to his wife.

He pulled her arms up, yanking her thin camisole off over her head. Damn, he'd forgotten how perfect her breasts were. He thought he'd memorized everything about her, but seeing her now, he knew his memory had done her no justice.

She trembled beneath him, her back arching underneath his gaze. Her nipples hardened to sharp little points.

He reached down and tweaked one. Her sharp gasp, followed by a breathy moan was almost his undoing. But no. This was important.

"What do you want, goddess?"

"I want you."

Fuck but that felt good to hear. He awarded her with a smile. "Tell me what you want *first*." He reared up over her, teasing his lips near to her mouth but not quite touching.

She arched her back, obviously needy with frustration. "Your mouth on me."

He dropped his lips to her skin, down her throat and ever so softly to her breasts, the barest whisper of a breath.

"Marcus," she moaned. "Take over. Tell me what to do."

"Say my name," he whispered. "Say my name again." He felt vulnerable the second it came out of his mouth but he couldn't help it. His name on her lips was everything. Her acknowledging who she belonged to while she was completely clear-headed.

"Marcus. Marcus. *Marcus.*"

He dragged her nipple into his mouth, biting and suckling with all his might.

She screamed and bucked beneath him, her legs wrapping around his waist. Oh, his goddess liked that, did she?

He moved to the other nipple even as he reached his hand down between them. He slipped his fingers into her drenched panties. Always so eager for him, so ready.

His fingers were quickly slippery with her juices. His cock grew even harder, though he wouldn't have thought that was possible.

She writhed beneath him. "Please, I'll do anything."

"Anything? Then let go baby." He used his fingers, strumming her like an instrument until she broke perfectly under him. "Because all I ever wanted was you. Just as you are."

She was breathing hard when he shoved his pants down enough to glide into her.

Fuck but she was tight. So hot and so fucking tight. Made for him.

"Yes," she breathed in obvious satisfaction. "Marcus, *yes*."

He moved and all the world was perfect, there was never any wrong in it, as long as he was pounding into her. Imprinting himself on her.

"Who do you belong to?"

Cora threw her head back. "You," she cried. "*You*, Marcus."

"You better fucking believe it," he growled and grabbed the back of her neck, lifting her so that when his kiss landed, she felt it throughout her entire body as he continued his rhythmic attack on her senses. He grabbed her ass and shifted her position so he slid in deeper than ever.

She moaned into his mouth and clawed his scalp as her pleasure rose.

That's it. That's it, goddess. Give it all to me.

And she did. She didn't hold back a single damn thing. She screamed his name as she came and thrust her hips against his, shamelessly seeking her own pleasure in a way that drove him absolutely crazy.

His own climax was lit by her going wild beneath him. He shoved into the hilt and as his seed shot out of him to coat her innermost depths, there was only one thing on his mind.

He crushed his wife close to him and whispered in her ear, over and over, "I love you."

She threw her arms around him and squeezed so hard he could barely breathe but he didn't care.

Because the next words that came out of her mouth were, "I love you too."

Four sweeter words had never been invented in the English language.

Marcus pulled back, needing to look her in the eye. She

was smiling but it was tentative, like she didn't trust this happiness.

"You done running, baby? Because if you come back to me, I don't know if I'll ever let you go." It had about killed him the first time and he wasn't sure if he'd be strong enough to ever do it again.

But her eyes were clear of doubt when she said, "I want to be with you. I want you back."

Marcus couldn't remember feeling such stunning happiness ever before. He grinned. "I know."

She laughed and shook her head. "Cocky."

"Very cocky." He jerked his hips.

Her eyes widened at the reminder that he was still inside her.

She arched an eyebrow. "Ready for round two already?"

"Shoot me if my answer to that question is ever no." He dropped back down to kiss his wife. Once wasn't really enough to truly remind her of his claim. It might take all night.

TWENTY-SEVEN

ARMAND LAY in his canopy bed, messing on his phone. When he looked up, Olympia was standing in his bedroom doorway, wearing another one of her long silky robes and looking like an ancient priestess.

"You're up late," he said. When she came and sat on the side of his bed, he set his phone aside. "Worried about your ex?" She and Zeke had been married for years, no matter how acrimonious the divorce.

"I didn't realize how much I still miss the bastard," Olympia admitted.

"Aww, come here, Armand will make it better." He opened his arms and she leaned into them. "I know something that will help you sleep," he whispered into the dark shell of her ear.

She pressed into him, fire in her tawny eyes.

Impishly, he plucked a bag of white pills out from under his pillow. "Sleepy time?" He shook them.

"Those aren't sleeping pills, *mon petit*." She laughed at his confused look.

"I thought... I was wondering why you had sleeping

pills at our little party." He studied the bag. "What are they?"

She dipped her head closer to his lips. "Ambrosia. Food of the gods."

Armand blinked at her, still not sure what she meant, when she took the bag from him and tossed it on the bedside table. "But we don't need those tonight."

Putting a hand to his chest, she pushed him down to the pillows.

"Take off your pants, *mon petit*. Mistress is hungry."

TWENTY-EIGHT

FOR ONCE CORA woke up before Marcus. She lay there a long while studying his face, her eyes tracing the strong jawline and the sexy hollows of his cheeks. He was masculinity personified. And how she loved him.

Being with him here, now, his big body so warm next to hers... She never wanted this moment to end.

But it would, wouldn't it? She bit her lip. Why hadn't she told him everything last night when they were finally opening up to one another?

It had been on the tip of her tongue numerous times. But after everything with Anna... And then his arms were around her and it felt so good, so right, she wanted a little more, for it to last a little longer...

She wanted it still. She wanted to bury herself in her husband and hide away from the world for a little while more. Was that so wrong? To steal a little happiness while they could?

Marcus frowned and stirred in his sleep.

She wanted to soothe him and promise she'd make it all

better. But that was a promise she couldn't keep, so she did the next best thing.

Ever so gently, she tugged the bedsheet down. Her eyes immediately widened. Because while Marcus might still be asleep, his cock certainly was not. The tent in his boxers was so tall, she was surprised the fabric was still containing him at all.

She was happy to remedy the situation.

She reached in through the slit in his boxers and tugged his shaft out. He stirred slightly but still didn't wake. She grinned as she bent over and took the tip of him in her mouth.

His hips shifted, effectively thrusting him several inches deeper. She smiled around him. What sort of dream was he having? It had better be about her.

She applied suction and bobbed up and down several times before bottoming out as far as she could take him down her throat.

Marcus groaned. He shot up to a sitting position, his hand going to her head and tangling in her hair. "Fuck the Fates, you're real. You are actually here."

A wicked smile curled her mouth as she looked up his stomach to his face. "You bet your ass I am, baby."

"Alright." Sweat beaded a little on his forehead as his hips raised up involuntarily and he forced them back down to lie passively under her. He fell back to his pillow.

She pulled off of him and he closed his eyes as a muscle jerked in his cheek. She took him in her hand, working him slowly up and down. "You like that?"

He groaned. "I love it."

"I've missed this," she spoke to his dick, wet with her saliva. "I dreamt about it at night. I felt it in me."

She dropped her mouth back to the head of his cock and

gave it a little suck, flicking her tongue along the slit the way he liked.

"Look at me," she ordered, and was thrilled when he obeyed.

Marcus hands fisted in the sheets. She didn't take her eyes off his gray ones, knowing he was promising her retribution.

She opened her mouth and took him as far as she could go.

"Fuck," Marcus squeezed out, his head thrown back. He was too thick for her to take all the way down, but she slid her mouth up and back, trying her best to go deeper.

"You're going to kill me," he groaned.

She came off with a pop, still holding him at the base. "Where do you want to come?"

"Inside you."

"Inside my mouth? Or inside my pussy?"

"Inside your pussy. I have plans for that mouth."

Turning so she faced his feet, she slid down on his cock, sighing with satisfaction. She canted her ass up and down, looking back at him with a sexy tilt of her mouth. "Like the view?"

"Oh yes." His hips were moving opposite hers and she could hear herself squelching around him.

"I'm so wet for you." She ground down.

"Yes, you are, baby." He gripped her hips, steadying her. "Ready for me?"

She tipped herself forward, steadying herself on her hands between his legs. "Ready, Daddy."

He drove his cock up into her and she lurched forward at the vehemence of his thrusts, shouting her pleasure to the ceiling when her climax hit.

It was over quickly; he came and pushed himself up

hard, then fell back, breathing hard. He pulled her back to him, lifting her sweaty hair from her neck to kiss it. They lay together quietly, his hands stroking her pale breasts and belly.

She half thought he'd fallen back asleep when he finally asked, "Well, Mrs. Ubeli, where do we go from here?"

Cora spiraled back into reality. "I have questions," she said. "Can you answer them for me, with total honesty?"

Even as she asked it, she felt her chest tighten. *Are you going to give* him *total honesty in return?*

Marcus thought they'd cleared the air of what had happened the night she'd run. But he still had no clue what had set all the events into motion.

Her.

Her actions. Making the deal with AJ, leaving the Estate, trying to rescue Iris with the help of the cops. How all of it had blown up in her face and resulted in his shipment being confiscated by the cops.

Marcus sighed. "I can. For you, I can. I'll tell you when there's something that might not be good for you to know. But if you want, I'll tell you everything." He tugged her hair gently. "You gonna return the favor? Are you gonna talk to me?"

There it was. He was asking her straight out.

And instead of giving him a straight answer, she curved her hand around his face. "I missed you," she whispered. "I saw that man in the penthouse pool, dead, and I thought it was you."

There. That was the truth.

"Babe, you gotta be honest with me. You can't hold this all in." He stroked her hair and she closed her eyes, it felt so good. Being with him, in his arms, it all felt so good. Was it wrong of her to want to hold onto it for just a little longer? "You're going to keep getting bad dreams."

"I know," she whispered. Her brow furrowed. "Where's Slim?"

Marcus matched her grim expression, but didn't answer right away. "We're looking."

"He's not dead?"

Marcus pulled her back close and stroked her hair, a sweet, gentle act that belied their dark conversation.

"We have reason to believe Waters is holding him." The way they were positioned, she couldn't see Marcus's face. But she could feel the tension in his body beneath hers.

"Why?"

"Power play. Maybe thinks he can turn Slim against me, or wants some collateral when we next go to talk."

"You're going to talk to him?"

A sharp shake of his dark head told her everything he felt about the subject.

"But...I thought you needed to ally with him. I thought it was the only way you could win a fight against the Titans." She lifted off of him so she could look him in the face, but he was staring off into the distance. "You can't let them win."

When he finally turned his attention back to her, his gray eyes looked straight through her, and she knew he was seeing something else.

"Marcus," she said, and he snapped out of it.

"We can get through this, you and me," he said, changing the subject. "No matter what is ahead. I was taught that being married is for life, and you gotta control yourself, be faithful. But being married means you have each other's back, for all time."

"You may not feel like it," his eyes searched hers, "but

I'll always, always have your best interest in mind. I'm not perfect, I'll make mistakes. So will you. We'll make them together and we'll talk them through."

"Okay, Marcus," she said.

"You going to run from me?"

"Only if you chase me." She smiled, remembering the time he'd chased her at the art museum.

"Oh, I'll chase you," he growled, and smacked her ass lightly. "We'll play. We have two months of play to catch up on." He leaned in close and slid his nose along hers. "But right now, I need to hear it from you straight."

She froze. Did he know? Was this a test?

"I need to know that you meant what you said last night. No more running?"

She let out a breath of relief. "I'm done running. I think I was running from myself as much as you."

"Alright, babe." He kissed her lips. "How about we get some food?"

"Can we go to the hospital? I want to check up on Anna."

Cora would tell him everything. She would. She just wanted to soak in this happiness for a little while longer. A little while longer. Then she'd come clean.

"As long as you're doing it with me," he smiled at her, dimple appearing in a rare show, "we can do whatever you want, babe."

TWENTY-NINE

"Who's that?" Anna craned her head after greeting Cora, obviously having caught sight of Marcus, or at least the shape of him through the hallway window. Cora's shy smile must have told her the rest. "Marcus. You two back together?"

Cora nodded, and lifted a bag. "Fresh t-shirt, jeans, underwear, the works." She rummaged around and held up a bright yellow makeup bag.

"Thank you," Anna sighed.

"When are you getting out?"

"Soon. Today. My producer friend is actually coming by to pick me up."

Cora nodded. "So everything's still okay with the movie? Even though you'll have to go back to work with—"

"Max Mars," Anna grimaced. "Don't remind me. He's been calling and texting nonstop."

Cora glowered. "If he's not getting the message, Marcus can—"

Anna waved her hand. "No, it's fine. I can handle him."

"And your attacker? What did the police say is happening to him?"

"He's still in lockup." Shadows played across Anna's bruised face. "Apparently Max pulled some strings so he's not getting out on bail. It's something, anyway. They say he could serve up to five years for assault and battery."

Swallowing hard, Cora took her friend's hand. The bastard deserved worse than five years. She couldn't think of anything more despicable than a man hitting a woman or child. "And the movie? What do you want to do?"

"I've wanted to be an actress all my life. I dragged my mom around to auditions, practiced for hours in front of a mirror. It's all I ever dreamed about." Anna closed her eyes, her forehead creasing.

"There are other movies, other directors."

"Other asshole actors?" Anna grimaced, shaking her head. "Not for me. You don't get it, Cora. There's a time limit to my success. I need to break out now, while I'm young, and beautiful enough to let my looks make up for my lack of experience."

"If Max doesn't back off or if he gives you a hard time in any way—"

"I've been taking care of myself a long time. I promise I'll be fine."

"But if you aren't, we can—"

"I said I'll be fine."

Cora backed off at Anna's sharp words, not wanting to upset her any more. But no way was she letting her deal with this alone. She was family now.

Anna set her jaw and even bruised, her face was still lovely in a cold, untouchable way. When she spoke, Cora had to listen hard to hear. "I'm going to do it. I'll do the movie and make my career. And then..."

"And then?" Cora prompted. Even though she was looking straight at her friend, she saw a totally different woman.

"No one will ever touch me again."

A nurse stopped in, and the burning intensity in Anna's eyes disappeared as she smiled and spoke charmingly to the woman.

When Cora left the hospital room, she found Marcus standing in the hall.

"All good, babe?"

Crossing the hall to him, she leaned close and took a deep breath.

"Babe?"

"Can your guys keep an eye on Max Mars? And... maybe send him a message to leave Anna alone?"

Marcus nodded. "He bothering her?"

"She broke up with him after what happened. But he's having a hard time taking no for an answer." She hurriedly added. "But he needs his face for the movie. So..."

"Got it." She thought she could see the ghost of a smile hovering around his mouth. "Anything else?"

"No." She came forward, put her arms around his suit-clad body, and pressed her cheek to his strong chest. He held her, while a few orderlies passed by and averted their eyes.

"Love you, babe."

She sighed, so content it hardly felt real. "I love you too."

"Well, if it isn't the two love birds. Marriage ain't killed your romance yet?"

Cora jerked her head around to see a familiar figure in a dirty coat.

Pete. The cop who'd betrayed her.

He approached slowly, at a slight angle, as if he expected Marcus to attack if he came at them straight on.

Which was exactly what he'd done when Cora had last called him—he'd come in sideways and found Marcus's weak spot—her. Pete had played her. And let a woman die so he could make his big bust. She wanted to claw his eyes out but she held back. Marcus didn't know and he couldn't find out, not this way.

Pete slouched against the wall, tilting his shaved head towards them. "What'd you get her for an anniversary, Ubeli? The rest of AJ's dead body? I hear his head showed up in a gang zone in Metropolis. Right on the Titan's doorstep, so to speak."

Cora couldn't help it; she gasped, and Marcus's arms got tighter. "Let's go," he muttered.

"Aww, what's the matter? No respect for the man who busted ya?" Pete flashed his badge and smirked. "How 'bout you, Cora? Haven't heard from you in a while."

"I'll thank you not to address my wife informally," Marcus said to the man over her head. "Or at all."

"Let's go," Cora said, ducking her head as her husband steered her away.

Pete loped along next to them, keeping his distance but staying close enough that Cora could hear him plainly. "Last conversation I had with her, she was real friendly."

Marcus stopped dead, but Cora stepped between him and the detective. "You're despicable," she snapped.

"Your friends get in a bind again, you can always call me." Pete gave a mirthless smile and Cora realized he was almost as tall as her husband.

Whirling, she tucked herself into Marcus's side and marched with him down the hall. Marcus's arms squeezed her a bit tighter, but other than that, he didn't acknowledge the man watching them retreat.

Cora slid into the backseat of the car, feeling sick to her stomach. The nerve of the detective, after he didn't offer any backup. He didn't care about the women in need, about Iris *dying* on his watch, just his own career enhancement.

It took a while to realize there was stony silence coming from the other side of the back seat.

"Marcus?"

Her husband stared out the window. "How does that dick know you?" he asked, voice deceptively quiet.

Cora felt her heart drop out. "I—uh—met with him once. Well, twice. The first time, he cornered me with Anna. He knew her. The second time...I asked him to help me find Iris. The Orphan's fiancée." Cora could still see the picture of the lovely young woman and the angelic looking singer, both dead now. Two beautiful lives snuffed out.

Her husband breathed in hard through his nose. "That all?"

Cora breathed out as her eyes fell closed. *Now or never.* She couldn't sit here and continue to lie to him. Honesty. He'd asked her for complete honesty only this morning and there was no more putting it off. "I may have called him before I went to find Anna and Iris."

"I see," Marcus said.

"I was trying to do the right thing. I never meant for any of it to—"

Marcus raised a hand and she fell silent. He leaned forward and ordered the driver, "Crown Hotel. Now."

"Marcus, please—"

"*Enough.*"

Cora jumped at the barked word. They drove on in silence for five minutes. Ten minutes. Fifteen.

Marcus stared out the window. Why wouldn't he say anything else? What was he thinking? She wanted to explain it all. The words were tumbling inside her, spilling over one another to get out. If she could just explain it right, she could make him understand.

Her stomach twisted in knots as they arrived at the Crown and Marcus took her elbow in a vice-like grip as he led her up to the penthouse.

The whole time, she prayed silently. He had to forgive her. He *had* to.

Finally, they were in the apartment and the door slammed behind them.

Someone had removed the flowers that usually graced the foyer without bothering to replace them. Even though the place was clean, the shades were drawn over the tinted glass, making the place dim and stuffy, a shell instead of a home.

Marcus went and poured a Scotch, neat, and now studied the amber liquid. "I think you better tell me what happened the night you ran. Starting with when I left, please."

Her eyes darted around the penthouse. She wanted to look anywhere but at him. Instead, she forced her gaze to meet his.

The truth had weighed heavy as a lead ball in her stomach for months, stealing her sleep, sullying her dreams. She had to tell him everything and hold nothing back, even if, when she was done, he hated her.

"You said you *went* to find Anna and Iris?"

"Y-yes," she whispered, hating the tremble in her voice. "AJ took them. Iris and Anna. He called me and said if I didn't come with the ransom money right away, he'd kill them and—"

Shit, she wasn't explaining this right. "I wasn't going to go like he ordered. I knew it was a trap. But Olivia had cracked Iris's phone and we had his address. You were gone and I thought I could get ahead of AJ, surprise him at his safe house and have the police with me to bust him—" She broke off, hating how stupid and naïve she sounded. It had all seemed like such a brilliant plan at the time. Fail proof.

She took a deep breath. If she didn't get it all out now, she never would. "When I got there, I was supposed to go inside, to offer myself in exchange for Anna and Iris, and as soon I said the safe word, the cops were supposed to come in and bust AJ."

Marcus studied the empty glass in his hand. He still hadn't looked at her, she realized, not since the car. "You gambled with your life."

"I knew AJ would be too afraid of you to hurt me. And the cops were right there," she broke off, swallowing hard. She outlined what had happened when she reached AJ's house.

"But the cops didn't come to the rescue?" Marcus was at the bar, refilling his drink. Cora still hadn't moved from the small landing in front of the door.

"They were listening in but when they heard AJ call you, they obviously decided they wanted a bigger bust. I used the safe word over and over but it didn't matter." Cora's voice cracked. "They let her die. They left Iris to die, right in front of me."

"So let me get this straight. You left the Estate of your own volition. You called a cop, thinking he'd keep you safe from a psycho who'd already taken two women."

Cora licked her lips, staring at her husband's dark silhouette.

"Is that right?" Marcus prompted.

"He had a SWAT team with him," she offered weakly. "I tried to take as many precautions as I could."

"Except at no point did you tell me, your husband!" He put his glass down hard, not violent enough to break it, but she jumped when it clunked against the cabinet. "At no point did you share."

"You were busy with the shipment—"

"You didn't trust me. My own *wife*."

"I'm sorry," she cried. "Gods, I'd change it if I could. It's my fault the cops came. It's my fault..." She couldn't finish, thinking of the way the blood poured from Iris's wound. How her eyes went vacant as her soul left her body.

"This is why you ran. You were afraid to tell me." She couldn't see Marcus's expression in the shadows.

"Yes," she whispered. She'd lied to herself about it—his violence had given her an excuse—but ultimately, this was why she'd run.

"It's getting late," he said. "I got things to do. I'll get someone to take you back." Already his phone was out.

Cora's heart thudded slowly, painfully. "Back where?"

"Your apartment."

"Marcus, I'm sorry." The words burned in her throat. Everything she'd wanted to say, but couldn't bring herself to. "I never should have gone to AJ. I should've trusted you."

She wanted to go to him, to convince him, to beg him to believe her. But he was now standing by the windows, drink in hand, and her feet were rooted to the spot. "I'll tell Waters it was my fault the cops were there. It was an accident."

"You stay away from Waters," Marcus whirled and snarled so violently her feet came unstuck and, even though she was across the room, she took a step back. "It's over. You've done enough."

The door opened behind her, startling her, and a Shade walked in, glancing back and forth between the two Ubelis, before focusing on the one who gave him orders.

"Yeah, boss?"

"Please escort Ms. Cora back to her apartment. Or anywhere she wants."

"Yes, sir." The Shade held the door open, waiting.

"Marcus," Cora whispered.

"Ma'am," the Shade called. He was obviously picking up on the tension in the room and thought it wise to give her a hint.

With one last look at her husband's straight back, Cora took her exit.

In two days, time would run out. They didn't have Waters' shipment. At least Marcus finally knew the truth. The fact was cold comfort. Especially when it hit her, in the car halfway to her place, that Marcus had called her Ms. Cora.

Not Mrs. Ubeli.

THIRTY

THE REST of the day Cora wandered around her apartment in a daze, analyzing Marcus's every move.

It's over. You've done enough.

At dusk, she lost the battle with herself and dialed his private number. "Marcus, we need to talk. I can explain." She stopped there because she didn't know if she *could* explain. Did it matter if she'd been trying to do the right thing when it all turned out so wrong? "Please call me," she finished lamely.

Pacing restlessly, she checked the fridge for anything appetizing. No luck. She started drawing open a bottle of wine. When her phone buzzed with a text message alert, she dropped the wine opener to grab it.

M. Ubeli not at this number. It's being monitored. Emergencies only.

She slapped her phone down with more force than necessary. Her husband was gone, disappeared behind the faceless Shades he used as an army. When she ran, she had to fight for her space, but he changes his number and, boom, she was cut off from him.

It wasn't fair.

"What can I do?" she ranted as Brutus watched. "He holds all the cards in the relationship."

Her dog cocked his head and rubbed against her, trying to offer comfort. She scratched his ears. "It's okay, boy, I'm not mad at you. You sit and stay when you're told."

She laughed at this as she finished opening the wine.

A FEW HOURS later there came a rap at her door.

"Who is it?" Cora paused in her slightly off-key rendition of the song playing on her phone's radio.

The heavy knock sounded again and Cora groaned, not wanting to move from her spot. She'd just gotten comfortable.

Marcus. What if it was Marcus? Her drink sloshed as she set it on the floor.

In a wine-induced haze, she barely remembered to peek through the peephole.

The man outside was so tall she could only see his neck.

"No," Cora said. Oops. She said that out loud. Shit. Maybe she could hide in the bedroom until Sharo went away.

"Open the door," Sharo commanded, in a voice that made it clear that he shouldn't have to ask twice. Had Marcus dispatched his second-in-command to kill her for ruining his business? She giggled, the wine making that thought more fascinating than scary.

She opened the door and looked up, and then up some more. Sharo was tall, like *really* tall. "Hey," she hiccuped. "What do you want?"

"Came to check on you."

"Did Marcus send you?" She squinted up into the midnight black face.

"He doesn't know I'm here."

That gave her pause. Sharo was intensely loyal, and as far as she knew nothing would entice him to go behind Marcus's back.

Marcus. Who hadn't sent him to check up on her. Who'd sent her away without even a backward glance.

"Well, I'm alive. Thanks for checking." She started to swing the door shut but Sharo's foot stopped it.

"Sharo, I want to be alone." He didn't budge at all and it only made her madder. "I can't believe you. Move, you big mountain."

But Sharo just herded her back into the apartment until he could close the door.

Brutus ambled over and sniffed the big man's hand.

"Fantastic guard dog you are." Cora glared at the Great Dane, who gave a *woof* and went to lie down on the hearth.

Meanwhile, Sharo was stalking through her apartment, first heading to her sound dock and cutting off the music.

"Hey!" she cried, but he ignored her, going to the balcony and looking out. He pulled the curtains firmly together, went back to the front door, and reached around her to dim the overhead light. The dimmer had been magically installed after she moved in, part of the 'upgrades' the super had instituted at the new building owner's—aka Marcus's—command.

"What the hell—" she sputtered.

Sharo leaned down and got in her face.

"People can see in here when you have the light on," he rumbled, looking down at her.

Cora stared up at him with wide eyes. Losing all sense, she shoved him in the chest with both her hands. "I was having a nice, quiet," she grunted as she pushed, not caring that she didn't make a dent of difference, "night in. Alone!"

"Not so quiet. I could hear you singing down the hall."

With a final grunt, Cora gave up pushing and stalked away. "Well, what am I supposed to do now that Marcus has decided we're on a break? Sit in the corner and knit?" She flopped onto the couch and fished around on the floor for her wine glass, nearly tipping it and herself over when Sharo sat down beside her. When he settled on his own cushion, she noticed he took up almost half the couch.

Lifting the bottle to inspect it, he gave her an amused glance. There was only about a glass and a half missing.

She raised her chin. "What? So I'm a lightweight."

Shaking his head, he leaned over and, before she knew it, he'd relieved her of her glass.

"Hey, I was drinking that." She struggled but was no match for him. He held her off with one large hand planted on her chest while he drained the rest of the red liquid in one gulp.

"I don't believe this," she fumed. "What are you even doing here?"

"Got your message."

She swallowed hard. "I thought that was Marcus's line."

"It is, but he's gone to ground again."

"Did... Did something else happen?"

"More threats. Waters is on the move. A few of our men have been attacked, but he seems to prefer kidnapping over murder. No demands yet."

Cora's temples were starting to pound with another one of the headaches she'd been getting lately and ugh, she felt like she was going to throw up. She rubbed her forehead and tried to focus on what Sharo was telling her.

"Waters is holed up somewhere, but he's in the city.

Gotta be. There's a warrant for his arrest in connection to the Mayor's poisoning." Sharo grabbed the wine bottle and poured himself a glass. She'd never seen him drink before. "We think he's working with the Titans."

"The Titans want back in don't they?" she whispered. "She won't stop, will she? My mother?"

He looked her in the eye and shook his head. "The Titans want back in and they're gonna get in, unless we can get Waters to join us. But with him scooping up Shades, it's not looking good."

"What can I do to help?"

"Nothing. Unless you can magically produce Waters."

She bit her lip.

Stay away from Waters. It's over. You've done enough. It's over.

"Why are you telling me this?" Cora tried not to sound sad and failed. Her mother was up to no good as always, trying to hurt her husband. She winced, the pain slicing deep. *Was* Marcus even still her husband? Did he want to be? "He doesn't want me involved."

"You gonna give up that easy?"

She stared at Sharo but he didn't look at her.

"What do you mean? I hurt him, I know that. I know he feels betrayed. But he won't even *talk* to me."

Sharo chuckled without mirth. "Not fun being shut out, is it?"

"No," she said, chin dropping to her chest. She'd given Marcus the same treatment for months after she'd left him.

"Two months gone and you grew a backbone. But you still haven't grown up."

Would she break her hand if she punched him? She'd probably break her hand. "Maybe when you all stop treating me like a child."

Sharo just shook his head, taking a long drink. "You wanna know what he's thinking? You wanna know everything?"

Cora frowned but nodded, tucking her legs underneath her on the couch, making her into the smallest ball possible. Brutus sat close by, looking unhappy until she reached out and stroked his soft gray head.

"You sure?" Sharo finally looked at her and the warning in his dark eyes was serious.

"Yes."

"You sure you wanna wake up? After this you may never sleep again."

Somehow she knew he wasn't talking about literal sleep. She nodded.

"Alright." He toyed with his empty glass, pausing for so long that she wondered if he forgot she was there. But she didn't dare break the silence. "You know Marcus's sister?"

"Chiara."

"You know how she died?" He picked up the wine, refilling his drink and keeping his hand on the bottle's neck.

Cora looked at her hands. "My mom killed her."

Sharo downed his second drink. "That wasn't till after. First the Titan brothers raped her. All three of them. She was stabbed, multiple times—I guess when your mom came in and found what they'd done. Maybe she was mad at Karl for cheating on her. Maybe she hated old man Ubeli that much. Or maybe it was for the power. But Chiara bled out on the mattress where they had her chained up."

Cora sat frozen, her hand still on Brutus's head. She'd never thought through the particulars of that night so long ago. She hadn't wanted to, she saw now. She was going to be sick.

But Sharo wasn't having any mercy on her. He was

going to tell the story no matter how much it hurt either of them. And it hurt him, that was clear enough to see by the glaze in his eyes and the hitch in his voice.

"Chiara was safe at the Estate, but she got a wild hair and took off. That's when they snatched her. We knew she was missing, pulled every fucking string we could to find her. In the end, a snitch found her. Too late. She'd been dead for a day. Fuckers left her alone to die, stabbed, covered in their filth."

Sharo's hand shook a bit on the bottle, a gold ring he wore on his right hand's ring finger clinking against the glass until he clenched it, hard enough for his knuckles to pale.

"Marcus saw her and lost it. He was still a kid." Sharo looked across the couch at her, his eyes filled with black memories. "But that was the day he grew up. Not the day they took his parents, not the year after. It was the day we found Chiara, that was when he left. Didn't even wait until she was laid to rest. Cried, last time I'd see him cry, and disappeared."

Cora gripped her arms around her legs to keep from shaking. Her eyes were dry; she had no tears for this. Sharo kept speaking, his deep voice echoing in the pit of this bottomless night.

"Took me a year to find him. He was fucking homeless for months before he found his way. Trained as a fighter, and came back to New Olympus. By that time, the Titans had been in power two years, and most of Old Man Ubeli's empire was gone. Marcus built it back, and didn't stop until the last one of them was driven out."

Silence.

So this was why he'd left her. "I betrayed him and gave the Titans an in."

"Woman." Sharo shook his head at her like she was

dense. "He sent you away because he can't deal. Everything he's done has been to protect you. And you leave your safe home—just like Chiara—and run to the bad guys. Doesn't matter why you did it. He already lost his family once. He can't lose you too."

Cora didn't know what to say to that. He was wrong, though. He didn't see the look on Marcus's face. He didn't hear how cold Marcus's voice was when he told her it was over. Marcus was a man who valued loyalty above all else. And she'd betrayed him. Without trust, what was left?

"You remind me of her, you know?" Sharo said, breaking the silence. "Chiara. She was sweet, but underneath was fire." His voice dropped, so she strained to hear. "We'd do anything to protect that."

The tenderness in his deep voice made her turn to look at him. Sharo's muscular form was balanced, rigid, but he'd let the mask slip from his face enough for her to see the man beneath, the years of pain and torment.

Cora leaned against the arm of the couch, suddenly seeing so much.

"You loved her," she whispered. Her stomach swam with nausea. "How can you even stand to look at me, Sharo?"

"Get some rest, Cora," he murmured. And that was it. He walked out the door.

But all Cora could see was that young girl, violated over and over again by Cora's uncles...by her *father*. And Mom had finished the job by...

Cora barely made it to the toilet before emptying the contents of her stomach.

THIRTY-ONE

ZEKE STURM EYED the male nurse with thick, curly hair and enough muscles in his arms to suggest a fine body lay under his scrubs. He had to applaud his concierge medical care service—they'd hired a young man who was exactly his type. Watching the curly-headed lad move around the room, he contemplated pushing away the portable desk that was hiding his erection so that the nurse—Paul was his name—wouldn't be able to miss it. With these young bucks, that was sometimes all it took.

"Sir, it's almost midnight. You need to rest." The nurse bent to pick up some clothes that had fallen to the floor and Zeke got a glimpse of his bright red thong peeking out from his turquoise scrubs. *Bingo.*

"I've been resting all day," Sturm said, and it was true. The doctors had released him from the ICU and he'd done a photo shoot meant to assure the public their mayor was on the road to health, but that was about it for the day. He'd insisted on coming home to sleep in his own bed, under the care of his private doctor. "I have so much to do...it's hard for me to relax."

The nurse—Paul—straightened slowly and grinned at him.

Voices outside the room interrupted.

Zeke frowned and jerked his head. "Go find out what that's all about."

The nurse only had time to open the door before an aide popped in. "Sir, Armand Merche is here to see you."

Zeke lifted an eyebrow. What was the young Merche doing here? "Send him in. And, take the night off, Jones. I'm in good hands here."

"Yessir." The aide disappeared and Armand popped into his place, his thick hair wild over his more staid suit.

"Am I interrupting something?" Armand wore his usual mischievous grin.

Zeke sighed. "No, no, come on in." He watched the young nurse leave along with his aide and didn't bother to hide his disappointment.

As usual, Armand picked up on it. "Glad to see you're feeling better. Any luck on nailing the bastard who did this to you?"

"We have a warrant out for Waters. We traced things back enough to charge him, but for the life of me I can't think why he'd want me dead."

"I can." Armand sashayed up to the bed, drawing off his suit jacket and tossing it on a chair. Underneath he wore a lavender shirt, its slim cut outlining his lean, attractive torso. He held up a bag of white pills and Zeke immediately snapped to attention.

"Are those what I think they are?" Sturm held out his hand and Armand dutifully gave him the bag.

"Ambrosia. Brew, or Bro, they call it on the streets now."

"Have you tried them?"

"I have actually. I thought they were sleeping pills.

Took one and..." Armand smiled coyly. "Well, it turned into a pretty good night actually, but that's neither here nor there."

"I see." Zeke wasn't in the mood. The fact that Armand had this contraband was a problem. "And how did you come by these?"

Eschewing the chair, Armand seated himself right on the Zeke's bed, facing him. "Your own police office. You have a breach."

Dammit. Zeke frowned. "Who?"

"Your charming ex-wife."

"Olympia?" Zeke tried to lift off his bed, but then groaned and laid back. "I guess I shouldn't be surprised. She used to treat the evidence room as her own personal locker."

He tossed the pills down the bed and Armand picked them up again. "Why'd she risk it?" Zeke asked. "Stealing evidence isn't a great career move for a former D.A., especially if she has designs on running for my office."

Armand shrugged, fingering the bag longingly. "I guess she still cares about you. She knew they were Waters' and returned them to him."

"Waters has the pills back? Is he distributing?" The news just got worse and worse.

"Last I heard he's in talks with the Titans to distribute."

Zeke closed his eyes, feeling a headache coming on. Most of the effects of the poison had worn off, but he felt as exhausted as if he'd run a marathon or two. And now all of this was coming to a head while he was waylaid. "Bypassing Ubeli will mean war."

Zeke stared off for a second, thinking about the Titans moving in on New Olympus again. What would that mean for him and his office?

Armand's face was carefully blank. "You know my

personal stake in the dark lord's success. Speaking of which, how'd the meeting with the Ubelis go?"

"Oh, fine." Zeke pushed his desk back a little. "He sent his pretty little wife alone. I couldn't produce the drugs, and she got me to agree to do some stupid fundraiser that was the pretext for the meeting. Which reminds me, I have to wriggle out of that." He leaned forward to make a note.

"Don't even think about it." Armand leaned forward and caught Zeke's hand with the pen. "You're putting in an appearance at the fashion show. I'm also helping with it."

"She's got you wrapped around her little finger, too?" Zeke might be tired but it didn't mean he was off his game. He arched an eyebrow at Armand. "Too bad Ubeli's got his claws into her. Of course," he mused, "she said they were separated, and I'm sure, in light of the recent death threat, Ubeli's gone 'to the mattresses.' We should invite her up here so she's not lonely. Put her on all fours, our own private dog show. Remember how we used to—"

"I remember," Armand cut him off, looking cross, and Zeke grinned to himself. So Armand had a soft spot for Mrs. Ubeli. Zeke filed this information away for later.

"What are you going to do about Waters?"

Zeke went along with the subject change without comment. "Ball's in his court. He has his shipment back. When did you say Olympia returned it?"

"Thursday morning, I believe."

"But—" Zeke thought rapidly. "Who ordered the hit on me and Ubeli's look alike Thursday night? If Waters already had his product back by then?"

Armand shrugged. "Your guess is as good as mine."

"What do you know?" Zeke narrowed his eyes.

Armand laughed. "Only what Olympia tells me. She

wanted me to give these pills to you, and let you know Waters has the rest back. Minus a few she took as her cut."

Zeke studied Armand, but found no clues on the winsome face. Coming here hadn't been a social call, or even to check on his health. Armand wanted him to know that it wasn't Waters who'd ordered the hit. Interesting. What exactly was his stake in all this? "Be sure to thank Olympia. How is she, by the way?"

"She misses you, but most days she won't admit it. Just like you."

Zeke harrumphed and Armand chuckled. "So cranky. There's still one part of you that's honest, though, isn't there?"

Armand lifted the portable desk away, taking care not to let any of the papers spill. Zeke's erection was clearly outlined under the thin sheet and he didn't try to hide it.

"Ah, there it is. Although it looks cranky, too."

"It misses you." Zeke stared Armand directly in the eye. Armand hadn't come here for this, or at least not *only* for this, but with their history, things usually always ended up here. Armand was a beautiful boy who'd grown into a beautiful man.

A smile played around Armand's mouth and his nostrils flared. "I missed him too, which is why I thought I'd pay a little visit. Of course, it's more fun when there's a third, so I invited a friend to play. Paul?" Armand raised his voice to call the nurse's name.

The curly-headed nurse came back in, this time wearing nothing but his red thong. As Zeke stared, Paul shut the door and Armand stood back, looking mischievous.

"Mr. Mayor," Paul posed for a moment before crawling up from the bottom of the bed. "Let's see if we can get you started on tonight's physical therapy."

THIRTY-TWO

MONDAY MORNING CAME, and Cora woke, hearing the ghost echo of the phone ringing. But when she checked it: nothing.

She padded out of the bedroom to be greeted by Brutus. No Shade stood guard in her apartment, no bodyguard blocked her door.

She checked her phone again: no messages.

Anna would be getting out of the hospital soon, and Olivia returning from her trip. It was Monday, the deadline Waters had set for Marcus to return his shipment to him. What was happening? Would Waters make another move against Marcus when he couldn't deliver? Or would he simply go to the Titans immediately to strike a deal with them? Worry had her pacing, wearing a trail in her hardwood floors.

An hour later, there was a knock on the door. Cora checked the peephole and opened it. A line of Shades poured through, carrying boxes upon boxes.

"What on earth—?"

"From the penthouse, Miss. Mr. Ubeli wanted you to have them."

Finding a box with a loose strip of tape, she peeked in and recognized her clothes. Stunned, she ducked around the Shades swarming around her and shut herself in the bathroom.

She called the number she had for Sharo, and the emergency line she thought was Marcus's, Sharo's rang and rang until she hung up, and the emergency line gave her a dial tone.

Every hope she had drained away at that empty sound. She dialed it again, confirming she hadn't made a mistake. Nope. No one there. She slammed her phone on the sink.

So that was it. It was that easy.

Marcus had cut her out of his life. Cut off her very access to him.

You didn't trust me. My own wife.

All this time, she'd been running, and she hadn't known what she was running from. It hadn't been from Marcus, but from this. This was her worst fear made real. But once he knew, he could never forgive her. She'd broken the bond between them and could never go back.

It's over.

It hit her as she exited the bathroom and made her way across her apartment through a sea of brown boxes. She was finally alone.

"You got what you wanted," she whispered to herself

Locking the door after the Shades, she slid down to the floor, tears spilling over faster than Brutus could lick.

$\sim$

"CORA!"

Cora's head flew up as Olivia charged into her office. "Is everything alright?"

"Fine, move." Olivia leaned over Cora and grabbed her mouse. She was back from her trip and as much of volcanic force as ever.

"What's going on?" Cora leaned back and watched Olivia surf the web at lightning speed, pulling up a popular news blog.

"Max Mars didn't show up on set today." Anna sashayed in, looking lovely and well rested. Two weeks since she'd been released from the hospital, and her bruises had healed. Glowing and glamorous, she looked like the fledgling movie star she was.

"Here it is," Olivia navigated to the side news bar, reading the headline, "Max Mars beaten in bar brawl. Unknown assailant, man in black."

"Oh my gods," Anna pushed her way closer to the computer screen and commandeered the mouse to click around the article. "He got totally busted up."

"There goes the movie," Olivia muttered.

"Not necessarily," Anna kept reading. "Says here they were careful not to touch his face."

Cora thought of her conversation with Marcus in the hospital hall, and allowed herself a private smile.

Two weeks, and she hadn't seen Sharo or her husband, or even evidence of a bodyguard following her.

Her anger had subsided into a dull ache as she watched and waited for the silence to break. Reading about Marcus's activities and knowing they were his felt like a secret message, an inside joke between lovers. It hurt and gave her hope at the same time.

"Thank the gods we've already shot his topless scenes. He'll be in pain, but he can work through it," Anna said.

Olivia snorted. "He looked like he was in pain through the entire God of War movie. Either that or he was constipated."

"No, that's his acting face," Anna said. "Oh, look, Cora, there's a picture of you here."

"Really?" Cora leaned forward but suddenly Olivia and Anna were blocking her way.

"Never mind, I was wrong," Anna said hurriedly, facing Cora while Olivia clicked furiously, navigating away.

"Yeah, it's not that flattering at all," Olivia muttered.

"Stop it, guys, let me see." Cora elbowed Olivia out of the way.

Anna and Olivia exchanged worried looks.

"You can't hide it from me; I'll just pull it up on my phone." Cora rolled her eyes at them.

Reluctantly, both stepped away and Cora clicked back until she saw what made them cringe.

It was a candid picture of her and Marcus, with a line down the middle. "Known crime boss and his wife split."

Another picture of her looking depressed and lonely, walking Brutus on the tree-lined sidewalk outside her apartment. She kept scrolling down, unable to stop herself.

"Who cheated on who?" she read the histrionic red text, and clicked on the thumbnails to see a picture of her with Philip Waters at Armand's party. The two of them had been standing close enough to talk, and their pose in the lavish setting did look rather intimate, especially with his hand hovering near her arm protectively.

She clicked to the next picture and saw Marcus walking with a tall, buxom blonde. His hand was at her elbow, helping her down the red line steps outside the Crown Hotel.

"What the fuck?" Cora hissed.

"Damn," Olivia said. "I never heard you swear before."

"You're rubbing off on her," Anna said. "Cora, honey, are you okay?"

"Seen exiting the Crown Hotel last night, Marcus Ubeli and on again off again flame, Lucinda Charles." Cora read the last words with a shriek.

"Oh no, he didn't." Olivia ducked closer to read the article.

"Maybe it's best if we don't jump to conclusions." Anna leaned over Cora's opposite shoulder.

"I can't believe this," Cora shouted. "I'm going to kill that bitch! And put Marcus's nutsack through the shredder!"

"There you go, that's the spirit," Olivia encouraged.

"Stop," Anna reached around Cora to poke Olivia. "Maybe it's a misunderstanding. An old picture like the one of you and Philip Waters."

But Cora was already shaking her head, her whole body trembling as she yanked her phone out of her purse. "He's wearing the tie I gave him for Christmas. That picture is recent."

Cora was so furious she could barely dial the number she knew would reach Sharo. She leapt up and paced while her friends watched, and ended the call with a curse. "Oh no, he does not get to do this to me."

"What are you going to do?" Anna said.

Hesitating, Cora was saved from having to answer by her phone ringing. "Sharo?"

"What?" She couldn't read Sharo's deep voice.

"I need a meet with Marcus."

"Not gonna happen. Shit's going down; he's buried deep."

"Then why am I looking at a picture of him and fucking *Lucinda* outside the Crown?"

A pause. "Fuck."

"Yeah, that's right," Cora ranted. "I want to speak with him, and I mean now."

Another pause, this one longer, like Sharo was speaking to someone close by.

"Uh oh," Cora heard Anna say, and turned to see that Olivia had pulled another picture up on screen, this one of Cora standing between Armand and Philip Waters, again from the party two months ago. *Ménage a trois?* the caption read.

"Aww, they cropped me out," Olivia huffed.

"Sharo?" Cora called, her eyes on the two men flanking her in the picture, one white tux, one black.

"Yeah." The underboss's voice was muffled now.

"Did you find Armand?" He'd all but disappeared after the orgy. Maybe a good thing considering Marcus had wanted to tear him apart once they'd realized the so-called 'sleeping pills' he'd given Cora had actually been Ambrosia.

"In the wind. We didn't get to pick him up and he hasn't returned to his place."

"What happened with Waters when the deadline passed?"

Sharo didn't answer.

"And Marcus?" she pressed.

"He's...busy."

The image of Marcus and that bottle blonde bitch flashed through her mind's eye. "Fuck that. You tell him," her vision swam a little as she swayed with anger, "Tell him that, after this, he'll be lucky if I ever want him back." And she hung up.

Her two friends stood at her desk, staring at her.

Olivia snorted. "Somebody grew a backbone."

"Men." Anna shook her head. "They're all assholes."

"Oh shit," Cora said, her anger draining from her. "Does this mean it's really over? What am I going to do?"

"Get drunk," Olivia suggested. "Have an orgy."

"Been there, got the T-shirt," Cora muttered, and plopped into her desk chair.

"You want to go get coffee and talk about it?" Anna asked.

"No, no, I have stuff to do. The shelter fundraiser is less than two weeks away, and the mayor is scheduled to show up. I have to get cracking."

"You sure you don't want to go out and get wasted?" Olivia sounded hopeful, but Anna was already pulling her towards the door.

"Come on, Olivia. Leave her alone. We have to finish recording my vocals for your computer game, anyway."

"It's not a game, it's a software program we're designing to be capable of recursive self-improvement so it can achieve singularity..."

"Oooh," Anna cooed. "talk nerdy to me..."

As her office door closed on her friends' banter, Cora pulled up the article on her and Marcus. She stared at the picture of Marcus and Lucinda until it hurt too much to look. Two weeks? Was that really all it took for him to replace her with someone else to warm his bed?

She started to click away from the site, but her mouse slipped and a picture of Philip Waters from the party popped up instead. In the white tux his midnight skin was all the more striking, and the large onyx ring he wore caught her eye.

Wait a second. She froze and squinted at the screen. She zoomed in.

Holy shit.

She remembered that ring. She remembered it from the long hours of her abduction, but she'd seen it again, hadn't she? At Olympia's place on the second most unforgettable night of her life.

The one that began with an orgy.

THIRTY-THREE

AFTER PAUSING a minute on Olympia's doorstep, Cora finally rang the doorbell. With the sound still chiming throughout the large row house, she pounded on the door for good measure.

The heavy door opened and the mistress of the house herself opened the front door. Olympia wore a tight red leather top and black skirt. Barefoot, she still had enough height to look down her nose at Cora.

"Mrs. Ubeli. Do you need something? I'm getting ready and need to be on my way to court."

"I need to speak with your guest. Andrea Doria." Cora kept her backbone ramrod straight. At this point, she had everything and nothing to lose.

"What business do you have with her?" Olympia's tone was borderline rude.

"Personal business. I mean her no harm. I just want to talk." Then Cora tilted her head. "Although I do wonder what would happen to a lawyer if they found a fugitive hiding in her home..."

Olympia's nostril's flared at the threat but she opened the door.

Cora stalked past her into the house, straight down the hall and into the large living/dining room that had been the scene of an orgy the last time she'd been here.

"Darling, do you have anything besides dairy milk?" A voice called from the kitchen. A pleasant tenor voice that could be modified either up or down.

The voice of Philip Waters.

The person who appeared in the doorway had a bald head, but full makeup. Andrea Doria, halfway to her full persona.

The drag queen stopped when she saw Cora approaching.

"Hello, Ms. Doria. Or do you prefer Mr. Waters?"

Olympia had followed Cora into the room. "I told you not to shit where you eat," Olympia said to the tall cross-dresser, then glared again at Cora. "I need to get to court. Flax milk's in the fridge." She stalked away.

"I'm not here to hurt you," Cora said to Philip Waters/Andrea Doria. "You paid me the same courtesy."

Philip/Andrea asked, "How could you have known who I was?"

"Your ring. The one with the large onyx stone. You wore it the night of the party. There was a lot going on, but I never forget a statement accessory."

Philip/Andrea raised one perfectly penciled eyebrow. "Are you mocking me?"

"Not at all. I don't mock people, especially if I'm planning to ask them for makeup tips." Cora smiled.

A small smile appeared on the fabulously contoured face. "So why are you here?"

"You said it yourself when you kidnapped me. I'm easy

to talk to. I'm here to lay some things out in the open and see if we can come to an agreement."

The smile disappeared. "Your husband sent you."

"No, he didn't. We are very much separated, and I am very much alone." She held up a printout of the picture of Marcus and Lucinda and handed it over. "This was taken yesterday. I haven't seen my husband in a couple of weeks."

The queen studied the picture and flashed Cora a look of pity. "Very well. Let's talk. Coffee?"

"Please." Cora followed the cross-dresser into Olympia's kitchen, and leaned on the beautiful quartz countertop of the large island as her former kidnapper went to the cabinet and took down two mugs.

"For the time being, I'd appreciate it if we kept to my disguise. I never thought my recreational activities would serve a serious purpose, but then I found myself hunted by my allies and wanted for double homicide." Philip/Andrea poured the coffee and winked at Cora. "So call me Andrea."

"Pleased to meet you, Andrea."

"You're rather brave to come here, after the last time." Andrea placed a steaming mug on the island close enough for Cora to reach it.

Cora studied Andrea. "I don't think you ever meant to hurt me. Although, FYI, kidnapping me didn't give you any points with Marcus. He killed the last guy who did that."

"I'll keep it in mind."

"So, you're wanted by the police." Cora took her mug and fixed it with flax milk and honey.

"You going to turn me in?"

Cora shook her head, tested her impromptu flax-milk latte, and then added more honey. "Turn you in, Ms. Doria? For what? They want Philip Waters."

"So this is a game." Andrea paced along the long island, keeping it between them.

"The more I thought about it...I don't think you did it. Poisoning the mayor, threatening Marcus—any of it. I think someone's setting you up." Cora sipped her creation again and smiled. "Perfect."

Andrea fixed her with an intense stare. "Who do you think did it?"

"Someone who stands to gain from Marcus and the mayor fighting with you."

"That could be any number of players."

"Who stands to gain the most from Marcus and Zeke cutting ties with you?"

"Who would you guess?" Andrea didn't touch her drink, but folded her long arms across her chest.

"My mother."

Andrea did a double take. "Fuck the Fates, how did I not see it? Apart from the blonde hair..." She shook her head. "I assumed she died along with Karl. They always send Ivan as their contact when they try to negotiate with me."

"She didn't die. She took me into hiding. When I came out, Marcus found me."

Andrea's sculpted eyebrows all but hit her hairline as she took a drink from her mug. "And you ended up married to him? I bet that's some story."

"For another day," Cora said. "What's important now is that my mother is back. She's the brains behind the Titans, she hates Marcus, and she wants to regain control of the New Olympus rackets."

"Well, young lady, you've figured it all out. You a gangster now?"

"Nope, just married to one." Cora shrugged. "And the

daughter of another. But I'm neutral ground. No one expects anything from me. That is my weakness, and my strength." She watched Andrea ponder this. "Why didn't you tell us you found the rest of the shipment?"

"I found it Thursday night, at Olympia's party. She'd recovered it for me. By morning, I was a wanted fugitive."

Andrea sighed. "And now Ubeli is pressing me on all sides, not to mention the mayor's legal arm. Our only hope of holding New Olympus from the Titans is to align our interests. Yet I am stuck here. I can't return to my ships."

Her eyes glittered and Cora was reminded of how dangerous this person was. Andrea/Philip owned the seas and had for decades. "It's been too long already. If things don't break, I will give my men orders to extract me with whatever level of violence is necessary. Lives will be lost on both sides, and your husband and Sturm will hold me responsible. Then I will be forced to deal with the Titans."

"Which is exactly what my mother wants."

Andrea nodded. "At the same time, I'm prevented from extending an olive branch to Ubeli, because then the Titans will know I've chosen sides."

Cora thought about this. "Is that why you're snatching Shades and going through the motions of war? To look like you're fighting with Marcus, when you're really not hurting anyone, just keeping his men prisoner somewhere?"

Andrea's face was scarily blank. "How do you know I didn't kill them?"

"I don't. Except that Slim's body hasn't been found anywhere. And if I were you and wanted to threaten Marcus, I'd leave a body. So..." Cora met Andrea's stare head-on with one of her own. "Where is he?"

Andrea laughed. "You're certainly giving new meaning to the phrase, 'Out of the mouth of babes.'" She leaned forward on the island opposite Cora. "I suspect you only *look* like a babe, though."

"My aura of innocence helps. And it'll work to your favor. I can be a bridge between you and Marcus, and I'm here to tell you that's what I'm willing to do."

"Your husband has broken ties with you."

"I still have his ear. And I have it on good authority that he prefers an alliance with you to all-out war. He will listen to reason." At least, she hoped he would. At this point, Cora thought more of dealing with Sharo than Marcus, the lying two-faced SOB.

"Very well." Andrea drummed her fingers against the quartz countertop. "If you were me, how would you go about breaching the gap between you and Ubeli, as well as the mayor, when we can hardly be in the same room together without killing each other or our enemies finding out?"

Cora put down her mug and smiled. "I thought you'd never ask."

THIRTY-FOUR

Cora and Andrea had just finished their conversation when Armand walked in.

Son of a— So this was where he'd been hiding out all this time? His hair was adorably tousled, adding to his sleepy dishevelment Bare-chested and barefoot, he stopped when he saw Cora standing in the kitchen with Andrea.

"Cora, what are you doing here?"

She didn't think, she just threw her empty coffee mug straight at him. Fortunately for him, her aim was horrible.

Armand jerked out of the way as the mug hit the rug near his foot and bounced. Open mouthed, he gaped at her.

Smiling, Andrea left for the dining room. "I see you two have some things to talk through."

Cora stood glaring at Armand.

"Did you just throw a mug at me? Who are you and what have you done with Cora?" Armand moved forward but she threw a hand up.

"Sleeping pills, Armand?"

He stopped dead in his tracks and turned white. "Oh,

gods, I forgot I gave you some. I didn't know they weren't sleeping pills, I swear."

"Well I trusted you and I took them. Once even when I was still at Olivia's." She could feel the blush coming over her face, but didn't lose her grip on her pique. "And had... dreams. Crazy, crazy dreams. I thought I was going out of my mind. Another night I even sleepwalked!" Right to her estranged husband's apartment.

"So...nothing happened? With Anna, or even Olivia?" he perked up, and Cora could see the lesbian fantasy start up in his mind's eye. To stall it, she looked around for another mug to throw.

He came at her, and she tried to dodge him, then wrestled with him as he grappled with her. Even with his lean build, he still had enough strength to catch her questing hands, and force them down.

"Are you really very mad at me?" He gave her hurt, puppy dog eyes.

She tried to stomp on his foot and missed when he jumped away. "Yes!"

"Cora, I didn't know. I swear. Olympia had them, and I raided them, thinking they were her sleeping pills. They looked the same. I'm sorry."

"You're lucky nothing happened when I took them."

"Nothing? Not even with Marcus?" He looked hopeful.

She wriggled away and he let her, but watched her in case she lunged again for a mug. He didn't deserve an answer. Especially one that was too painful to give right now. "Haven't you seen the news? He left me for his old flame. That Lucinda bitch."

"No way," Armand gasped.

She pushed the photo of Marcus and the woman towards him.

"This has got to be photoshopped. There's no way... damn. He's wearing the tie you gave him for Christmas." Armand rubbed his hand through his unruly hair, making it stand up even further.

"Marcus is looking for you," she told him quietly. "After what happened that night at Olympia's party, Marcus put it together... Remember when I told you I'd sleepwalked? Well I walked right to Marcus's door and...wasn't behaving like myself."

Cora felt her cheeks blaze hot. "Anyway, Marcus made the connection after I told him I'd gotten the pills from you. He connected you to the shipment."

"I know. I heard he was looking for me. That's why I'm hiding out here with Andrea. Olympia's being a good sport about all of it."

"What Marcus *doesn't* know is that Waters already has his missing shipment back. I'm going to tell Sharo today. So you'll be off the hook."

"The Mayor knows, too," Armand said. "Waters allowed me to tell him."

"Good. So you'll help me with the next phase of the plan."

"Operation Win Back Marcus?" Armand said, and lunged to grab Cora's wrists again when she started to go for her ceramic weapon of choice. This time he whirled her around so her arms were crossed in front of her. For a moment she struggled but he just crushed her tighter with his wiry biceps on either side of her arms.

She sagged forward.

"I want to help you." His voice was muffled in her hair. "That, and I bet Olivia a grand that you two would be back together within a month of the party."

Cora couldn't help it, she laughed. He let her go,

crossing to the other side of the island, keeping it between them. His hair was wild, sticking up in every direction, but his brown eyes were wary.

"Will you forgive me?"

"Not a chance," she said. "You invite me to a party, I get drunk and wake up to an orgy!"

He winced.

"Before that you accidentally drug me! And help my husband corner me at a party I helped you throw." The more she spoke the more she was geared up to charge around the island and tackle him. "And you tip my husband off to my new address and he ends up buying the entire building..."

"Now, that, I'll take credit for. Also, you're welcome."

"Just shut up," she said. "I don't know whether to hug you or put a hit out on you."

"Definitely all for hugs here."

"At this point, you're too valuable to kill."

"Good to know." He leaned on the island across from her, back to his shit-eating-grin. "Seriously, I'm sorry. Tell me what I can do to make it up to you."

"Well, other than never giving me medical help ever again, there's one thing."

"Name it."

She sobered. "I need to pull off this fundraiser."

"Done. My design team is working on it as we speak."

"That's not all I need help with." She bit her lip, wondering how far to bring Armand in.

"There's two sides to this fundraiser," Andrea Doria said from the door. She stalked towards the coffee pot for a warm-up. "One is for the dogs. The other," she motioned with the coffee pot, "is for the city." She looked pointedly at Cora, who sighed and explained to her friend.

"Are you on board with the plan?" Armand asked Andrea when Cora was finished.

Andrea nodded. "It's risky. And we only have two weeks to pull everything together, and to make sure it doesn't fall apart. No easy feat."

"Yes," Cora said, "but it's going to work." *It has to.*

"For all our sakes," Andrea said. "I hope you're right."

THIRTY-FIVE

CORA PACED her apartment while waiting for Sharo to answer his phone, then said, "Waters found the missing shipment two weeks ago. Zeke Sturm can confirm. Also, Waters is keeping the Shades alive. He can't communicate with you because he's stringing the Titans along until you can meet. You need to act like you're at war with Waters to fool the Titans, but don't escalate things further." She took a deep breath to finish. "Don't ask me how I know all this."

A pause, then, "Why didn't Sturm report this to us sooner?"

"Why do you think?" Cora retorted. Waters and Armand had discussed the Mayor at length with her. Apparently Zeke Sturm was a consummate politician, waiting to see which way the wind blew before doing anything or choosing sides.

Sharo's sigh told her that he understood.

"Give me two weeks," she said. "I'll have more for you then."

"Woman, what are you planning?"

"Two weeks," she repeated and hung up.

The phone rang again and she let it go to voicemail, bustling around her apartment. When her door buzzer went off she shook her head and muttered to Brutus, "See? Can't just sit and do as they're told, but they expect me to..."

She checked the peephole and froze when she recognized the spiky blond head.

"I know you're in there," Waters' bodyguard breathed.

"Did Andrea send you?" she called through the door.

"Poor Cora. Husband left her all alone." Spike Hair tilted his head and she saw his bloodshot eyes. Checking the locks, she leaned against the door, heart pounding. She jumped when he rapped on the door. "Open up, little girl. I'll keep you company."

"Please, please go away," she whispered to herself. Her cell phone lay on the countertop, but she couldn't bring herself to move and get it.

Sensing her tension, Brutus came to her side. She curled into him, but he stood at attention, vibrating with alertness. When Spike Hair spoke again, the dog barked, three times. A warning.

Shaking, Cora kept hold of her dog. Had Waters sent his thug to threaten her? Could he be trusted to follow through on the plan, or was he playing her? If so, why send Spike Hair to threaten her like this?

As she waited for him to leave, she ran through all her memories of Waters. In every instance he'd acted like a gentleman, a man of his word. But he'd said it himself—with the Titans closing in, he'd be forced to turn against Marcus. Did that include her? Damn it, she should never have volunteered the information about who her mother was. What if he'd contacted Demi and made a deal that included turning Cora over to her?

"You can't hide forever," the thug outside the door said

finally, and when Brutus relaxed, Cora knew the threat was gone. She squeezed her eyes shut. Maybe Waters wasn't backing out of their deal and his man was acting independently? Or was she just deluding herself like the naïve idiot she'd always been? Still, it was ages before she would feel safe enough to open the door.

"Two weeks." She hugged Brutus, and hoped she would last that long without her husband's protection.

THIRTY-SIX

"You ready, belle?" Armand called, and Cora straightened from the front of the rented stage where she was pinning up bunting.

"Looks good," Armand said. "And it's almost three. Just enough time to go home, take a nap, and get ready for tonight."

Easing backwards, Cora took in the product of a month's planning. The large tent took up half the new dog park. Three hundred chairs faced the long T shaped stage—a real cat walk. Or should she say, *dog* walk.

Behind the stage, Cora knew, the models were getting ready, both human and canine. Maeve was back there somewhere, along with Brutus and about fifty volunteers.

"Okay," Cora said. "Just a sec."

Two weeks had flown by. After the incident in her apartment, Olivia had inexplicably volunteered to pick her up and take her to and from the office. That meant Cora worked eighteen-hour days, but Maeve was only too willing to check in on Brutus, sometimes even taking him to visit the shelter and all his old doggie friends.

Armand had also been exceptionally sweet, flitting in and out of her life, showing up at her apartment with Chinese takeout, leaning against the fireplace and cracking jokes about the Shades, watching her closely to make sure she ate.

She didn't tell anyone about Spike Hair, or his threats. The truce between Waters and the rest of the city leaders was too important for her or a wild card bodyguard to muddle it. She kept her head down, worked outrageous hours to draw every detail of the fundraiser together, and didn't go anywhere without at least one friend by her side.

Now the work and the wait would pay off. At least she hoped so. Everything hung on the success of tonight.

"What are you still doing here?" Maeve came out from behind the stage curtain, holding an adorable, tiny mutt. "You need to go change. You can't be the belle of the ball smelling like dog."

"Everything is going to smell like dog tonight. That's the whole point," Armand joked. "Besides, she's not the belle of the ball. That would be Queenie."

The little dog barked when she heard her name, part Chihuahua, part terrier: all attitude.

Maeve laughed, and Cora tried to smile, but it crumpled quickly under the weight of everything she had on her mind.

"Go on home, Cora," Armand spoke up. "We have it under control, at least until things get underway at seven."

"All right." She gave the bunting a final frown and straightened. "Are you my ride?"

"I've got my stuff here to change into. I was going to check out the old theater."

Cora nodded absently. The theater was a brick building at the end of the park. Too small for the fashion show, it played an important role in the second half of the night's events—the events that would make or break the alliance between three powerful players and decide the fate of New Olympus.

"Cora," Maeve called, and Cora realized her friend had called her name twice. "There's someone here to pick you up." Armand motioned her out of the tent.

"Fine." Cora headed out of the tent, ignoring the worried looks her friends exchanged over her head. She knew she wasn't acting like herself, and everyone who knew her had picked up on it, but she couldn't help it.

A month and she hadn't seen or heard from the man whose last name she still bore. Divorce papers hadn't arrived, but then, he'd been busy fighting a mock war with Waters.

At least there were no more pictures of Marcus in the paper with his arm around other women.

Other than reports of escalating violence between New Olympus and Metropolis gangs—street confrontations, drive by shootings, and vandalized buildings owned by Marcus's holding companies—she'd had no sight or sound from her husband, not even from Sharo.

Which is why, when she saw the large black man hulking behind the wheel of a car, she stopped short. Sharo got out of the car and opened the door. Habit propelled her forward into the back seat, until she sat secure behind bulletproof glass. Her heart ached, being this close to her past life.

"How have you been?" Sharo's dark sunglasses wrapped around his head and she couldn't see his face.

"Fine."

Sharo turned the car into traffic, pulling out of it a minute later to cut down a back alley. "You eating?"

"Yes. Did you get my last message?" She'd left a voice-mail last night. "Are we on?"

"All systems go." He stayed silent for the few miles the car crawled through thick traffic. "He's doing well."

She let out a breath. Now tears came, pooling in the corners of her eyes and stinging. Crap. She couldn't afford puffy eyes today. But Sharo sitting there made the loss too fresh, too raw. She took several deep breaths, though, and managed to get herself under control.

After parking, Sharo followed her into her apartment. Brutus was already at the pavilion, a lead in the doggie fashion show.

Her thoughts on Marcus, Cora left Sharo in the living room while she showered. Her dress, an ethereal blue, lay on the bed.

She dried her hair quickly, then pulled it back in an antique silver clip, curling the ends. She put on just enough make up to give her a dewy glow. She looked like a teen ready for prom, except for the distant look in her eyes.

The dress came on like a second skin, the neckline plunging to the point where she couldn't wear a bra. Try as she might, leaning over and shifting, the final few inches of the dress's zipper escaped her. The last time she'd worn it, she'd been on Marcus's arm. He'd helped her with it. She felt a twinge of pain at the memory.

Trotting out of the bedroom, heels in hand, she waited until Sharo turned away from the balcony doors.

"Will you zip me? I can't reach it." She went to him and turned, head bowed. A pause, then the dress bodice tightened as he obliged. For such a big man, his hands were nimble, zipping her up and hooking the little hook without so much as touching her.

Once she felt the hook catch, she stepped away and

bowed to slip on her shoes, heels like skyscrapers. She'd be among powerful men tonight, and she needed the height, the authority.

The dress's baby blue color gave her an innocent air, complemented by the pink of her cheeks. An approachable sweetness, until someone got close and realized the fit was so tight they could pick out the goosebumps on her legs if they wanted to, and just one twitch to the side and her nipples would be exposed. All the more sexy, because it was unexpected.

Sharo must have felt the effect, because as she straightened, she felt large hands brushing her back, lifting her curls and fixing them so they flowed down her back. It felt nice.

"You were right," Sharo said out of the blue. "I loved Chiara. We were engaged."

Sharo's voice was so deep, and he was usually so quiet, she almost thought she'd imagined it.

She kept her head bowed, hoping he'd take the hint and keep talking and fussing with her hair.

"We kept it a secret. People didn't need to know. We knew. From the first time we saw each other, we knew we would be together."

His hands on her shoulders turned her gently to face him. Even in her skyscraper heels, he dwarfed her. "She was in danger, just because she was born. Her father had so many enemies. And she was just this little, shy thing, until you got to know her. Then she was feisty."

He looked like he was about to laugh, and he tugged one of Cora's curls. Then his face darkened. "I was young. Cocky. I thought I was strong enough to keep her safe."

He paused so long, Cora wrapped her hands around his wrists, as if her touch would bring him back to her.

"You hate it when we keep you in the dark, or on a

pedestal. But I'm telling you, if I could bring Chiara back, I'd take her far, far away and lock her in a tower if that's what it took to keep her safe."

Oh Sharo. Cora wanted to reach out and comfort him, but she didn't want to break the spell. He was opening up to her and she saw the truth, that inside the large, brutal man before her, there was a gentle giant. Or at least, there once had been. Was there anything left of the boy who had once loved a girl, before he'd lost her so brutally?

Her eyes searched his black ones. She found nothing but darkness.

And suddenly, she was crying. She felt like she'd cried an ocean of tears lately. But how could she not? First Marcus, then Sharo. How was it possible for two men to lose so much?

Sharo shushed her, pulling her to him and holding her in a giant hug. His heat wrapped around her as she pressed her face to his suit as if that would stop her tears. She'd need to redo her makeup but she didn't care.

A big hand cupped her head. "I had a childhood growing up with her. Watching over her. And when we were older, we had a year together. A good year. Then her parents died, and she got shut up at the Estate. One good year, and one bad. Then she died."

He put his head close to Cora's, making sure she heard him. "She was sneaking out of the Estate, trying to meet me."

"Oh, gods." The image played in Cora's head, immediate and full of color: sweet Chiara, young Chiara, running over the green lawn to meet her love. Then— Then—

Cora's stomach spun and she squeezed her eyes shut. No. She couldn't lose it now. Sharo deserved for her to hear him out.

"Marcus and I found her a week later." Sharo reached out and took her hand. "We'd told her it wasn't safe. She knew that and went anyway, no guard on her, no protection, she just got a just a mad idea and ran off to find me."

Cora wiped her eyes, pressing her fingers to her skin as if they could hold back tears. "So when I snuck out—"

"It was Chiara all over again. And her death is something he's never dealt with. It was too much. It could've been Chiara all over again, and it was too much."

She dropped heavily on the couch. "Then why aren't *you* mad at me? You of all people have every reason. My parents—"

"Aren't you," he said firmly, sitting beside her. "And I've dealt with her death, Cora. I buried her. I loved her, and she died, but she's not gone. Not while I have my memory. She was the love of my life and I'll never lose her."

He sighed. "But Marcus fights it. He thinks if he works hard enough, long enough, wraps up every inch of this city so tight that nothing happens without his say so, that he'll somehow save Chiara, and bring her and his parents back. He's spent all these years running."

Cora sat up beside him, searching his face. "What does that mean?"

Sharo tilted his head towards her. "Means he needs a woman by his side who understands, and who can be there for him. In his world, men destroy, women heal. He needs you."

"He sent me away."

He squeezed her hand. "He needs you."

"Will I ever see him again?" she whispered.

Sharo let his features soften into a smile. A happy ache went through her at the tender sight. The gentle giant was still there. That boy who'd once loved a girl remained inside the man today. "That can be arranged."

Cora's lower lip trembled, but she nodded. "Okay."

His wrapped a big arm around her, and she relaxed into the hug, letting his steady heartbeat calm her.

He said Marcus needed her. Wrapped in Sharo's warmth, she felt like anything was possible.

A thought struck her.

"What about you, Sharo? Are you going to fall in love again?"

He turned and lightly—very lightly—kissed the top of her head.

Her cheek pressed to his huge chest, she blinked. She let him hold her for a beat, then, she shifted away, avoiding his eyes.

"I should fix my makeup." When she let her eyes drift up to his face, she could barely look at his tender expression. He looked ten years younger, closer to her age.

With a nod, he let her up and she stood up.

Back in the car, they shared a taut silence. Sharo's large hand rested on his leg; she reached forward and touched the gold band he wore on his right ring finger.

He looked down at her, eyes still gentle.

"Thank you," she said, touching the ring she now knew he wore for Chiara. Her throat closed before she could elaborate—*thank you for sharing, for watching over me.*

His eyes crinkled into a smile and she knew he heard her unspoken words.

Then his gaze slid down to her cleavage and back up. "I've got your back tonight," he said, and he didn't sound happy. "Don't let anyone get too close."

She read his displeasure and couldn't help smiling.

"Marcus bought me this dress," she reminded him, and his nostrils flared.

"You were mine, I wouldn't let you out of the house in that thing."

"Good thing I'm my own woman then," she said. "Because you boys couldn't pull this off without me."

THIRTY-SEVEN

THE FIRST HALF of the night went well. The dogs paraded next to the models, and everyone was on their best behavior.

"Are they all house-trained?" Cora looked up at Andrea Doria, who'd joined her backstage.

"The dogs are. Can't say for sure about the models." Andrea smiled. Her blonde wig was glorious, teased around her perfectly made up face.

"You look amazing," Cora told her honestly.

"Thanks, darling. You're sweet."

"I'm serious. And I was serious about getting a makeup lesson, I want to know all your secrets." Cora admired the contours of Andrea's cheekbones, then turned back around to watch the mayor give his speech.

"It's my honor to dedicate this park to our four-legged friends. My father taught me that you measure a man's humanity by how he treats his fellow creatures."

"Talks a good game, doesn't he?" Andrea muttered.

"Mmhmm," Cora agreed.

"And so we are here to honor the most loving and loyal of creatures. My friends, I never thought I'd say this with any pride, but here I am to tell you: this city is going...to the dogs!" Zeke said to the crowd's happy applause.

"See you after half time," Andrea said, and when Cora turned around, she was gone.

Striding carefully in her high heels, Cora met the mayor backstage.

"That went well," Sturm said briskly.

"Yes, thank you, Mr. Mayor." Cora stepped forward before his aides could intervene. "Could we trouble you for a quick photo op in the back building, where the light is good? The photographer has a setup back there."

The mayor blinked at her, and Cora realized he didn't completely recognize her. "Just back here," she repeated. "There's someone I want to introduce you to."

"Sure, sure," Zeke said, waving at his aides. "Just a few minutes."

"Certainly." Cora smiled and led the entourage across the park lawn to the old theater. Inside, she led them to the stage. The space was big and open, which was the main point. There were few hidden corners other than backstage —but Waters' men had secured it beforehand, and otherwise, everything was out in the open.

"Interesting spot," Zeke commented. He and his aides slowed when they saw Andrea Doria's tall form flanked by two guard. Andrea also held Brutus's leash; Cora hurried to take it and then positioned herself between the two parties.

"Mr. Mayor, meet Andrea Doria."

Zeke barely hesitated, extending his hand for the tall drag queen to shake. "A pleasure, ma'am."

"All mine, Mayor Sturm." Andrea didn't bother to alter her voice's smooth tenor. "I'm so glad you have recovered so well after the poisoning."

"Yes, bit of a scare, but all's well that ends well." The

mayor gave his fake chuckle and looked around. "Where are the cameras?"

"I believe you know Ms. Doria under a different name," Cora said, stepping between the two.

The mayor's eyes narrowed and Cora knew then he recognized her. He opened his mouth, but Philip Waters stole the show by removing his platinum blonde wig and stating his name clearly.

The mayor's people reacted immediately, drawing their weapons and forming a hedge around Sturm. Cora found herself at the center of a deadly circle as Waters' men also responded.

"Stop, just stop," she cried out. Stretching out her hands in a 'stop' sign, Cora looked from one powerful man to the other. "This is neutral territory. We are just going to talk."

"Well, well," Zeke said, staring at the tall black man. "This is an interesting way to get my attention. Although you had it as soon as you tried to poison me."

"I'm innocent of that," Waters said. The wig lay at his feet, and even wearing a dress and backed by only two men, he looked more than a match for the mayor's posse. "You're the one who allowed my shipment to be taken, and then reneged on our deal."

"Enough," Cora said and, at her feet, Brutus barked—a deep, dangerous sound that stilled the men who heard it. "Waters never tried to kill you, or my husband. And the matter of the shipment has been settled, are we agreed?" She glared at all of them. "The real issue is that you're being played."

"The only issue I have—" Zeke began but Cora quickly cut him off.

"Don't you get it? The Titans are setting you against each other. They'd like nothing better than to watch you take each other out. Then they can take the city with no one in their way."

Cora's outburst seemed to silence the mayor, if only because he wasn't used to being interrupted.

"Mr. Mayor, look at him," Cora snapped. "Does he look like he's hiding anything from you?"

Ezekiel Sturm took in Philip Waters from head to toe. Then, to everybody's shock, he laughed, and it was a genuine, pleasant sound.

"Lower your weapons," Zeke ordered his men, and Waters' men mirrored them.

"This is unbelievable," the mayor shook his head, but he had a smile on his face. "You planned this ambush?"

Waters also grinned. "Mrs. Ubeli did. I come in peace."

"An alliance, eh? You, me, and Ubeli, all united against the Titans?"

"So says the lady," Waters nodded.

The mayor studied Cora. "Do you speak for your husband?"

"She does," a voice echoed from near the ceiling, and Marcus Ubeli sauntered down the stairs at the side of the stage, flanked by several Shades.

At the sight of him, all the air rushed out of Cora's lungs. Down at the base of the stairs, the curtain rippled and Sharo stepped out of his hiding place, nodding to her. She nodded back and retreated from center stage to watch the mayor, the shipping mogul and the mob boss converse.

"An alliance, then." Zeke Sturm actually sounded pleased. "Me in office, Waters controlling the sea and Ubeli," he waved his hand as if that would encompass Ubeli's activities on both sides of the law.

"Agreed," Philip Waters said, and looked to Marcus, who fixed him with a dark stare.

"Return my men."

"Done," Waters said. "Although I'd like to hire them as muscle. The Titans took their shots at offing the two of you. Once they know I have no intention of aligning myself with them, they will come for me."

"Very well," Marcus said. "I'll give the orders. We'll keep staging skirmishes to get the Titans thinking we're at war. Then, when the timing's right, we strike."

Cora turned in a slow circle, looking at all three of the men, almost disbelieving at how well this was all turning out.

"So, if we're all agreed—" Zeke began, when movement caught Cora's eye.

"Get down," she shrieked, and the men around the mayor reacted instantly, pulling him to the floor and raising their weapons.

They were too slow for Spike Hair, who darted out of the wings and fired before any of the mayor's men could react.

But he didn't aim for the mayor.

"Marcus," Cora cried and Sharo threw himself forward, but he was too late. The gun went off, and Marcus dropped.

Someone jerked Cora back. "Come, Mrs. Ubeli, I've got to get you out of here."

It was a Shade, Angelo she thought his name was. But she had to get to Marcus, to see if he was okay—

But no matter how she struggled, Angelo pulled her backwards from the scene, stronger than he looked. Sharo had rolled off Marcus but she couldn't see— She couldn't see if—

Spike Hair continued to fire. Bullets ricocheted around the stage. It had all happened in seconds and Cora couldn't, she couldn't—

Angelo was pulling her from the room and out down a hallway. "I have orders to get you to the back exit if anything happens," he said, dragging her away from Marcus and Sharo.

She wanted to wrench away from him and run back, but gods, she could still hear the gunfire. What good would she really do Marcus if she went back in there, though? She'd only be a distraction from him getting himself to safety.

He'd ordered his Shades to get her out should something happen. For once in her life, she could obey and not screw things up worse.

So no matter how much she wanted to punch Angelo in the face and run back to help the others, she went along with him as he hurried her down the hallway and out the exit into the warm evening air.

And right into an alley where her mother, Demi Titan, stood with half a dozen armed guards waiting.

"Baby, it's so good to finally see you again."

THIRTY-EIGHT

In the blink of an eye, Cora saw it also clearly. How her mother had manipulated them all. She'd only had to flip two men after all—one inside Philip Waters' camp, and one inside Marcus's. Spike Hair and Angelo, who, now that Cora thought about it, Marcus had mentioned had been troublesome in the past.

And now here she was. Caught like a fly in a spider's web.

"Call off the attack," Cora said. "You have me."

Demi laughed. She looked nothing like the woman Cora had grown up with, who wore overalls and rarely conditioned her hair.

Now Demi's dark brown hair was styled in big curls, she wore dramatic makeup, and she had on a power skirt-suit. "Not that you aren't special, darling, but this is about so much more than you. This is about history. And righting wrongs. Ubeli stole this city from me and I mean to have it back."

"Righting wrongs?" Cora scoffed. "Sixteen years ago,

you murdered an innocent girl. After my father and uncles *raped* her."

Demi's face went cold. "I thought I knew what I was getting into when I married a Titan brother. But I was young. Karl was handsome and said he loved me. I never had a real home or real family so marrying into his seemed like a dream come true. But he was weak."

Demi took a step towards her. "So I did what needed doing while he drank and whored his way across town. Then he finally managed to do something right—he caught the Ubeli girl, but of course he couldn't keep his dick in his pants."

Demi shook her head in disgust. "So again I had to come in and clean up his mess."

"You stabbed her over and over!" Cora shouted. "You're as much a monster as he was."

Demi crossed the last of the space between them and grabbed Cora's wrist in a painful, bruising grip. "You will not disrespect me in front of my men. You've embarrassed me long enough, running around and consorting with the enemy. It ends here. Today."

"What are you going to do?" Cora glared hatefully, only inches from her mother's face. "Kill me in cold blood? That's what you're good at, right?"

"I do what has to be done," Demi said through gritted teeth. "Something a girl like you would never understand. But you will. I'll take you home and you will get an introduction to the way the real world works. You are my daughter and one way or another, you will behave as such."

"Never—" Cora started to shout, right as the back door to the theater swung open and a deep voice called, "Cora!"

"No!" Cora shouted but it was too late. The shooting had already begun.

"Sharo!" Cora cried.

He had his weapon out and managed to take down three of Demi's guards before falling to his knees, blood gushing from several wounds on his chest.

"No, Sharo!"

Cora fought to get away from her mother but Demi caught her from behind in a chokehold and started dragging her towards the SUV parked several feet away.

Cora wheezed and tried to scream, but she couldn't get any breath, her mother's hold on her was too tight.

How many times do I have to tell you to turn your head to the side to free your airway?

The self-defense lessons with Marcus.

Cora swung her head to the right, immediately freeing her airway, just like Marcus said. She sucked in a deep breath, then she elbowed her mother hard in the side, once, twice, three times, until Demi's hold loosened. For good measure, Cora stomped on her instep, then, when Demi was wheezing, Cora grabbed one of Demi's arms and planted her feet, using her firm stance as a fulcrum to launch Demi to the ground.

Demi screamed as her face slammed into the pavement and she rolled over once. She landed right by Sharo. He'd been immobile, Cora feared dead, but he suddenly reared up and slammed a knife straight through Demi's heart. And then he collapsed.

"Sharo!" Cora cried, right as the back door of the theater opened and a handful of more Shades poured out. They made quick work of the rest of Demi's guards, but all Cora could see was Sharo.

"Sharo, please," she sobbed, crouched at his side, pressing her hands to the wound on his chest. They had to stop the bleeding. There was so much *blood*. It was like Iris all over again. "You're going to be all right."

He lifted his hand to caress her face. "Loved—"

"You loved her, I know. You told me. You're going to be okay. You're going to love again, you'll see." She choked on her tears as the big man's eyes closed. "No. No! Help me! Someone! Help me!"

Marcus was beside her, prying her hands away as several Shades moved in to put pressure on Sharo's wounds.

"Marcus?" She grabbed him with bloody hands. "You're alive?"

At the same time, an ambulance pulled into the back alley and sped their direction. Its lights weren't flashing and the sirens didn't sound, but as soon as it came to a stop, several EMTs poured from the back and Marcus barked orders at them.

Sharo was immediately put on a gurney and wheeled inside where the EMTs started working on him.

Cora looked on in stark shock.

Marcus finally took her hand as the ambulance sped away, this time with lights flashing.

"I had an ambulance nearby in case things went wrong. And I was wearing a vest," Marcus said gently as she finally turned to him, parting his shirt and touching the Kevlar. "I should have insisted Sharo wear one, too."

Cora heard the pain in his voice but she was too raw to be able to comfort him.

"Come with me, now, Cora—"

He tried to put his arm around her but she wrenched away. "Will they be able to save him? Sharo saved me, he killed my mother. He has to be okay—"

"It's over. Honey, it's over now."

She glared up at him, fury and grief warring within her. "No, it's not. But it will be."

THIRTY-NINE

CORA SAT on the edge of the limo seat, tense as they passed a long line of drab, squat buildings marked with graffiti. If New Olympus was the glittering belle of the ball, Metropolis was its ugly step-sister.

"Almost there," Fats said from the driver's seat.

"Any sign they're on to us?" Cora straightened her wig.

"Not if we've come this far." Philip Waters shooed Cora's hands away and fixed her dark brown curls. Andrea had given Cora a makeup lesson after all. Heavy makeup designed to make her look older.

Like her mother.

"How do I look?" Cora smiled at Philip carefully so the thick makeup wouldn't crack.

"Like a mob mistress."

"Good. Because that's what I am."

"Checkpoint ahead. Get your game faces on," Fats instructed as he slowed the car. Two men with machine guns blocked the road as a third approached the driver's side.

"Confidence," Waters murmured to Cora as Fats rolled his window down.

"Mrs. Titan and guest," Fats announced.

"Mrs. Titan?" the guard asked.

Cora leaned forward so the Titan's men saw her. "Of course it's me," she snapped in her mother's voice.

"What's with the tail?" The man motioned to the three cars following them.

"They're mine." Cora waved a hand.

"I don't recognize them."

"They're new. My personal guard died in New Olympus. Once we forged our alliance, Mr. Waters was kind enough to loan me a few of his." Cora's heart pounded as she waited for the guard to call her on her lie.

"I got orders not to let anyone I don't recognize through. The Titan brothers won't like it."

"They really won't like it when they find out Philip Waters withdrew his offer of alliance because you wouldn't let him through to the meet."

On cue, Philip Waters rolled his window down.

"You're wasting my time," Waters informed the man in his deep, grave voice. The checkpoint guard paled.

Cora sat back, sliding a large pair of sunglasses on and looking straight ahead as if the checkpoint didn't exist.

"Hurry up and drive," she barked at Fats. "Alex and Ivan are waiting."

Cora remained in 'Demi Titan' mode as the guard waved them on. As soon as Fats drove past the machine guns, Philip chuckled. "That was perfect."

Cora squeezed his big hand. The next stage of the plan wouldn't be so easy.

"We're here," Fats reported as the car stopped in front of an old church. "The Titans holed up here three days ago.

Both are inside, expecting Demi and Waters. They're meeting with their capos in an hour."

"Plenty of time to take out the trash." Philip straightened his collar and exited the car, offering a hand to help 'Demi' out.

As they strode ahead, arm and arm, three more black cars pulled up to the church. Men poured out—some Shades, some Waters' men. They'd infiltrate the church, quietly taking out any of the Titan's men and assuming their places.

Cora and Waters waited in the foyer until Slim strode in. "All clear. Your uncles are in the basement, oblivious. Alone."

This is it. Cora kept the big sunglasses on and let Waters guide her with a hand on her back down the stairs.

"Ready?" he rumbled when she paused to stare at the doors leading to the basement hall. In a second she'd meet both her uncles for the first and last time.

"Ready," she said finally, and pushed the doors open.

The basement was hot and stuffy, smelling of onions and sausage. Two blond men sat at a plastic table, playing cards in their shirt sleeves. They stopped when she marched in, a phalanx of guards fanning out around her, and Philip at her side.

"Demi? About fuckin' time." One of the blond men turned. Ivan. She recognized him from an old photo. "Philip," he said, getting to his feet. "Glad to see you here. It's good that you've come to see reason. Your product will be safe in our hands."

Cora stopped just inside the door, keeping to the shadows, and let her and Waters' guards surround the room. "Yes, he and I have come to an agreement," she said.

"The alliance is a done deal, then?" the second Titan

asked, also standing. Her uncle Alexander. He glared at Fats and Slim and the rest, obviously suspecting something, but not going for his gun.

He wouldn't dare in front of Philip Waters.

"The alliance is done." Cora said. "But you two and I have unfinished business." She slowly pulled her sunglasses off and put them in her pocket.

Alex scowled. "What's that supposed to—" He stopped short when Philip pulled a gun from his pocket and, before he could even blink, shot him. He slumped forward.

"What the fuck?" Ivan shouted and went for his gun, but every man in the room pulled a gun on him before he could.

"Stand down," Cora said coolly.

There was a riot of action as the Shades swarmed the table, securing Ivan and Alex, who was moaning in pain.

"You're not Demi," Ivan snarled.

"Hello, uncle," she greeted him, tugging off the wig. "Nice of you to join me for this family reunion."

Her uncle's eyes bulged. "Where's Demi?"

"My mother is busy at the moment." Busy being dead. "She sent me."

"You bitch—" Ivan started, only to choke when Slim looped a belt around his neck and tightened it.

Meanwhile two Shades had bound and gagged Alex. "What should we do with this one?"

"Is he dead?" Waters asked, coming to join Cora.

"Nope," Fats reported. "You got him in the stomach."

"I'm getting rusty." Waters grinned. "But then again, belly shots are so perfectly painful."

"Make sure he gets to my husband in one piece," Cora instructed and turned to Slim and the Shades who held Ivan. "Him too."

Ivan gurgled something and Cora motioned for his throat to be freed.

"What's the meaning of this?" Ivan rasped. On his knees, surrounded by her thugs with guns, he didn't look so big.

"In a minute, I'll explain everything," she informed him sweetly. "But not to you. Your reign is over. You're going away for a while. At least, until Sharo can hold a knife again. I'm sure he'll recover faster, knowing he has you waiting for him to take his revenge out on."

Before Ivan could shout anything else, Slim stuffed a gag into his mouth and dragged him off with his brother.

The doors closed, leaving her and Waters alone. Cora let her shoulders slump.

"Well done," Waters said. "That went quicker than I expected." He bent to study her face. "You didn't want to talk to your uncles?"

She shook her head. "Honestly, I had nothing to say to them."

The doors opened and one of Waters' men reported, "The Titan capos are starting to gather in the sanctuary. Do you want us to relieve them of their weapons?"

Waters nodded and the man disappeared. He watched Cora wander around the room, lost in thought, touching the table where her uncles had sat.

"You talk to Marcus yet?"

Cora blinked as if coming awake. "Not yet. Time was of the essence. We had to get here before they got too suspicious when Demi didn't get into contact."

Philip tilted his head. "He wants to talk to you."

"He will. I have to do this first."

Waters' man returned. "We're ready for you."

"The capos are unarmed?" Waters asked.

"Not all of them were happy but we used that Aurum pulse thing Mrs. Ubeli picked up for us on the way, and their guns jammed. Excuse me, I meant Mrs. Titan."

"Ms. Titan," Cora corrected. "Tell them the Titans are now allied with Philip Waters and loyalty will be greatly rewarded. We'll be with them shortly."

The man scuttled off and Cora smiled. Turned out she liked giving orders.

"Ms. Titan?" Waters asked. "You taking back your maiden name?"

"I've never been a Titan, actually." Cora took his offered arm. "But it's my birthright, so I better get used to it. So will everyone else."

With a smile of his own, Waters nodded. Cora let him escort her to the sanctuary before pulling away.

"I have to do this alone."

He nodded again. She reached up and touched his cheek. "Thank you," she said simply, before dropping her hand and striding into the sanctuary. Waters covered his cheek with his hand.

The capos sat in the front pews like oversized, disgruntled altar boys in ill-fitting suits. Above them, in the balcony and choir loft, Shades and Waters' men stood guard, outfitted with special guns that Olivia had designed to withstand her patented weapon-jamming device. Turned out Olivia had been up to more on her West Coast adventures than just pestering suppliers. She'd come home bearing new toys.

With a nod to Fats and Slim, Cora climbed the stage to address her new capos.

"Welcome," she called and waited while they all took her in.

"Who da fuck are you?" one man called.

"We've never met. I'm Cora Titan. You will treat me with respect."

"Or?"

"You die," Slim shot back.

Cora smiled. "I understand you have questions," she said. "In a minute I will answer them, but for now know this. There's a new Titan in town. As of now, I'm running the show."

The capos murmured to each other. "Who died and put you in charge?" another asked.

"My mother and uncles, actually. If they're not dead, they will be soon." Beeping sounds filled the room and the capos patted their pockets, pulling out their vibrating cell-phones en masse.

Thank you, Olivia.

"You've just been texted pictures of my deceased mother. Note the resemblance." Cora tilted her head to the side, giving them a profile.

"Fucking spittin' image," an older capo murmured. "Demi and the old man, what's his face, Karl."

"You'll find I have a lot in common with both my parents," Cora said. "With one difference. While they enjoyed war, I prefer the alternative. Peace."

"Peace," a capo echoed.

"Indeed. After all, it's so much better for business." Cora spread her hands. "Imagine this. A city at peace. Men and women visiting your brothels. Hordes of partygoers sampling Ambrosia, returning again and again to buy from your distributors. We have a new alliance with our good friend, Philip Waters."

She turned to smile at Philip as he ambled in. She paused a moment to let him greet the capos and shake a few hands. He took a seat at the end of one pew, his great height dwarfing the rest.

"With Waters at our side and unlimited access to overseas imports, profits will roll in. Imagine the streets alive with people who've come for the party. New Olympus is where they do business. Metropolis is where they come to have fun."

"I like it," the older capo said. "Especially the part about the profits, and alliance with ole Waters here. I knew your father," he said to Waters.

"What about the cops?" another capo called.

Cora dropped her next bombshell. "Tomorrow the mayor of New Olympus introduces a proposal to make Ambrosia legal. A controlled substance. It'll be the new Viagra, but recreational, and for both men and women. We can expect the mayor of Metropolis to follow suit."

Yep, the mayor was on her side too, and she saw the impact the news had on the crowd. It hadn't taken much convincing to get Sturm and Waters to throw in behind her, once she explained that her assuming control of the Titan gang was the quickest way to bring lasting peace to the streets. "With a few bribes, we'll buy all the rights to distribute. Legally."

"This true?" a capo demanded of Waters.

"Every word," he confirmed, and the murmurs got louder.

"Damn. Never thought I'd go straight in my old age," the gray-haired capo muttered. "But if there's profit in it, who cares?"

"This is bull." One capo shot to his feet. "You're a lying whore." His shout echoed to the rafters. So did the sound of a hundred guns trained on him.

Cora raised a hand. "Stand down," she drawled. "I like a

rigorous debate among my leaders. As long as they remember their place."

Fats and Slim grabbed the man and brought him cursing before her, forcing him to his knees. "But there's no room for men who don't see my vision."

A glint of metal and she had a knife at the man's throat. "Do you pledge your loyalty to the Titans?"

"You ain't no Titan," the man spat, and then died with a gurgle as she slit his jugular.

Her stomach rebelled at the sight. But this one act of violence now could stop endless violence later. She had to prove she was strong and ruthless or these men would never respect her rule. She understood now some of the choices and sacrifices Marcus had to make every day to hold his city in check. She would now do the same.

Waters strolled to her side and offered a white handkerchief. Cora wiped the blood from her face and hands, but didn't bother with her white dress. She'd expected to be christened tonight. Once she'd handed back the handkerchief, she fixed the capos with a cold stare she'd learned from her husband. "Anyone else?"

Dead silence answered her until the older capo chuckled. "She's a Titan all right. Fuckin' visionary, like her parents. Spittin' image."

"Any other questions?"

"What about Ubeli? With all due respect," the capo added. "We just gonna roll over and let him win?"

Cora smiled. "Not at all. From now consider war at an end between us. You handle business as usual. I'll handle my husband."

Another chuckle from the oldest capo. He elbowed his neighbor while the others exchanged knowing glances.

"I know a few of you won't be happy with the new

arrangements," Cora continued. "I expect you to come discuss things with me. Respectfully. Otherwise, you'll feel the full force of the Shades and Waters' men, not to mention the trouble you'll get into with the law. Oh yes, the cops have orders to back me. The mayor of New Olympus introduced me to the Metropolis chief of police, and we're fast friends." She laughed lightly.

Another chorus of beeps had the capos checking their phones again.

Slim held out a screen to show Cora the grisly image.

"Looks like my husband got my little peace offering. A sign of goodwill. Alexander Titan had some use after all. He was your main leader, correct?"

A few of the capos had turned green.

"I don't have to warn you what will happen if you ever cross me," Cora said. "I expect we'll all get along beautifully, especially when profits start rolling in. I'll be by to visit each of your businesses this week. Expect me. I'll expect you to be on your best behavior. Behave and you won't get on my bad side."

A bark broke the silence. Brutus broke from his handler in the back, and bounded to Cora's side. She knelt to stroke his head a moment before rising. Slim came to her side with a red coat. With his help, she shrugged it on over her dress.

"Now, Philip and I are going to dinner. You're all invited to pay your respects." She'd know who was loyal if they came to kiss her ring. "If not, I'll see you later this week."

Signaling Brutus, she strode down the aisle, her guards at her back and her dog at her side. Waters paused a moment before following.

"The king is dead," he rumbled. "Long live the queen."

FORTY

A WEEK LATER, Slim pulled the limo up to the docks.

"You gonna be all right?" Waters asked. They'd spent the week in Metropolis, cementing Cora's rule over the Titan's businesses.

Cora raised her chin. "Don't worry about me." The capos weren't all happy she'd moved in, but they'd put down the ones most likely to betray her, and placated the rest with a bigger cut of profits.

"That's the spirit." He chucked her under the chin. "You let me know if anyone causes you trouble."

"I will. Thank you, for everything."

"Don't thank me yet," he announced as he got out and went around to open her door. "In a minute you're gonna want to yell at me."

"What? Why?"

"This is my limo. Your ride's over there." He stepped away and she looked down the pier to a black car idling at the curb. A familiar form waited, hands in pockets, dark head bent.

Marcus.

Cora drew in a sharp breath.

"He's been calling me like crazy," Waters grumbled. "Demanding proof that you were okay. Me and Slim and Fats all had to report hourly."

Cora put a hand to her neck, gaze fixed on the dark form of her husband. "I don't...we didn't leave things in a good place. I know he came through at the theater, but I don't know..."

"He's here, isn't he?" Waters put out a hand and Cora automatically took it. When she was out of the car, he gave her a little push. "Go get him, kid."

She started across the blacktop. Marcus looked so sober, leaning against his car. She'd talked to him on the phone over the past week, but only about Sharo's progress after his multiple surgeries. Whenever he tried to turn the conversation to deeper topics, she made excuses and hung up.

There was so much between them. So many lies. So many scars. Could he forgive her? If he really had been with Lucinda, could she forgive him? Had he moved on? Did he even want her?

She wobbled on her heels and stopped.

"Cora." He called her name and her head snapped up. His arms opened.

Kicking off her high heels, she ran.

MARCUS HUGGED her as soon as she'd jumped into his arms, but she'd turned her head aside when he lowered his mouth for a kiss.

She might have completed her coup in Metropolis, but there was unfinished business between them.

"Thanks for the ride," Cora said from her side of the

limo. She made no move to bridge the awkward space between them.

Easy. Gently. Give her time, Marcus could practically hear Sharo coaching him. He missed his friend more than he could say. Sharo had been put in a medically induced coma, but the doctor said all indications were positive that he would have a full recovery. But they wouldn't know for sure until he woke up. It had been days, though, and he still hadn't opened his eyes.

You better not die, brother. I don't need you haunting me. Marcus could almost hear Sharo's chuckle filling the car.

They'd spent hours talking in the weeks Marcus was separated from Cora and Marcus tried to muster all of that advice now.

All right, brother. We'll try it your way.

"You were magnificent." Marcus drank in his wife's slim form, barely believing she was real. She looked different. Older. Not hard or jaded, just wiser somehow. "Waters and the Shades told me everything. I made them get footage."

She shrugged, then looked at him anxiously. "How's Sharo?"

"No change. Yet."

She bit her lip and he had to clench his hand into a fist to keep from brushing his thumb against it until she relaxed. Then she asked, "You really think so? You really think I can do this? Lead the Titans?"

"Don't believe me. Check it out." He grabbed the paper on the seat and showed her. "*Queen of the Underworld.* You're gonna have to get used to getting dogged by the press."

"I'm already used to it. I married you, remember."

"Mmm." He'd always hated being called King of the

Underworld but he'd embrace the term as long as she was by his side as his Queen.

His Queen looked exhausted, though, as she glanced his way. And she was sitting much too far away, almost hugging the opposite door.

"Come here." He held out his arm.

She sighed. "Marcus, just because this is all over…" She shook her head and looked out the window, her expression far away. "It doesn't mean—" She broke off, hands going to her face.

She'd been as powerful as any general back there demanding her due as head of the Titan Empire but here with him, she was as vulnerable as always.

And he was done allowing her to put distance between them. He went to her and gathered her in his arms. "I almost lost you and I'll be damned if I spend another minute apart from you."

She struggled, though, and when she pushed away from him, her eyes flashed fire. "It was easy enough for you to walk away from me three weeks ago. And I saw the picture of you with that woman. Your lover."

She had to mean Lucinda. Marcus had raged when he first saw the picture but now he grinned. "Jealous, kitten?" He could stand anything but her indifference.

If he thought her eyes were fiery before, it was nothing to the fury that sparked at his words.

"Get off of me, you oversized oaf." She shoved ineffectually at him but he only tightened his arms around her.

"I didn't touch her. I ran into her outside the Crown and she stumbled into me. Probably on purpose. Come to think of it, it was probably her who'd called the paparazzi. She always was an attention whore. I steadied her and then continued on my way. That was the full extent of our interaction."

Nice work, Sharo said. *Now tell her the truth.*

Get out of my head, Marcus almost muttered aloud before taking his advice. Tilting his head at his beautiful wife, he said, "There's no replacing you, love. There never could be."

Her countenance immediately changed. Instead of pushing him away, she gripped the lapels of his suit coat. "I was so scared. When you went down, I was so scared." Her eyes filled with tears. "And then Sharo."

"We're heading to New Olympus General now. I knew you'd want to see him, first thing."

"Good." Cora sank against him, her head to his chest. "Is it really over?"

He squeezed her close to him and breathed in the sweet aroma of her hair. "Yes, goddess. It's over. But the rest of our life is just beginning."

He felt her nod against his chest. But the next second she was pulling away. "Sharo tried to explain. I'm sorry. I'm sorry that I left the Estate like that and headed straight into danger. I had no idea about Chiara."

Tears spilled down her cheeks and he cupped them, shaking his head. "You couldn't have known. I just— I just couldn't—" He looked down and huffed out a frustrated breath.

But then he forced himself to meet her gaze again. "I swore to protect you. No matter what. Even if it meant the safest place for you was away from me. It killed me, being away from you. Worse than the first time. So much worse, because I was afraid it was forever."

He didn't want to think about what the past three weeks

had been like. He'd thrown himself into his work but not even that could distract him from missing her. Or from wondering, every hour of every day, every minute, if she was okay, what she was doing, if she hated him. If she was moving on. His sleep had been tormented by nightmares of her happy—in the arms of another man, wearing another man's ring.

Ten times a day, he'd had to wrestle himself back from saying fuck it, and getting in his car and breaking every traffic law known to man to go back to her. All his discipline, all his control, none of it counted when it came to her.

Maybe she saw something of his torment on his face because she lifted a hand to his cheek and whispered, "Never again. From here on out, it's you and me together. Always. No more secrets. No more lies. No matter if you think it's for my good or not. We're partners in everything now. Swear it?"

He met her eyes solemnly. "I vow to you, Cora Ubeli, never to lie to you again."

"Not even if you think it's for my own good? I need you to say it, Marcus."

He smiled at her tenacity. "I will never leave you nor forsake you. I will never lie to you again or keep secrets, even if I think it's for your own good. Now your turn."

She clasped his hands and there was no smile on her face. She was taking this dead seriously.

"I, Cora Ubeli, vow to never leave nor forsake you, and I will never lie to you or keep secrets from you again, even if I think it's for your own good."

"Now all that's left is to seal it with a kiss," Marcus said, moving his head slowly towards hers.

She rose to him and when their lips met, Marcus thought he might just die after all at the angel soft touch of her lips.

In his worst moments, he thought he'd never get to experience this again. Even remembering how that felt made him crazy. He couldn't do gentle, not right now. Not after all they'd been through and their separation.

He crushed her to him and she threw her arms around his neck, apparently just as desperate for him in return. Their mouths met in a hungry tangle. Lips, tongues, teeth. He couldn't get enough of her. He needed all of her. Now.

But just as he shifted her to straddle him, the SUV came to a stop and the driver's voice sounded over the speaker. "We're here."

Cora broke from Marcus's mouth, eyes wide. "Sharo."

She barely bothered to rearrange her clothing before shoving open the door. Marcus had to run after her; she was halfway to the hospital entrance by the time he got out his own door.

THEY SPENT TWO DAYS' vigil at Sharo's bedside before he finally opened his eyes.

It was sunset when his large brow finally scrunched and he blinked his eyes open.

"Sharo!" Cora cried, jumping up and grabbing his huge hand in her tiny one. "You're awake. Marcus, he's awake!"

Marcus stood behind Cora, smiling down at his oldest friend, at his brother. "Thank the Fates," he breathed out. Sharo had been such a study constant in his life. He couldn't imagine going on without him. He was family.

Sharo looked around, obviously confused.

"Here." Cora let go of his hand only long enough to grab a cup of water with a straw in it from the bedside table to hold it up to Sharo's mouth.

He took several swallows before leaning back on his pillows. "What— Happened?"

Cora took his hand again. "You saved the day. You saved my *life*." She squeezed his hand.

"And for that, you have my eternal gratitude, brother," Marcus said.

Sharo met his eyes over Cora's head and they shared a silent look. Sharo nodded and Marcus knew he understood. Marcus owed him everything. It was a debt Marcus could never repay but he'd spend the rest of his life trying anyway.

"My mother would've gotten away with all of it if you hadn't showed up when you did," Cora continued. "And then you got shot. So many times," her voice broke. "I thought you were dead. The doctor says we're lucky that you're alive. If one of the bullets had even been half an inch closer to the left." She broke off, shaking her head, tears falling down her cheeks.

"I'm okay," Sharo croaked, and Cora immediately held the water back up to his lips.

Then Cora swung around to look at Marcus. "He's awake. We need to get the doctor. They said to call him when he woke up."

Marcus nodded and pressed the button for the nurse to come in.

The nurse and then doctor arrived several minutes later. Marcus and Cora were hustled out of the room while the doctor attended to Sharo.

As soon as they left the room, Cora's shoulders slumped. She was exhausted. No matter how Marcus had tried to coax her to go home to get some rest, she'd refused to leave. She'd gotten a few hours sleep on a little cot they'd set up in the room, but not much.

Now that Sharo was awake, though, he was insisting. She'd go home and get a full night's rest.

Her hand slid into his, fingers intertwining.

"I love you, Marcus." She paused in the middle of the hospital hallway and looked up at him. "Thank you for giving me this life. Thank you for everything. You know how much I love you? Can you even fathom it?"

Marcus smiled down at her, the woman he loved more than life itself.

He was about to leaned down to kiss her when her eyes suddenly rolled back in her head and she collapsed. He barely had time to catch her before she hit the ground.

FORTY-ONE

All was dark and there were no stars.

"Hello?" Cora called into the darkness.

No one responded.

Cora stretched her arms out and felt all around her. Nothing. There was nothing.

"Marcus? Marcus?" Her voice was high-pitched, nearing on frantic. Where was she? Why couldn't she see anything? She spun around but there was only more nothingness, until, arms outstretched, her hand finally ran into a brick wall.

The air smelled sour and dank and that was when Cora knew.

Mama had locked her in the cellar again.

It had all been a dream. Marcus. New Olympus. None of it had ever been real.

Marcus had never been real. He'd never loved her. He never would. Because he didn't exist. None of it had. Olivia. Anna. Sharo. Armand. She'd made them all up in her head.

How many days had she been down here? How long since she'd had food or water? How long since she'd slept?

She'd experienced it before, the delirium that came with being confined in the solitary space for long stretches.

She sank to her knees.

She was alone.

Unloved.

Her mother had finally driven her mad.

"Noooooo!" she cried, banging her fists on the earthen ground. "Please!" She didn't know what she was begging for. Maybe for the earth to open and swallow her up whole.

But then she froze. Because she heard something.

She sat up and craned her ears.

"Cora. Cora!"

The sound was coming from so far away, Cora could barely hear it. But it was there. Either that, or it was an auditory hallucination.

But she was so desperate, she didn't care.

"Hello?" She stumbled towards the sound. "Hello?"

"Cora," came the voice, louder this time. "Cora, baby, come back to me."

Marcus. It was Marcus's voice.

Cora started running towards it. She should have run into the back wall of the cellar but she didn't. The darkness just went on and on and as she ran, it began to lighten. First to a dark gray and then...and then...

Cora blinked her eyes open and winced at the painfully bright lights.

"Cora!" Marcus's blurry face loomed over hers. He was smiling and crying at the same time. She'd never seen Marcus cry in the entire time she'd known him.

Wait. Was this real? Or was it just another hallucination?

But when Marcus dropped his lips to hers, she decided she didn't give a damn. She was staying.

FORTY-TWO

CORA HAD TAKEN about ten years off Marcus's life when she collapsed in the hospital hallway.

But then she was blinking up at him, awake, only ten minutes later. And if she had to pass out, she couldn't have picked a better place to do it.

Nurses and doctors had immediately rushed to their aid and gotten her on a gurney and into a room.

She was dehydrated, something Marcus would never forgive himself for—he should have been making sure she'd drank more fluids while they watched over Sharo, especially after the traumatic events of the days beforehand.

The doctors had taken some blood and they were waiting on the results. Marcus had never been a praying man but he prayed now, to every god he knew and even those he didn't, that the bloodwork would come back fine and nothing was wrong with her.

They'd been waiting for what felt like hours even though he'd threatened the doctor to prioritize Cora's blood-work with his most menacing face. In reality, it was only a little over 45 minutes before the doctor came pushing through the door.

Marcus leapt to his feet. The doctor was carrying a folder and he was smiling. Smiling had to mean good news, right? If it didn't, Marcus would do more than smash this guy's face in.

"What is it?" Marcus demanded. "Tell us."

"Marcus." Cora squeezed his hand gently. "Give the man a chance to take a breath."

Marcus looked down at his wife in the hospital bed. She was too pale for his liking. And ever since she woke up, she kept asking him if he was real and clutching his hand like he would disappear if she let go even for a second.

"Other than the slight dehydration issue, you are in wonderful health," the doctor said to Cora, avoiding Marcus's gaze and walking to the other side of her bed.

"And I have good news." Cora frowned up at him but then he continued, "You're pregnant!"

"What?" both Cora and Marcus said at the same time.

Cora gasped and stared at the doctor in shock. Then she looked up at Marcus with a tremulous smile on her face. She clasped his hand even tighter as she blinked rapidly. "I guess, I mean— I forgot to re-up my birth control shot because—"

Because they'd been separated.

Cora shook her head and let out a little laugh. "And then I didn't even think about it but I should have gotten my period three weeks ago. Everything has just been so nuts preparing for the fundraiser and everything else." She broke off with another laugh.

But Marcus wasn't laughing. He looked at the doctor. "So how far along is she?"

"When was the date of your last period?" the doctor asked Cora.

She was still shaking her head in wonder, and then her eyes went to the ceiling as she calculated. "Um, about six weeks ago? Maybe seven? The second week of last month, I think."

Marcus did the math in his head. He wasn't that well-versed in women's reproductive health but he'd had a woman once try to falsely claim he'd fathered her child and had learned a little about it. If her last period was seven weeks ago, that meant the baby had been conceived five weeks ago...right around the time they'd first gotten back together and first had sex.

But if she was off, even by a little bit.., They'd been separated for months. She'd left him and he never asked if there was any one else during that time.

Frankly, he hadn't wanted to know. Okay, that was a lie. He had wanted to know, with a vengeance, but he also knew himself too well. If any other man had touched Cora, whether she welcomed it or not, that man would not remain breathing for long after Marcus discovered his name.

But now there was a child...

His jaw locked and he could hear his heartbeat racing in his ears. There was a child. No matter what, the child was half Cora's. And anything that was half of her, he would love until his dying breath.

He reached down and retook her hand. "I will love this child as my own, no matter what."

Cora blinked up at him in confusion. "What do you mean? It *is* your child." Then understanding seemed to dawn on her. And she threw his hand away. "I didn't sleep with anyone else while we were separated. Did *you*?" Her eyes spit fire and color flushed back into her previously pale cheeks. "So help me, if you so much as—"

Marcus roared with laughter and then sat down on the bed, pulling her into his arms. "No. Never. Never anyone but you."

He kissed her hard. At first she was unresponsive but then her lips softened and she gave in to him. His sweet Cora. His powerful, ball-busting Queen.

He pulled back from her and pressed his forehead to hers. "We're going to have a baby," he whispered.

Her big blue eyes blinked up at him, wide with astonishment. Her hand slid between them to her stomach. "A baby," she said in awe. "Your baby."

"You've made me the happiest man alive. I love you. Forever." The words were an understatement. They always would be.

But he would spend the rest of his life proving them to his wife. His beloved. His Queen.

EPILOGUE

THREE YEARS LATER...

CORA KNEW the moment her husband entered the ballroom. Her spine prickled. Behind her, close to the door, the murmuring crowd quieted.

"Incoming, twelve o'clock," Armand waggled his brows at her. Cora pivoted in her gold dress and instantly picked Marcus out. He was suave and knee-weakeningly handsome in his tux.

"No costume?" Armand pouted, putting a fake-monocle to his eye. Cora swatted his arm.

"He wouldn't wear it. But does he even need one?"

Marcus had caught sight of her. His stubbled jaw creased into a smile. Mmm, five-o'clock shadow, her favorite. He had been working a lot lately, and hadn't had time to shave before the ball. He'd make it up to her later with the burn of his beard against her thighs...

Pressing two fingers to his lips, Marcus blew her a kiss.

"Damn. He makes an entrance." Armand dropped his monocle.

"I know," Cora murmured.

"I was talking about Waters."

"Oh." The big shipping tycoon had just wandered in with a group of giggling women in skimpy sea foam green costumes.

"Water nymphs. Very, very clever," Armand admired their costumes. "Shall we go greet your husband?"

"I think not," Cora said. "Let him placate his supplicants." As usual, Marcus was surrounded by people wanting to shake his hand and whisper in his ear.

"You make him sound like he's an emperor," Armand lifted a critical brow. "What does that make you?"

"A goddess." Cora smiled into her drink. "Leave Marcus alone. He'll come to me."

"Of course he will. You two are glued to the hip. Or...other parts." He cast a pointed glance at her rounded belly.

"Armand!" She put a hand to her baby bump.

"Aaaand you're blushing. I still got it."

"You're worse than Olivia." Cora pretended to look prim.

"Thank you. What number is this?" Armand hovered his hand over her belly. "Two of ten? Eleven?"

"Two of two, thank you very much. We wanted a boy and a girl."

"You already have little Vito, so that makes this one..."

"A girl." Cora's flushed skin seemed to glow. "We found out last week."

"Mrs. Ubeli!"

Both Cora and Armand turned to greet a gray-haired man in a white coat.

"Dr. Laurel," the man reminded them, raising bushy eyebrows that'd make Einstein jealous. "We met at the last gala. I can't tell you how grateful we are for all your charity. We're on the brink of a breakthrough."

"Dr. Laurel," Cora murmured, letting him pump her hand. "Of course I remember."

A willowy young woman in a white toga and a headband of green leaves hovered at the Dr.'s elbow until he dragged her forward. "Allow me to introduce my daughter, Daphne."

"Hello." Daphne gave a shy little wave, laughing when Armand executed a bow.

"Please to meet you, dear," Cora said. The girl was a beauty with olive skin and almond shaped green eyes. She looked barely out of high school. "Are you in college?"

Daphne flushed as her dad guffawed. "College? My girl graduated already. On track for a Ph.D. Genius. Takes after her mother."

"And you as well, Dr. Laurel, I'm sure." Cora smiled gently at the young woman. "Would you mind spinning around and showing us your costume? Let me guess what you are."

With a graceful nod, Daphne spun on her heel,

"Her specialty is biochemistry," Dr. Laurel was telling Armand. "Her research is already making waves. Youngest recipient of the Avicennius grant."

"Very impressive," Armand said.

"She didn't want to come," her father announced. "But she's spent too much time cooped up behind a microscope. You're still young." He waggled a finger at his daughter.

"You look beautiful," Cora told Daphne. "I'm still trying to guess what you are. White robes and a wreath on your head?"

"I'm an ancient Olympic athlete," Daphne explained. "A winner. These are my laurels."

"Clever," Armand said and Daphne blushed further.

"You can't be an Olympic athlete," a deep voice interrupted. A tall, dark-haired man stepped between Daphne and everyone else. "Olympic athletes performed naked."

"Oh my," Armand raised his fake monocle to his eye and peered at the newcomer. "Hello there."

"Logan, stop being such a stuffed shirt," Dr. Laurel chided with a grin. "Mrs. Ubeli, may I introduce Dr. Logan Wulfe, unparalleled medical researcher and apparently an expert on ancient sports customs."

"Not an expert," Dr. Wulfe said. His face was stern but there was a mischievous tilt to his lips. His fingers traced the edge of Daphne's laurel leaves. "You could be Daphne, chased by Apollo, who turned into a laurel tree."

"That's a sad story," Daphne said, a bit breathlessly. She gazed up at Logan Wulfe as if he was a god come to life.

And no wonder. With his height, dark hair, and rawboned features, he wasn't handsome but overwhelmingly masculine. Perfect to play the part of a brooding gothic hero. Daphne wasn't the only one under his spell. Armand didn't rip his gaze away until Cora elbowed him in the ribs. Everyone looked at him when he sputtered.

"She could be a military conqueror," Armand covered smoothly. "The Romans stole the practice of crowning winners with laurels, and gave wreaths to their successful generals."

"That fits," Logan nodded to Daphne, who looked like she might faint with happiness. She had hearts in her eyes.

"Do you want to dance?" she asked and a shadow fell over the tall man's face.

"I don't dance. Not even for you."

"I'll dance with you."

The shadows on Logan's face deepened as a model-handsome blond broke into the circle.

"Here's my other star student. Adam Archer, of Archer Industries," Dr. Laurel babbled as the blond and Logan glared at each other. "His partnership has been essential to the success of our company."

"Happy to be of service." Adam flashed a toothpaste smile to everyone but Logan. "Daphne, shall we?"

The young woman put her hand in his outstretched one, letting him lead her away. But as the song began, her eyes drifted back to Logan.

"Excuse me," Logan muttered, pushing a hand through his thick hair before walking off.

"Forgive my protege's rudeness," Dr. Laurel said to break the awkward silence. "Logan and Adam used to be like brothers, but recently had a...a falling out."

"Business or personal?" Armand asked, studying how Logan glared at Daphne and Adam on the dance floor.

Dr. Laurel blinked. "Business, of course."

"A bitter rivalry. How delicious," Armand murmured and Cora nudged him again. "Excuse me, I must go...see if I can offer comfort." He and the doctor wandered off in Logan's direction.

A strong hand on Cora's back made her turn.

"Marcus," she exclaimed. There were a few silver hairs at her husband's temple but he was even more handsome than ever.

"My love," he dropped a kiss on her shoulder. "Are you feeling all right?"

"Better, now you're here." Cora cupped his cheek. They exchanged what Olivia called an "ooey-gooey" look.

"I got away as soon as I could. Waters has a new delivery for us. Sharo's overseeing it now."

"He's not coming to the party?"

"He says he's too busy." After Sharo recovered, he insisted on helping Cora secure her hold on Metropolis. He hunted out dissenters and put down any coups. With his responsibilities in two cities, he did nothing but work.

Cora frowned. "He needs a girl."

"That's what I told him. That cute little physical therapist he mentioned a few times. I could get the Shades to pick her up, deliver her to him..."

"You are not going to kidnap Sharo a bride."

"Why not? Worked out well for me." His hands slid over her hips, tugging her flush to him.

"Marcus, not here, people will see..."

"Like I care." But he pulled her into a private alcove before claiming her mouth.

"Marcus," Cora gasped when he let her come up for air. "You're mussing my hair."

"I'll muss more than that." With a shark's grin he reached for her again. "I can't get enough of you, woman." But once he had her in his arms, he simply held her.

Cora rubbed her chafe cheeks. Stubble burn. Perfect.

"Just wait until your daughter gets here. She's gonna have you wrapped around her little finger."

Marcus's hands framed her belly.

"Have you thought about a name?" he whispered huskily in her ear.

"Of course. Chiara."

"You sure?"

Cora turned to face her husband fully. "Are you okay with that?"

"I am if you are." He toyed with a strand of her hair.

"Marcus," she covered his hand. "What is it?"

"I wanna name our daughter something good. Something happy and light. Untainted."

"Your sister was all those things." Cora pressed her forehead against her husband's. "My love, the past will always be with us. A part of us. The pain will never go away. But we are strong. We can remember the good and bring it with us. Let's name our daughter after your beautiful sister, and remember Chiara the way she'd want."

Holding her husband close, Cora rubbed her face against his. And if her cheek came away wet, there was no way to tell who cried the tears.

"You're so beautiful," Marcus whispered. His thumb rubbed circles on her flawless skin. "How is it you're also so wise?"

"Are you implying beautiful women don't have brains?" Cora raised a brow. Marcus shook his head. "I'm kidding. I know you're in awe of me."

"Of you. And the fact you're with a guy like me. Why is that anyway?"

"Hmmm," Cora twined her arms around his neck. "I thought I had a few reasons but I don't know. You better kiss me before I forget."

"I'll do more than kiss you," Marcus bent her back in his arms, claiming her mouth as she laughed, moving his lips down her throat until she gasped.

"We're missing the party," she murmured as he tugged her zipper down.

"Fuck the party."

"Marcus." She laughed and gave in. With any luck, no one would come investigate her disappearance. If they did, the happy sounds emanating from the alcove would give her away. "Marcus," she panted.

After a moment he raised his head. "Yes, my love?"

"I love you."

"And I love you," he said.

"Say it again."

"I love you. *Per sempre.* Forever." He whispered it over and over, imprinting his kisses on her cheeks, her eyelids, her fingers and fluttering pulse. He had forever to make her feel his love for her.

Forever started now.

TALES OF OLYMPUS will continue with Daphne's story in *The Beauty & the Rose.*

Add *Beauty & the Rose* to your Goodreads TBR

A NOTE FROM THE AUTHORS

A note from Lee:

Whew! What a ride! Stasia and I are so glad you made it to the end of Marcus & Cora's story. Without our readers and fans, none of this would be possible. Big fat thanks to our author friends who cheer us on and provide moral support through the writing doldrums.

When I first started writing Marcus & Cora's story in college, I had no idea what their books would become. New Olympus is a whole world Stasia and I can play in. If you have requests for which character's story we tell (*cough* *Sharo* *cough*) please let us know. :)

A note from Stasia:

I agree, writing this trilogy has been one insane, exciting ride!!! Thanks for coming along with us! We lived with these characters, cried with these characters, celebrated with them, almost killed some of them before days later, deciding, nooooooooo! We can't kill them!

So yay, most of them have survived and yes, we will be

writing another trilogy, in the world telling Daphne's story (mixing mythology with a little bit of our favorite fairytale, Beauty & the Beast), and zomg, already the ideas are stirring and soon we'll begin outlining and starting all over again!!!

THE PANTHEON: WHO'S WHO

A note from Lee: *I've always loved Greek and Roman mythology. 'Innocence' is a retelling of the myth of Persephone and Hades. 'Awakening' goes further, using the story of Orpheus and Euridice as a subplot, and introducing more of the re-imagined Pantheon. I held nothing sacred and pulled from Ovid, Hesiod, Shakespeare, Homer, and even the Bible ('cause why not?). Some of the references are super oblique, but if you're a nerd about this stuff like me, you'll appreciate this cheat sheet (if you don't give a whoop about allegories, ignore this):*

THE UNDERWORLD:

Cora Vestian: Persephone, Proserpina. First name comes from *Kore*. Last name inspired by the *Vestal Virgins*.

Marcus Ubeli: Hades. Last name inspired by the chthonic god *Eubuleus*.

Demi Titan: Demeter. Last name taken from the Titans, the old gods who were the enemies of the Zeus-led pantheon.

Sharo: Charon. Nicknamed *The Undertaker*.

The Shades: Marcus's criminal army.

The Styx: a crime ridden area of New Olympus

Brutus: Cerberus.

The Chariot: Marcus's private club where he conducts most of his business. Contains the office where he and Cora met.

The Orphan: Orpheus.

Iris: Eurydice.

The rest of the Pantheon:

AJ: Ajax the Lesser.

Anna: Aphrodite. Her stage name is *Venus*.

Armand: Hermes. He has wing tattoos and owns a business called *Metamorphoses*, a reference to Ovid.

Elysium: the popular club and music venue, owned by Marcus. The place to see and be seen in New Olympus.

Hype and Thane: Hypnos and Thanatos. God of Sleep and Death, respectively. They run club Elysium.

Maeve: Hectate, goddess of the Crossroads. She advises Cora.

Max Mars: Mars. God of war = volatile action movie star.

Oliva: Athena. Her company is *Aurum*, the Latin word for gold. Inspired by Steve Jobs. Aurum plus Apple = golden apple.

Philip Waters: Poseidon. Controls the shipping corridors into New Olympus.

Zeke Sturm: Zeus. The esteemed mayor of New Olympus. Last name (Storm) inspired by the lightning bolts Zeus used.

ALSO BY STASIA BLACK

DARK CONTEMPORARY ROMANCES

Innocence

Awakening

Queen of the Underworld

Cut So Deep

Break So Soft

Hurt So Good

The Virgin and the Beast: a Beauty and the Beast Tale

Hunter: a Snow White Romance

The Virgin Next Door: a Ménage Romance

Daddy's Sweet Girl (freebie)

COMPLETE MARRIAGE RAFFLE SERIES

Theirs to Protect

Theirs to Pleasure

Their Bride

Theirs to Defy

Theirs to Ransom

ABOUT STASIA BLACK

STASIA BLACK grew up in Texas, recently spent a freezing five-year stint in Minnesota, and now is happily planted in sunny California, which she will never, ever leave.

She loves writing, reading, listening to podcasts, and has recently taken up biking after a twenty-year sabbatical (and has the bumps and bruises to prove it). She lives with her own personal cheerleader, aka, her handsome husband, and their teenage son. Wow. Typing that makes her feel old. And writing about herself in the third person makes her feel a little like a nutjob, but ahem! Where were we?

Stasia's drawn to romantic stories that don't take the easy way out. She wants to see beneath people's veneer and poke into their dark places, their twisted motives, and their deepest desires. Basically, she wants to create characters that make readers alternately laugh, cry ugly tears, want to toss their kindles across the room, and then declare they have a new FBB (forever book boyfriend).

Join Stasia's Facebook Group for Readers for access to deleted scenes, to chat with me and other fans and also get access to exclusive giveaways:
Stasia's Facebook Reader Group

 twitter.com/stasiawritesmut

instagram.com/stasiablackauthor

ABOUT LEE SAVINO

LEE SAVINO has grandiose goals but most days can't find her wallet or her keys so she just stays at home and writes. While she was studying creative writing at Hollins University, her first manuscript won the Hollins Fiction Prize.

She lives in the USA with her awesome family. You can find her on Facebook in the **Goddess Group**(which you totally should join).

 instagram.com/intothedarkromance

Made in the USA
Middletown, DE
05 November 2019